A Christmas Promise

Barbara McMahon

&

Barbara Hannay

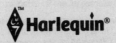

Harlequin®

TORONTO NEW YORK LONDON
AMSTERDAM PARIS SYDNEY HAMBURG
STOCKHOLM ATHENS TOKYO MILAN MADRID
PRAGUE WARSAW BUDAPEST AUCKLAND

Recycling programs
for this product may
not exist in your area.

ISBN-13: 978-0-373-68840-1

A CHRISTMAS PROMISE

Copyright © 2011 by Harlequin Books S.A.

The publisher acknowledges the copyright holders
of the individual works as follows:

SNOWBOUND REUNION
Copyright © 2006 by Barbara McMahon

CHRISTMAS GIFT: A FAMILY
Copyright © 2005 by Barbara Hannay

This edition published by arrangement with Harlequin Books S.A.

For questions and comments about the quality of this book
please contact us at Customer_eCare@Harlequin.ca.

® and TM are trademarks of the publisher. Trademarks indicated with
® are registered in the United States Patent and Trademark Office, the
Canadian Trade Marks Office and in other countries.

www.Harlequin.com

Printed in U.S.A.

BARBARA McMAHON

was born and raised in the southern U.S.A., but settled in California after spending a year flying around the world for an international airline. After settling down to raise a family and work for a computer firm, she began writing when her children started school. Now, feeling fortunate in being able to realize a long-held dream of quitting her "day job" and writing full-time, she and her husband have moved to the Sierra Nevada mountains of California, where she finds her desire to write is stronger than ever. With the beauty of the mountains visible from her windows, and the pace of life slower than the hectic San Francisco Bay area where they previously resided, she finds more time than ever to think up stories and characters and share them with others through writing. Barbara loves to hear from readers. You can reach her at P.O. Box 977, Pioneer, CA 95666-0977, U.S.A. Readers can also contact Barbara at her website, www.barbaramcmahon.com.

BARBARA HANNAY

was born in Sydney, educated in Brisbane and has spent most of her adult life living in tropical north Queensland, where she and her husband have raised four children. While she has enjoyed many happy times camping and canoeing in the bush, she also delights in an urban lifestyle—chamber music, contemporary dance, movies and dining out. An English teacher, she has always loved writing, and now, by having her stories published, she is living her most cherished fantasy.

In 2007 Barbara won a RITA® Award for Best Traditional Romance with *Claiming His Family. Adopted: Outback Baby* was a 2009 RITA® Award finalist.

To catch up on all Barbara's latest news, visit www.barbarahannay.com.

TABLE OF CONTENTS

SNOWBOUND REUNION

Barbara McMahon

Chapter 1

Cath Morgan drove through the Virginia countryside anxious to reach her destination. She ignored the stand of trees lining the road, raising their barren branches to the winter sky. It was a beautiful day, cold and sunny. She should have been enjoying the scenery, but heartache was her companion and she never gave a thought to anything but reaching the house at the end of the journey. Sanctuary. The place she had loved as a child, and wanted to escape to now that things were unraveling.

She'd left Washington, D.C., that morning, after months of soul searching. It wasn't easy walking out on a marriage. But for a woman married six years, it had not been as hard as she had expected. Out of all that time, her husband had only been home a total of one year, seven months, two weeks and three days. She'd counted it up.

She'd spent two summers in Europe, to be closer to where Jake was. But even then, he'd rarely been able to spend more than a few days with her.

What kind of marriage was that? For all intents and purposes she was a single person unable to have a normal social life because of a legal tie to a man half a world away.

Time to change all that.

She felt as if she were cutting a part of herself out with a dull knife.

Cath noted on the highway sign flashing by that she was drawing closer to her turnoff. The exit that would take her to the house her aunt Sally had left to her when she died last summer.

Jake had come home for the funeral. That had added the three days to the tally. But then he'd left. She hadn't wanted him to go, had begged him to stay, but some skirmish captured the world's attention, and he went to report it.

Aunt Sally's death had been the catalyst for this change. She had been Cath's last living relative. There was no one else. If Cath wanted children to live on after her, she had to do something about it.

She'd talked to Jake several times on the phone, e-mailed him almost daily—at least at first. But he didn't want to discuss things long-distance. And would not return home.

Cath gripped the wheel tighter. She wasn't going to think about the past. For far too long she'd put her life on hold for Jake Morgan. Now she was taking it back.

She'd known when she married him that he was a reporter with a travel lust that took him all over the globe. From armed skirmishes to natural disasters, Jake Morgan always sought to be in the middle of the next late-breaking news. It had been exciting in those first months to be a part of his life, to tell friends and co-workers that her husband was Jake Morgan.

E-mail and phone calls had kept them connected. And she'd been thrilled each time he came home, hoping that this was the time he'd stay. Her summer in Athens and the one in Rome had seemed romantic at first. But she was as lonely there as at home, and didn't speak either language.

After six years, she was tired of their electronic relationship. She was tired of constant disappointments. She wanted a husband at home every night, someone to eat dinner with and discuss their respective days. Someone to share child raising with. Someone to give her the baby she longed for. Someone to grow old with.

Jake was not that man. The realization had come slow and hard. But she'd admitted it finally. And taken steps to change the status quo.

She recognized her exit approaching and slowed to turn off the highway onto a quiet country road. It soon narrowed and twisted as it meandered through the wooded area. Historic Williamsburg was not too far from the house on the James River that had once been her aunt's. Cath's parents had died of influenza when a particular virulent strain had swept through the country the winter of her senior year in college. Her mother's parents had been dead before she was born, her father's dying within months of each other when she was still a young child. Her birth had been a surprise to everyone, occurring when her parents were in their forties and had long given up any hope for a baby.

Cath began to recognize familiar landmarks. She smiled sadly as she rounded the last bend and saw the old house in solitary splendor on the banks of the historic river. She'd spent many summers here with her aunt. Even knowing Aunt Sally had died last summer, Cath halfway expected to find her peering through the windows, watching for her arrival.

She turned onto the dirt driveway, heading past the house toward the old carriage house in back. For a moment her imagination flickered to the past. The house had been built in the 1770s, had withstood the war for American independence, and then the bloody Civil War that almost tore the country asunder ninety years later. The clapboard structure had been renovated a time or two. The plumbing wasn't the best in the world, but sufficed. Electricity had been added long ago and probably needed to be updated to accommodate all the modern electric devices.

Cath wasn't sure if she'd be the one to handle that. One of the reasons for her visit was to decide what to do about the place.

She stopped near the back door and shut off the engine, looking around her. The grass lay dying in the winter sun, long and shaggy. She'd tried to get a caretaker for the grounds, but dealing with a firm long-distance wasn't the easiest way to handle things, and it looked as if they had neglected the job.

Cath thought she'd best sell it and get from under the responsibility. Yet every once in a while, she daydreamed about moving to Williamsburg and living in the old house.

She hadn't voiced that option to anyone, but it rose higher on her list of things to think about. She was a great teacher and would have no trouble finding a job wherever she went. Maybe a clean break from everything would be best. If she moved here, she'd have a place to live in that wouldn't have a single memory of Jake.

She planned to spend her entire school break working on the house—and considering her options. Sadly she was doing it alone.

Her aunt had been a spinster, never married. She'd loved Cath's visits and always made sure they toured Historic Williamsburg each summer and went many times to the beach. Cath remembered most fondly the lazy days lying in the grass in the backyard beneath the weeping willow tree, on the banks of the river, watching the water drift by. The trees had been in full leaf every summer, providing plenty of dapple shade in the hot Virginia summer. They looked bare and bleak without their leafy canopy.

Everything looked a little bleak in winter, reflecting the way she felt.

She and Jake had only managed one Christmas together, their second. Other years she had spent part of the day with her friend Abby and Abby's family. She'd been invited again this year, but Cath had wanted to spend it in the old house. She needed to get used to doing things by herself if she was serious about ending her marriage.

She climbed out of the car, studying the old, two-story clapboard house. It had been around for a couple of hundred years and Cath expected it would survive another couple of hundred.

She'd tried to keep up her spirits the last weeks of the school term. There was no sense letting anyone else know how difficult the past few months had been. Once her decision had been made, Cath thought it would become easier. It was not proving so. Her heart ached in longing and wishful thinking. But she was determined to see the change through, and make a different kind of life for herself in the future.

Cath had wished she could be a part of a large family when she'd been a child. But she'd been the only child of older parents. Her desire for siblings had faded as she grew up. And she found lots of joy in teaching her third-grade class every year.

But this year, with the death of Aunt Sally, the desire for children of her own had escalated. She'd tried to talk to Jake about it, but he'd pooh-poohed the idea, saying their lives were full the way they were.

His maybe, not so hers.

Others spent weeks shopping for Christmas, making cookies and pies and decorating their homes. She had finished her short list before Thanksgiving. And there wasn't much reason to decorate their condo when she was the only one there.

She needed to get this place sorted out and packed up. If not now, then it would have to wait until summer. That was a long time for the house to remain empty. She wondered what it would be like filled with childish laughter, the sound of running feet and shrieks of delight.

She drew a deep breath. She wasn't out of love with Jake, but she couldn't stay in a marriage that existed more on paper than in reality. One day she hoped to make a happy life with someone else. Once she got over Jake. If she ever did.

Opening the car door, she caught her breath at the cold air. Time to get inside and see about warming up the big old house before bedtime. There was plenty to do and not as much time as she wished to do it all. Could she have the place ready for sale by January first? The project gave her something to focus on. She would hardly notice another holiday was passing without her husband.

Her e-mails over the past several weeks had urged him to return home. Jake had always said things were too hot to leave. She tried to explain her unhappiness and the decision she was making, but couldn't come right out and tell him via e-mail. She wanted to tell him in person.

If he didn't return home, soon, however, she wasn't sure what she'd do. She'd have to write him, not let him find out from an attorney. She'd even written a practice note and left it at home. Not that she expected him to show up. It was more important to Jake to report the news from some hot spot than spend the holidays with his wife. She'd have to write him in January, when she returned home.

She had to tell him their marriage was over.

Tears filled her eyes. She dashed them away, blaming them on the cold wind. Time to get inside and warm up.

Jake Morgan let himself into the town house. He was exhausted. The flight home had been one delay and mishap after another. He should be thankful the plane hadn't crashed, but that was about the only holdup he hadn't experienced.

Maybe it had been a sign he wasn't supposed to come home for Christmas. But Cath's e-mails lately had been disturbing. She'd almost demanded he come home. She rarely even asked. Plus, he wanted to see her. His flying visit in August had been solely to attend her aunt's funeral. Not enough time to spend together beyond the duties of that sad event.

"Cath?" he called.

The place was silent. Jake headed for the bedroom. A quick shower, a nap and he'd be good to go. She must be out shopping. He knew school was out for the Christmas holidays, so she wasn't at work.

Maybe she was visiting her friend Abby. They could be baking Christmas cookies with Abby's kids. Cath always liked the season. Her notes were usually full of decorating at the school she'd done, or the treats she baked for colleagues.

The house felt cold and lonely with her absence.

He glanced into the living room as he passed, stopped by the envelope propped on the mantel, his name in large print.

A sickening dread took hold. His instincts had been honed by years of dangerous assignments. He knew better than to ignore them.

Dropping his duffel bag, he crossed the expansive living room and picked up the envelope. He ripped it open and stared at the words for endless moments. He crushed the letter, the words almost unfathomable—she wanted to end their marriage.

Cath had left him. She was gone. The house was empty and lifeless for a reason—the heart of it had gone.

Jake reread the words, as if doing so could change them. They remained the same, indelibly engraved in his mind. He felt sick. Disbelief warred with the words dancing before his eyes.

The woman he loved beyond all else had not loved him enough to stay.

Crushing the paper in his hand he turned, as if seeking her.

It was his fault, and he knew it. He'd deliberately stayed away this fall as if sensing the change in her, fearing this very thing. Why had he thought she wouldn't take such a step unless consulting him first? So they could *talk.* She always wanted to talk about things, nitpick them to death. She'd given enough hints all fall that he should have picked up on them. Subconsciously maybe he had. Why else change his plans at the last moment and return home for Christmas?

But he was home now, dammit. Where was Cath?

He ran up the stairs to their bedroom. Throwing open the closet door, he breathed a sigh of relief when he saw most of her clothes. She hadn't moved out. Not yet, at least.

Her suitcase was gone.

He went into the bathroom, assessing what was there

and what was not. She'd gone somewhere for Christmas, she was coming back. He could wait.

Jake shook his head and turned. He was not going to sit around while Cath ended their marriage. He wanted to set her straight on that. Only, he had to find her first.

Walking slowly downstairs, he tried to think. He was known for his coolness under fire, why couldn't he think now?

Abby would know. She was Cath's best friend.

It took a few moments to locate Cath's address book. Jake looked around the condo with impatience. It was his home, too. Just because he wasn't often here didn't mean he should feel like a stranger in his own home. He dialed Abby's number.

"Hello?"

"Abby?"

"Yes?"

"Jake Morgan here. Do you know where Cath is?"

"Where are you?"

"Home."

"She said you weren't coming home for the holidays."

"I planned to surprise her. Only she got the first surprise in."

"What do you mean?" Abby's voice was cautious.

"A letter."

There was silence on the other end.

"Where is she, Abby?"

"She says it's over, Jake. She's been agonizing over this all fall. Let her go."

"Like hell, I will. Where is she?"

"If she wanted you to know, she'd have left word. I can't help you, Jake."

She hung up.

Jake swore and slammed down the phone.

If she had not expected him home, Cath wouldn't have gone to stay at Abby's. They could drive over to each other's place in less than ten minutes. It meant she went somewhere else. But where?

Aunt Sally's house.

Her refuge, she'd once said.

He scooped up his duffel and headed out. A bath and sleep would have to wait. He needed to find his wife and talk her out of her plans to leave.

Cath finished the makeshift meal and cleared the kitchen. She still wore her jacket, the house was too cold to take it off. The old furnace had been difficult to start, but she'd finally managed. Now it was just a question of time before the coldness was dispelled.

She'd made up the bed in the room she'd always used. Aunt Sally's room was larger, but Cath wasn't ready to make that step yet. She wished her aunt had electric blankets. Something was needed to warm the bed if she wanted to sleep in it tonight. Maybe she could use the old-fashioned bed-warming pan that had hung in the cellar for as long as Cath could remember. Her aunt had told her how generations of Williamsons had used it to warm their beds before retiring. Long before central heating kept the house a comfortable temperature.

Tonight Cath knew how the early settlers felt. She didn't think she could take off her clothes to get into her nightgown without freezing. But she hesitated before going down in the dark old cellar. She didn't like going there in daylight, she really didn't want to go now, warming pan or not. Plus, she wasn't sure she knew how to use one.

The warm water felt good on her hands as she washed

the few dishes. She'd found the pilot light had remained on for the hot water heater, so she had instant hot water. Maybe she should take a bath. Wasn't there a small space heater in the bathroom? Aunt Sally hated to turn on the big furnace before it was needed, as she put it. She'd delayed the lighting of the furnace until way down in the fall, using the space heater in the bathroom, and letting the sunshine streaming in through tall windows warm the ambient temperature through the house during the day.

Cath wasn't as stouthearted. She liked comforts—at least heat and lights.

She'd brought some books to read, and considered heading for bed now just to get beneath the covers. But it was only seven-thirty—too early to go to bed.

Cath had dusted and vacuumed the main rooms downstairs, and cleaned the one bathroom and her bedroom since her arrival. Giving all a lick and a promise, as her aunt used to say. Too much to do in one day, but she had two weeks ahead of her. She was tired, still cold and lonely. She wished… No, don't go there. A good night's sleep would be just the thing. In the morning she'd start cleaning and clearing in the back bedroom and work her way through the second story and then the first to clear clutter and decide what to do with Aunt Sally's furnishings and mementos. Her clothing had been donated last summer. But there were still generations of things in the house to sort, if she included everything stored in the cellar.

She'd leave the cellar for last. No telling what was down there. It was dark, with faint illumination, and piles of boxes, trunks and old furniture. As a child, she'd found it spooky. The door often slammed shut, apparently for no reason. Aunt Sally said it contained the remnants of all the families who had lived in the house.

Cath had asked about ghosts when she'd been little. Nothing to be afraid of, her aunt assured her, just gentle reminders of ancestors long gone. Cath was not looking forward to that clearing job.

She checked the locks on the front door before going up to her bedroom. A sweep of headlights came in through the beveled glass. She stared at the driveway. Was someone lost and asking directions? Or was it a neighbor who had seen the lights and wanted to know who was in Sally Williamson's house?

The beveled glass distorted the man who got out of the car. He reached in for a bag and slammed the door. The night wasn't completely black. She could still make him out from the faint starlight, striding toward the house. He might not be clearly visible in the darkness, but she'd recognize that stride anywhere. It was Jake.

Her heart skipped a beat, then raced. For a split second, gladness filled her—then dismay. What was he doing here? Why hadn't he told her he was coming home for the holidays? How had he found her?

She stepped back from the door, to one side, out of sight, wanting to run to her bedroom and hide beneath the covers. Instead, like a deer caught in headlights, she watched as he approached the door. She hadn't seen him since last August. He e-mailed as regularly as he could, complaining if she didn't write to him often. But there wasn't as much to share as there used to be. And once she began thinking about leaving, she had found it difficult to communicate as if everything was fine.

He knocked on the door.

Do or die time, Cath thought. Why had Jake come? Surely he'd seen the letter she'd left just in case he arrived at home.

She opened the door a crack, standing slightly behind it. The cold air swept in.

"Hi, Jake. I didn't expect you."

He pushed gently and stepped inside, dumping the bag and glaring at her.

"What the hell kind of letter was that you left?"

"An explanatory one," she said. "I thought if you showed up and I wasn't there, you might worry."

"But not worry about your leaving me?"

"I'm safe."

"That's not the point and you know it," he said. "I busted my butt to get home for the holidays and you weren't even there. Instead I get some damn-fool letter saying you're calling it quits."

"That's right," she said evenly. She could do this. She just had to ignore the spark of feelings that flared at the sight of him. All the pain of her decision, the regrets and might-have-beens sprung up. She pushed the thoughts away.

He looked drawn and tired. There was a two-day's growth of beard on his cheeks and chin, and his eyes were bloodshot and weary-looking. His clothes were rumpled. Despite it all, her heart called out, unhappy with her choice.

"I didn't come all this way, through the worst connection of flights I think I've ever taken, to be dumped. I've come home to my wife," Jake said, reaching out, pulling her into his arms and kissing her.

Chapter 2

Cath resisted as long as she could, but his kisses always drove her wild. Despite her best intentions, she returned the kiss, reveling in the feel of the man holding her. It had been too long. She had missed him so much! She loved being held by him, being kissed. She felt alive, whole, complete. Why couldn't it always be like this?

Then reality returned. Common sense took over and slowly she pushed against his embrace. They'd always been terrific together in a physical sense. But it wasn't enough. No longer.

She couldn't stay married to Jake Morgan. She wanted more than to be a part-time wife. She deserved more!

She pushed harder and he released her. Breathing fast, he looked at her, his gaze intense and assessing.

"Nice of you to stop by," Cath said, opening the door. "Have a nice holiday."

He reached around her and slammed it shut. "I'm staying, get used to the idea."

"You can't stay here. I'm leaving you."

"So leave."

"This is my house. You leave."

Cath realized they were starting to sound like four-year-olds. She didn't need this.

"Not tonight. I've been up for more than twenty-four hours. I had planned to get some sleep this afternoon, but instead had to drive down here," he said, looking around.

"No one invited you," she said, glaring at him.

"I invited myself. It's cold in here."

"The heater's on, it was freezing before. It'll take a while to warm the entire house. You could have told me you were coming home. I asked you often enough in the past weeks."

"I didn't know for sure if I could make it and I didn't want to get your hopes up. No worries there, I guess," he said.

"We could have had this discussion in Washington if I'd known you were coming. I could have come down after talking with you," Cath said. She didn't want him to stay. She was too afraid her carefully constructed rationale would crumble around him. But it was late and he looked exhausted. Could he find a motel room in town? Williamsburg was bursting at the seams with all the tourists who came for the holidays. Most places had been booked solid months ago.

"We definitely need to discuss things, but not tonight. Where are we sleeping?" he asked.

"*I'm* sleeping in my old room. If you insist on staying, you can have Aunt Sally's room. I'm not sleeping with you. You read the letter, I'm calling it quits, Jake." For a moment, she hoped he'd sweep away all the points leading to her decision. But he picked up his duffel and started for the stairs.

"We'll talk in the morning. Isn't that what you like to do, talk things to death?" he asked

"Not this time," Cath said quietly. She had no words left. No hope.

Jake paused at the bottom of the stairs and looked back at her. In two strides he crossed the short distance, leaning over to kiss her. She clenched her hands into tight fists, resisting with all she was worth.

"We're not over, Cath," he said.

She watched as he climbed the stairs, her heart pounding. The wooden floors echoed his steps. She could trace his location by the sounds. He paused at her room then moved on down the hall to the next one. A breath escaped, she hadn't known she was holding. None of the other beds were made, he'd have to fend for himself. And leave in the morning. Tears threatened. His being here would make everything that much harder.

Cath couldn't believe Jake had shown up out of the blue. Nothing in his recent e-mails had even hinted he was thinking of coming home. The last she'd heard, he was someplace in the Middle East.

She hugged herself against the chill, and not just the temperature in the room. She couldn't go to bed now, her thoughts were a total mishmash, spinning and jangled.

His kiss had been all she could have ever hoped for. He could always make her feel like the queen of the world with one kiss.

But the important things—discussions of their future together, planning their family—he always sidestepped, only saying they'd deal with whatever fate decreed. She wasn't going to go along with that anymore. She wanted her freedom from this marriage, wanted to be able to forge new ties eventually, and even try for a baby. And she didn't plan to wait until she was in her forties as her parents had been!

It was late when Cath finally went upstairs. She had paced the living room until she couldn't stand it, exquisitely aware that Jake was asleep upstairs. She was halfway tempted to wake him up and have that discussion now. She'd been a long, agonizing time coming to this decision. She just hoped Jake accepted it with some grace.

But she was not going to wake him up. She'd be civilized and wait until morning. The house had warmed enough she was willing to try changing into her nightgown, glad she'd brought the long flannel one with rosebuds and pink ribbons. She needed the high neck, long sleeves and long length to keep her warm. And to keep from thinking romantic thoughts about her husband.

Sleep was the furthest thing from her mind, however, when she did get into bed. All she could think about was Jake in a room down the hall. She hoped he wasn't going to be difficult about this. He ought to be glad she'd started the ball rolling. He was never home. This way, he never even had to fly back to the U.S. between assignments. He could flit off to whatever late-breaking news spot drew him without any cares in the world.

Somehow she knew he wasn't seeing it quite that way.

When Cath awoke the next morning, she immediately thought about Jake. His being here was a complication she didn't need or expect. Why had he returned? He hadn't made it home for the past four Christmases, why this one? Had her pleas in her e-mails finally made a dent? Or was he planning another brief stay, like last August? She knew better than to get her hopes up. Six years of living on the periphery of Jake Morgan's life had taught her well.

Dressing rapidly in the large bathroom, she became convinced her aunt Sally had been of far sturdier stock than she. It was still cold enough to show her breath and Cath didn't like it one bit. She'd have to see about turning the heater higher. The small space heater wasn't up to the task of dispelling the chill.

Once dressed, she went downstairs without hearing any sound from Jake's room. He'd looked exhausted last night. If he'd been up for more than twenty-four hours, then maybe he'd sleep in late.

Or at least late enough to enable her to get her priorities straight and her ducks in a row. He'd want an explanation, she'd give him one—logically and calmly. He could rant and rave all he wanted, but her mind was made up. She just hoped she could keep from descending into a rant herself. She'd kept a lot of her disappointments and anger inside. Only lately had she allowed herself to admit to all the things wrong with their union. It wouldn't be fair to dump them on Jake all at once. She should have told him all along how she resented the time he spent away from her. How lonely she had been for years.

Looking into the empty refrigerator, Cath wondered what to do for breakfast. She'd originally planned to eat at one of the cafés in town and then go grocery shopping. Maybe she should follow through with her plan; no telling how long Jake would sleep. And if he did waken before she returned, it might show him she was serious about their ending their marriage. In the past she would have stayed to prepare him breakfast. Today he was on his own.

It was after eleven when Cath returned. The minute she opened the kitchen door, she knew Jake was up. The fragrance of fresh coffee filled the kitchen. Where had he unearthed that old percolator of her aunt's? And the coffee to go with it? She'd made do with instant yesterday when she'd arrived.

Cath placed two grocery bags on the counter and turned to get the rest.

"I'll help," Jake said, coming into the kitchen from the hall.

She shook her head. "No need, I can manage." She wasn't giving in an inch.

Jake ignored her, however, and followed her to the car, reaching in the trunk to withdraw two more bags. Cath took the last one and closed the trunk.

"I said I could manage," she said, following his longer stride to the house.

"I'm sure you can, but why not take help when it's offered?" he asked reasonably.

She placed her bag on the table and shrugged out of her coat. Did he realize how much she didn't want him there? Jake had always had a stubborn streak. Now was not the time for it to take hold.

Putting the things away, Cath geared herself up for the coming confrontation. She had to stay calm, she told herself over and over. Not let Jake rile her or make her angry or talk her out of her decision. She'd tried not to look at him, not wanting to worry that he looked almost gaunt and tired beyond belief.

She'd thought everything through all fall long. She would be rational and certain.

She looked across the room. Jake leaned against the counter, legs crossed at the ankles, arms crossed over his chest, his gaze steady-focused on her.

"Want to tell me what this is all about?" he asked.

She put the cans of corn and beans in the cupboard. "I thought the letter said it all. I'm ending our marriage." She almost smiled in relief at how calm she sounded, but she didn't feel like smiling. She felt like crying.

"Why?"

No outburst, no denial, just one quiet word.

Cath turned to him, taking a deep breath. Do or die time. "Our marriage is not working for me. I want more than what we have. This is nothing new. We've argued about the entire setup more than once. I say what I want, you say things that sound placating, then take off for another five months to someplace I've never heard of until it's so common on the nightly news it becomes part of everyday life. I worry about you, but you don't seem to worry about me. I want a family, you don't. Jake, there are dozens of reasons to end this. I can't think of one to keep on the way we've been."

"How about love?"

"What about it? Do you love me? You have a funny way of showing it. I think you're comfortable with me. You like having me in D.C. to keep a place for you to return to when you get stateside. But how much of a relationship do we really have? Do I know any of your co-workers? Do you know any of mine? What was I most worried about this fall? What was your happiest moment last month? We don't know any of that, because we aren't really a couple. We're two people bound by a marriage license, who don't even live in the same country most of the time."

Jake didn't say a word. Cath had thought about this long and hard and she wasn't going to make it easier for him. Her nerves shook, but she continued to put up the groceries. Sooner or later he'd say something. She was not going to be the first to break the silence. Not this time.

"You knew what my job was like before we were married," he said at last.

"Yes and no," she replied. She knew this would be one

argument. "I knew you worked for an international news bureau. But I had no idea of the reality of that. I didn't know until we lived it that you would be gone more than you're home. That I'd be so lonely and yet unable to do much about it. I certainly didn't know that when I was ready to think about a family, you wouldn't be as excited to start as I was."

"We never talked about having kids."

"Aunt Sally's death shook me up, more than I suspected at first. I want to have a family, be connected to others on the planet. We're not getting any younger. I don't want to be old like my parents were."

"I thought we wanted the same thing—living in the capital, having friends, doing things—"

"That's just it, Jake, we don't. Not together. We went to a concert at the Kennedy Center five years ago. Five years. Other than that, if I want to see a play or concert, I have to get Abby or another friend to go with me. What kind of marriage is that?"

His jaw clenched. Cath could tell he was keeping a tight leash on his emotions. Maybe, once, she'd like to see that leash slip. To really know what he was feeling. But Jake was too good a reporter to insert his feelings into things. Maybe that was part of the problem; she never felt he was totally involved, but was always observing. Or getting ready to make a commentary.

"Maybe there's room for improvement, but you don't just throw away six years of marriage without trying to save it," he countered.

"If you wanted this to work, you needed to do something before now. I haven't gone anywhere. What do you suggest, quitting your job? I don't see that. And if you don't, you won't be home nights, so we're in the same loop as always."

She folded the grocery bags, stuffed them in a cupboard

and turned to leave, her knees feeling weak, her heart racing, tears on the verge. But she'd done it. She'd maintained a cool facade. He'd never know how sick she felt inside, how her heart was truly breaking.

It was pointless to argue. Nothing was going to change. Her mind was made up. One day he'd admit she'd been right. She hoped she herself felt that way!

"Wait, Cath. I'll admit maybe things have been in a rut lately. But this is my career we're talking about. It takes me where the news is. I can't say I'll stay in D.C. and only report on what's happening in Washington."

She paused at the doorway and looked back at him. "It's more than a job, or even a career. It's your life, Jake. Face it. You love the adrenaline rush of plunging into a war zone, or daring mother nature when faced with catastrophes. A job is something you go to for a few hours a day and then go home and have a real life."

"Someone has to report the news, Cath."

"I'm not arguing that, I'm just saying I don't want to be the person contributing to it by giving up my husband. I want a man I can rely on to be there for me."

"I'm only a phone call away."

"How long did it take you to get back this trip? You said you'd been up more than twenty-four hours. You may be a phone call away, but it took you a long time to physically get back. What if there'd been an emergency? What if I really needed you?"

"What if you do in the future? I won't be there if we get divorced."

Cath stared at him for a moment. "I want to get married again."

Jake looked dumbfounded. Then anger flared. "Your letter said there wasn't another man."

"There's not, where would I meet someone? There's no one now, that's the truth. But I hope to find someone, a man who wants the same things I do—especially children. I feel I've wasted six years of my life hoping you'd want what I want and we could start a family. It's never going to happen, is it, Jake? You'll always have a dozen excuses and then be off to Beirut or Singapore."

"You and I need to work on things a bit more, maybe. No, wait." He held up a hand when she started to speak. "No maybe about it. I see where you're coming from. I can try to meet you partway, Cath, but to just chuck everything after all these years doesn't make sense."

"Only because you're just hearing about it now. I've been thinking about this since you left last August. I wasn't ready to be alone after Aunt Sally died. She was my last relative."

"I'm a relative. I'm your husband."

"I'm talking blood kin and you know it. I felt absolutely alone in the world. I needed you and you took off."

"I didn't realize that," he said slowly.

"I came to that conclusion several weeks later," she said, smiling sadly. "It's because you don't really know me anymore. I'm not the twenty-two-year-old, excited to be falling in love with a man of the world. I'm a responsible adult who has really been living on her own for most of the six years of our marriage. I've grown up. My goals and dreams have changed. I've changed."

Jake studied her a long moment. "Maybe I have as well."

"Maybe, but I wouldn't know, would I?"

"I don't want a divorce."

"It's not all about you anymore, Jake."

He looked startled at that. "It was never just about me," he said.

"Yes, it has been, but no more. I've made up my mind to take back my life and make it like I want."

Cath turned and walked down the hall to the stairs. She'd planned to start cleaning the upstairs bedrooms today. She only had four days until Christmas, and then a week after that before she had to return to Washington. If she did one room a day, she'd be finished on time. She had to focus on that and not what might have been.

Jake followed her. "Cath, that kiss last night should have told you something," he said.

She paused midway up the steps, holding on to the banister as she turned to look at him. "Sure, sex between us has always been great. But there's more to marriage than sex a few times a year. Don't you get it, Jake? It's over. I'm moving on. You can do what you want. Preferably from Washington. I think you should leave."

"We're not divorced yet, Cath. I'm staying."

Cath wanted to yell at him that she didn't want him around, that his mere proximity was disturbing, giving her ideas she had no business entertaining. She'd loved him so much, why couldn't he have seen that and offered more than what they'd shared? She needed to keep her goal firm and not be swayed by the dynamic presence of the man or her lost dreams.

"I don't want you to stay," she said.

"I don't want to leave. I don't think you can physically remove me."

Cath shook her head in frustration. "Of course not. Stay if you wish. Just keep out of my way."

"What are you doing here anyway? Running from Washington?" he asked, ignoring her last comment.

"I'm planning to sort through things. See what the house needs to fix it up. I'm not sure what I want to do with it."

She started to turn back up the stairs, but continued to look at him over her shoulder. "I may move here and get a job locally." How would he like that bit of news?

Jake scowled and began to climb the stairs. Cath didn't exactly run the rest of the way up, but she wanted to make sure she was firmly on the second floor before he could crowd her on the steps, or touch her. Or kiss her again. She needed to make sure there was none of that to muddle her thinking, or give her ideas that would fizzle to nothing as soon as the call of adventure summoned him back.

For a moment Cath felt a pain that almost doubled her over. She had loved Jake so much, had such high plans for their lives together. And it had come to this. Trying to be civil a week before Christmas. Tears threatened again.

"Can I help?" he asked.

"You should get started if you want to get to Washington before dark," she said.

"I'm staying, Cath. If you're serious about going through with a divorce, this will be our last Christmas together."

"Or second one, depending on how you look at it."

Jake sighed. "You're right and I'm sorry. I should have been home for Christmas every year."

"That surprises me to hear. You've never been sentimental. Why the change of heart?"

"Getting older, I guess. Doesn't everyone make decisions they later regret? I regret not spending more time with you. Especially in light of what you've just said. Don't you know the thought of you at home kept me going when times got rough?"

Cath had a boatload of regrets—that things had turned out the way they had, that she had spent so many lonely years wishing Jake had been with her watching TV together instead of her watching alone for glimpses of him. Wishing she'd shared more of her dreams with him. The biggest regret was that they'd not had any children. She could have stood the empty nights better if she'd had someone to lavish her love upon.

She stepped into the back bedroom. The curtains were dusty and closed. She pulled them open, dislodging a cascade of dust while letting in the cold winter light.

"I wish I could open the window to clear the air, but I had enough cold yesterday," she said, surveying the furnishing.

"Do you know anything about antiques?" Jake asked, stepping close enough beside her she could feel the radiant heat from his body.

"Not much. But I can recognize good quality furnishings. I'm only keeping things I like. I thought I'd ask a couple of antique dealers to come and give me an estimate on what things are worth." Hoping he wouldn't notice, she stepped to the side, putting a bit more distance between them.

"Tell them you're doing it for insurance purposes, you'll get a better reading," he suggested, stepping farther into the room and trailing a finger across a dusty table.

"Good idea. Good grief, where do I start?"

"With a vacuum and dust cloth. I'll help."

Cath tilted her head slightly. "You'll be late getting off for Washington."

He looked at her and grinned, the expression causing her heart to skip a beat. "I'm not going back to Washington without you. You might as well make up your mind to that. So I guess I'm here until the new year. Where are the dust cloths?"

Cath gave in. If the news bureau called, he'd be gone in a heartbeat. And she could use some help if other rooms looked like this one.

"Just as long as there's no misunderstanding," she cautioned.

"I'm clear on everything you've said," he replied, amusement lurking in his gaze. "But that doesn't mean I won't try to change your mind."

Cath smiled sweetly, though it took effort. "You can try. But I think you'll find I'm not the easily impressed young girl you married."

She didn't want him to try. She wanted him to make things easy for her for once. But he looked as if it would take a tank to budge him, so she gave up. She would remain strong. He'd give up soon, she'd bet on it.

"I'll get the dust cloths and vacuum," she said, turning to escape. There was enough work to keep them both too busy all day long to talk or think. He'd get tired of housework and yearn for the excitement of a natural catastrophe or some war skirmish.

Hell of a way to spend his homecoming, Jake thought as Cath left to get the cleaning supplies. He pushed the curtains wider apart, and was showered in dust. He thought about the fantasies he'd daydreamed on the flight across the Atlantic, him and Cath in bed, only getting up for food from time to time. It didn't look good for that scenario coming true anytime soon. He'd have to convince her what they had was worth saving. Even if it meant making changes on his end. God, he didn't know what he'd do if she really went through with a divorce. He'd been crazy about her from the first day they met.

He loved his job, but he loved his wife more. Didn't she know he'd love to come home every night to be with her? But unless she lived in the troubled spots of the world, that wasn't going to happen.

How many nights had he lain awake in bed, wishing she was there with him, just to hold, to talk to, to kiss? How many days had he taken a break from the grueling schedule and wished she'd shared the quiet afternoon, kicked back and doing nothing but being together?

Did she really think she didn't mean everything to him?

Maybe it was selfish on his part, but he wanted her to want him, be there for him. Want to share what they could together. And for him to be enough for her without having to have others to make a family.

Cath returned, lugging a vacuum and two dust cloths.

"I think you need more than a vacuum to clean these curtains," he said, slapping one. The cloud of dust almost enveloped him.

"I guess you're right," she said, frowning. "Can they be washed, do you think?"

He looked at the material. There were spots burned by the sun. The hem looked frayed.

"I'd chuck them and get new ones."

"Another thing to do. If you'll take them down, I'll go hunt up some trash bags."

"Let's pile everything in the yard for the time being. We'll see how much accumulates and then decide if we want to make a run to the dump or if the local trash company can come and pick it up," Jake suggested.

"You're saying you think there'll be a lot of trash?"

"Don't you?"

Cath looked around the room and shrugged. "Maybe. We'll know better after I assess each room."

"You're going through every room in this place?"

"Yes."

"Over this one holiday?"

"You have a problem with that?" she asked, giving him a look.

"It's Christmas, Cath, don't you want to celebrate?"

"Sure, I'll take Christmas Day off."

The past several years she'd spent the day with Abby and her family. Wouldn't she want to decorate and all this year?

"You'll need decorations," he said.

"Give me a break, Jake. When did you ever care about decorating for Christmas?"

"The year we shared it in Washington."

He could tell she remembered. She looked away with sadness. He should have come home for that holiday each year. He could have found a way. Regret began to eat at him for the lost opportunities. All the more reason to make this one special. To find a way to change her mind.

For a moment a touch of panic swept through him.

What if he was unable to change her mind?

"Whatever. If we get through this room today, I'll look for Aunt Sally's decorations. Funny, I never spent a Christmas with her. I only came in the summers. I wonder if she was lonely on Christmas. She didn't come to visit us. What did she do all those holidays?"

"What will you do over the holidays if we're not married?" he asked. Maybe thinking like a single person would give her a better picture of what life would be. He hoped she hated it.

"Visit with Abby like the last four, I guess," she replied. "Until I meet someone else to marry. Then we'll establish our own Christmas traditions."

He frowned and yanked on the curtains. They ripped at the top and came tumbling down. The dust made him cough. Served him right for letting his temper take control. He was usually cool under trying circumstances. The thought of Cath with someone else, however, made him see red. She was *his wife.* She loved him, he knew she did. He just had to get her to see that she wouldn't be happy with anyone else. He wasn't giving up on their marriage!

She began opening drawers in the dresser as he bundled the curtains up. Heading for the door, he hoped being outside for a few minutes would cool his temper and give him some insight in how to get Cath off the idea of divorce and back into his arms.

Two hours later they were almost finished. Jake was working on the windows, the outside could stand cleaning as well, but he'd need a ladder for that. The room sparkled. The dresser had held little. The closet was empty. The room had obviously been a little-used guest room.

He glanced at Cath, remembering the slinky nightie he'd picked up in Paris. He had planned to give it to her on Christmas Day, and then have her model it for him. That dream popped like a bubble. She was wearing sweats, on her hands and knees, washing down the dirty floor molding. Her blond hair was pulled back in a ponytail to keep it out of her eyes as she worked. There was nothing romantic or sexy about it, but just looking at her sparked a flare of desire. The thought that she no longer cared enough about him to fight for their marriage hurt. He had to find a way to ignite the flame that once blazed between them.

Chapter 3

Jake was driving her crazy, Cath thought as she surveyed the clean bedroom, glad to see how nice it looked. Even with the windows bare, it looked much better than when they'd started. Jake had worked as hard as she had. Which was causing problems. She'd believed by now he'd give up and wander away to do something else. But he'd surprised her. He hadn't complained once. Hadn't tried to get out of anything, from carrying the dirty curtains outside, to washing each tiny pane of glass in the tall windows.

Every so often she'd feel his gaze on her. It took all her self-control to keep from looking back. She swallowed hard. She didn't want that tingling awareness when he was near. She certainly didn't need the memories of them together in happier times crowding her mind, of the love that had flowed, the laughter shared. How long ago that seemed.

This was now. Nothing had changed with his arrival, except to throw her into confusion. She dare not believe in happy endings again. She would only be disappointed.

"That's that," he said. "Anything else left here?"

She looked around, loath to leave the task. What would they talk about without the room's work between them? She was too tired to start another room today, yet dreaded having to make conversation. Why couldn't he just leave?

"It looks nice," she said. "Thank you for helping."

"It's what husbands do," he said.

"Stop it, Jake. That's not going to change my mind. You're here for how long before being gone another six months? If you really wanted to change things, you'd start with your job."

"Or you could quit your job and come with me," he said.

She looked at him in disbelief. "I have no desire to go to war zones or spend my life traveling around after you. I did that twice. You were rarely there, and I was far from home and friends. I want a home to be a refuge each night to return to. I like the furnishings and the artwork I chose. I'm not a nomad and have no intentions of becoming one."

"I'm not a nomad. I have a home."

"No, Jake, you have a place to stay when you're in Washington." Cath gathered up the dirty dust rags and reached for the vacuum. She'd put it in the next room for tomorrow's work. Then she wanted to take a quick shower and get rid of the sixteen layers of dust that she'd accumulated during the cleaning.

Looking at Jake, she was surprised to find his expression thoughtful. She'd thought he'd come back with an instant reply, but for once he seemed to be thinking about what she said. And if he followed it through, he'd know she was right.

"I'm going to take a quick shower and then make something for dinner," she said.

"Early for dinner."

"We didn't have lunch and I'm starving."

"Go take a shower. I'll clean up after you're finished," Jake said. "Unless you wish to share the shower?"

The devilish gleam in his eyes caused Cath's heart rate to kick into high. She was not going to give in to temptation. She couldn't foresee a future where as former lovers they got together from time to time for old times' sake. The break had to be clean and sharp. And final.

"I'll hurry and try not to use all the water," she said, and turned and fled.

Cath put together sandwiches and heated some soup for dinner. It wasn't fancy, but was plenty for the two of them, and would have to do. She wasn't trying to impress anyone with her culinary skills. She was used to making do with abbreviated meals because she didn't feel like cooking at the end of the day when it was for herself alone.

They ate at the kitchen table. Cath was careful to set their places as far apart as practical. Jake said little, digging in to the food like a starving man. She realized that except for the coffee he'd made that morning, he'd had nothing to eat all day. She felt guilty and tried to squelch the feeling. Let him fend for himself. But saying it to herself didn't work. She should have offered him something earlier.

"We can look for the Christmas decorations when we finish," he said a few moments later.

"You're serious about decorating?"

"Don't you want to?" he asked.

Cath thought about it for a minute. The house would seem more welcoming if decked out for the holiday. "I guess. I don't know what Aunt Sally might have. And I didn't bring any of our ornaments."

"Is there an attic?"

"Just a small one. My guess is the decorations would be

stored in the cellar with everything else from the last two hundred years."

"That's some cellar."

"I remember going down there when I was a kid and being scared silly. There are cubicles and narrow passageways making it like a maze. Furniture and boxes and old trunks are everywhere, and cobwebs. Aunt Sally once said the family never threw anything away. I believe her. I guess if she had decorations that's where they'd be, but exactly where is anyone's guess."

"So we go exploring."

Cath wasn't thrilled with the idea, but her curiosity was roused. Aunt Sally must have decorated at the holidays, yet Cath would never know the significance of any of the ornaments. She wondered if her aunt's collection contained any very old baubles or if any had had special meaning to her. She regretted not spending any Christmases with the elderly woman. She should have insisted Aunt Sally spend the last several Christmases with her. Each time she'd invited her, Aunt Sally had given an excuse. Hadn't she been lonely spending the holiday alone?

The dim bulb over the bottom of the cellar steps did not provide much illumination when they started downstairs sometime later. Cath had propped the door open and let Jake lead the way. When they reached the cement floor, he looked around.

"We should have brought a flashlight," he said.

"There's lighting throughout, just not very bright. I don't know if the wiring can stand it, but I'd like to replace every bulb with a brighter one." She found the old light switch and flipped it up. Throughout the cellar lights went on, throwing deep shadows among the items stored there.

"Spooky," she said with a shiver.

He laughed, and reached out to take her hand. "I'll protect you from the bogeyman."

She snatched her hand back. "I can take care of myself." As if to prove that, she stepped to the right and started down one aisle. There were boxes and boxes stacked shoulder-high. None were labeled. If they had to look through each one, they could be here all week.

The thought of clearing the cellar was mind-boggling. Cath studied the items as she walked along. There was no way she could clear this area during the holiday break. It would take days to go through things. The furniture alone would be enough to furnish another house. She wandered down one aisle and over to another. The light cast odd shadows. She ran her fingertips over some of the tables, coming away dusty. There were old chests and armoires, chairs and tables. A cradle. She stopped at that and rocked it gently, imagining a baby of her own nestled snugly asleep beside her own bed. The cradle looked old, with hand carvings on the headboard and footboard. The wood was burnished from years of use.

She moved on, opening a drawer here and there, lifting the lids of some of the boxes—clothing from an earlier era, books long forgotten, mementos from ancestors long gone.

She lifted one lid of a very old trunk and saw lace and silk. To one side a small leather-bound book. She took it out and opened it. It looked like a journal of some kind.

"I found them," Jake's voice sounded from a distance.

"I'll be right there." She tucked the book under her arm and closed the trunk. She'd read through it later. Maybe it belonged to one of her ancestors.

"Call again so I can find you," she said.

"I went left from the stairs. You went right, so I'm probably directly across the cellar from you," he said.

She followed the sound of his voice and, rounding a corner, found him standing in an open area, two boxes of Christmas decorations opened at his feet.

"There're more," he said, pointing to the stack at his right.

"Let's take them upstairs and see what we can use." She reached for the closest box and the journal dropped to the floor.

"What's that?" Jake asked, reaching for it.

Cath scooped it up. "A book I found. It looks like a journal or something and I thought I'd read it."

His hand dropped. "Family history?"

"Maybe." She put it on top of the box, and lifted both. "I'll take these upstairs."

Jake stacked another two boxes on top of each other and followed.

Two more trips and all the boxes of decorations had been brought up to the dining room and put on the large table. Cath placed the journal away from the boxes, for some reason not wanting to share with Jake. Time they broke ties, not made them.

"We need a tree," he said, pulling out a string of lights. "Your aunt must have had a tree each year, and a large one to boot if the number of strings of lights is any indication."

"We don't need a tree."

"Sure we do. I know just the spot in the living room where it should go, in front of the two windows on the front wall," he said.

Cath knew where he meant. Shifting the furniture would center the tree as the focal point of the room.

It would be festive, and more like Christmas, with decorations and a tree. She loved Christmas. But to share it with Jake felt awkward. She wouldn't have bothered on her own. Why should she just because he came home unexpectedly?

"Maybe I'll see about getting one tomorrow," she said reluctantly.

"We'll go together. Let's cut one at a tree farm," he suggested.

Cath looked at Jake with surprise. The one Christmas they'd spent together, they'd picked up a tree at the Boy Scout lot. As she recalled, she'd done most of the decorating, he'd been on the phone with the news bureau.

"I don't know if they have any tree farms around," she said. Nor did she want to get the tree with Jake. It was bad enough having him here, but she didn't want to do things that would build memories. Even if he didn't agree at this moment, he would soon have to acknowledge their separating was the best thing.

"I'll check." He headed to the kitchen and the phone book beneath the telephone.

"Where's Windsor Drive?" he called.

"I have no idea."

"The exchange is the same as this one, so it can't be too far away. We'll call in the morning and find out," Jake said, returning to the dining room, phone book in hand.

"It says it's open seasonally, which has to mean now. And they open at ten. Shall we go there before tackling the next bedroom?" he asked.

Cath felt a shiver of awareness go through her at his tone. She wanted to turn and run away from the powerful attraction the man held for her. If she gave in, he'd only leave in a few days. Leave her with more regrets.

Could they have done things differently at some stage of their marriage?

She looked back at the decorations, many wrapped in tissue to protect them. A premonition shook her. She should not be going on any Christmas tree search with Jake. Either she wanted to end the marriage or not, and doing things together wasn't ending their relationship.

"I don't think so," she said.

"Why not?" he asked, closing the telephone book and putting it on the table.

He crossed to her and turned her slowly to face him. "It's only getting a tree, Cath, what can that hurt? It's not like it's going to change anything, is it?"

It would, but how to explain? He made it seem so innocuous, but she knew it could hold danger. To her recent decision. She remembered so many of the happy times together. There had not been enough of them. But in the end, Jake always left. And her heart broke a little with each departure. She needed to make this break clean, not linger, have second thoughts, or—

"Cath?"

She looked up, into once dear, familiar dark eyes. Eyes that seemed to see right down to the heart of her. Slowly Jake came closer. He leaned over her until his mouth touched hers, his lips warm and firm, pressing against hers.

For a heartbeat she was where she always longed to be. Then she remembered and pushed against him.

"No, Jake. Leave me alone." She broke away and stepped across the room.

"I don't want you staying here, you know that. But I can't force you to leave. I can insist on your keeping your distance from me, however. If you won't, then I will leave."

"And go where?"

"To Abby's. She invited me for Christmas, I'm sure she would be happy to have me visit."

And not Jake. The unspoken message was clear.

He held up his hands in surrender. "Fine. I'll keep my distance. You keep yours."

"What?" She blinked. She had done nothing.

"Just in case you get a case of the hots for me you can't control," he said audaciously.

Cath wished she were closer, she'd slug him one. He could be so annoying on occasion.

"I'm sure I can control myself," she said primly. Reaching for the diary, she turned and headed for her room. At least she could be alone there. She had a feeling delving into the past would be safer than dealing with the present.

"Wait," he called.

She paused, looking at him over her shoulder.

"What about tomorrow?"

"Get the tree yourself," she said.

She shut the door to her bedroom and went to climb into the bed. It was too early to go to sleep, but she could begin reading the old book. She was tired enough to relish lying down while she did it. Bending and reaching while cleaning had strained muscles beyond their normal use.

Cath covered herself with the top quilt, trying to ignore the fact Jake was downstairs going through Christmas decorations. This wasn't a real Christmas for them, just the last one they'd share together. How sad. Maybe she should spend it with him. He was alone, so was she.

But that would give him false hope. And she was firm in her decision to wrest back her life and put it on a different path.

She lifted the journal, snuggled down beneath the covers and opened the cover. The first words sent a chill through her.

Four days until Christmas. The handwriting was tiny,

but legible. Who had written it? Cath looked at the inside cover, but there was no name, no indication what year it was written. The person who wrote it knew who he or she was. The book probably had never been intended for anyone else to see.

Cath couldn't believe she was reading it four days before Christmas. How spooky was that?

I hate this war. At last I heard Jonathan is in North Carolina. Can he return home for Christmas? I pray so. He was at the battle at Kings Mountain, clear across the state. A great distance in the snow. I haven't heard from him since. I wish he'd send word. Or come home. Maybe he is on his way even as I write. I'd give anything for him to stride into our kitchen and say, 'Come here Tansy darlin' and give your husband a kiss'.

Was she talking about the Civil War? Cath tried to remember the battles of that war, but Gettysburg kept popping into mind. She'd have to look up Kings Mountain. She wished her memory of history was better.

Mrs. Talaiferro had her boy Ben bring me some butter this morning. He repaired that loose hinge on the hen house for me. I sent back some of the ham slaughtered from the hog a few weeks ago. Without neighbors helping out, I don't see how I could manage. Farming is really a man's job. Jonathan is so good at it. I hope he's home for the spring planting.

The nights are lonely. The days are so short and cold. I can scarcely go outside to gather eggs. My fingers were half frozen by the time I fed the hens and hogs. I hope Jonathan is warm. I sent him a new muffler I knitted, but haven't heard from him in so long, I don't know if he got it or not.

I miss my husband. Please, God, let this war end soon. Let the British be driven to the sea!

The British! Cath sat up at that. Was this diary from the time of the Revolutionary War? Who were Tansy and Jonathan? Early relatives of hers? They must be if her journal was in the cellar. As Aunt Sally had always said no one in the family seemed to throw anything away.

Eagerly Cath read more. The pages that followed related the loneliness Tansy felt with her husband absent. Cath wondered how old the writer had been, how long they'd been married. Why was there no other family mentioned? It appeared that Tansy lived alone. Would later pages reveal more? This was obviously not the first journal the woman had kept. Could she find the others? Coming to the end of the entry several pages later, Cath noted the next one started: *Three days until Christmas.*

Closing the book, Cath decided to read each day's entry as it matched her own countdown until Christmas. How odd to find the journal today—on the exact same day it was written. How could she find out about the Battle of Kings Mountain? That would give her an idea of what Christmas Tansy was writing about. Did Jonathan make it home in time for the holiday? She wanted to skip ahead, but refrained. It was tantalizing to have to wait until tomorrow to find out what happened next. But gave her something to look forward to.

She quickly got ready for bed and climbed back in. Drifting off to sleep a short time later, Cath was anxious to return to the cellar for the first time. She'd love to find out more about Tansy. To see if there were more journals, or a portrait or something. She bet her Aunt Sally could have told her about Tansy. If only she'd known about her earlier.

It was pitch-dark when Cath awoke. A nightmare frightened her awake. She lay in bed searching the blackness, feeling the tendrils of the horror reluctantly let her go.

She rolled to her side, eyes wide, straining to see something. The images of men on the battlefield wouldn't go completely away. Blown apart by guns and cannons, everyone had Jake's face.

She shuddered and pushed back the covers. She wanted to shake the fear that coursed through her at the nightmare. Jake was fine, sleeping down the hall. The old diary had sparked the dream—she knew that from the images of the men that had populated it—dressed as farmers and soldiers had so long ago. It was just a bad dream.

She pulled on a thick robe, found her slippers and headed for the kitchen. Some light, warm milk and semblance of normalcy were what she needed. Turning on the hall light, she descended the stairs and padded softly into the kitchen.

Flipping on that light, she was startled to discover Jake, sitting near the window, gazing out at the darkness. Beside him on the table was a bottle of scotch whiskey and a half empty glass.

He turned and looked at her, squinting slightly in the light.

"What are you doing up?" Cath asked. Glancing at the bottle, she raised her eyebrows in surprise. "Where did you get that?"

"Your aunt Sally had a stash." He raised the glass. "To Aunt Sally." Taking a hefty swallow, he carefully placed the glass beside the bottle.

"What time is it?" she asked, glancing at the kitchen clock. It was almost three o'clock in the morning!

"Why aren't you in bed?" she asked.

"Couldn't sleep. This homecoming isn't exactly what I was looking forward to, you know? Hell of a way to spend Christmas, get slapped in the face with a divorce demand." He turned away.

Cath stared at him. He stared out the window. What could he see in the dark?

"What are you doing up?" he asked a minute later.

"I had a nightmare. I thought some warm milk would help me go back to sleep. Want some?"

He laughed, but the sound held no humor. "No, this'll do me," he said, reaching for the glass again.

"I never knew you to be much of a drinker," Cath said, moving to the refrigerator to get the milk.

"Never had a need before. Trying to forget my sorrows," he mocked.

"Come on, Jake, don't be dramatic."

He slammed his hand down on the table and rose, turning to glare at her.

"Dramatic? Hell of a homecoming, Cath, to an empty condo and a cold note on the mantel. I drive like a maniac to get here and for what? An icy reception. This is not how I wanted to spend Christmas. I busted my butt getting here. You're talking about leaving me, giving me no chance to change things and blabbering on about finding another man when you're my wife! What do you expect me to do, just sit back and say have at it? Dammit, I'm not going to do that! You won't even go shopping for a blasted Christmas tree with me. What—do I have the plague or something? Cath, I love you. I married you because of that and nothing has changed!"

Cath stared at him, taken aback at his vehemence. She'd never seen Jake so angry, not even when talking about injustice in the world, which really riled him.

She looked at the whiskey bottle. Was that loosening his tongue? She'd wanted to understand how he felt about things. Maybe liquor was the way to go.

He followed her glance and picked up the bottle, holding it out for a moment, then took a healthy swig from it. "It's the only warm thing in the house right now," he said, setting the bottle back on the table.

Taken aback, Cath opened her mouth to defend herself. Then thought better of it. She tried to see things from his point of view. She'd been thinking of this separation all fall, had discussed it endlessly with Abby. But she'd only given him a vague clue in all her e-mails. Essentially he'd walked into the situation cold.

He'd expected Christmas at home, and she'd been gone.

Had he been as lonely as she during the months apart? Did he sometimes wish things would be different?

Guilt played on her. She should have told him in her letters which way she was thinking. Should have given him a chance to open a discussion before now. Cath tried to be fair, and if she were fair to Jake, she would ease up some. They were only together for another few days. She could be cordial during that time. They'd married thinking they'd be together forever. She'd known when she married him what his job was. Just because she couldn't cope wasn't a reason to condemn the man. The fault lay with her.

"Okay, I'll go get the tree with you," she said before she thought.

He looked at her, then at the bottle. "Gee, thanks a bunch for the mighty concession." He picked up the bottle and walked out of the room.

Cath stared at the place he'd stood, hearing the echo of his anger. Tears filled her eyes. She never thought he'd care. She thought she'd be the only one to mourn the ending of their marriage. But maybe she'd been wrong about Jake.

Turning to the stove, she blinked, trying to clear her vision. Once the milk heated, she added cinnamon and poured it into a mug. She left the pan soaking in the sink. Carefully carrying the mug of warmed milk, she turned off the lights behind her. She didn't hear anything from Jake's room. Her heart ached that he'd drink himself stupid because of her. It was so unlike the man. Or at least the man she thought she knew.

Going into her bedroom, she wondered what else she could have done. Written him sooner? But if he thought the letter on the mantel was cold, what would he have thought of an e-mail telling him they were through?

She could have discussed it with him—if he'd ever come home. Even today, when he'd tried to talk about it, she'd been stubbornly reticent—saying only she wanted it to end.

She slipped into bed and sipped her milk. She was feeling as melancholy as Tansy had sounded in her diary. She could relate to the loneliness Tansy wrote about. How many nights had she lain in bed wishing so hard that Jake was with her? How many days had she gone through the motions of living, always feeling a part of her was missing? Did Jonathan come back to Tansy? Did they have a long and happy life together? They were probably her great-great-great or more grandparents. She should find out about them before the end of the holiday.

As to what to do with the house, Cath was growing attached to it. She liked the location on the banks of the wide James River. She was in the country, yet only a short distance from Williamsburg, and not too far from the bigger cities of Norfolk and Richmond. It was a lovely, ideal setting in which to raise children.

A pang struck her. She'd so love to have a child with Jake, a little boy with his daddy's dark hair and eyes, or a small girl with Jake's determination and observation traits. But she didn't want to raise a child alone. She wanted its father actively involved. Home for school events, and soccer meets, to have the house filled with love and laughter. But it wasn't going to happen and she had to let go of those dreams and forge new ones.

She'd find a man to love. A man who wanted what she wanted, a home, a close-knit family that shared every aspect of living. And together they'd have a perfect future.

She just had to get through this holiday with Jake.

Chapter 4

The next morning was blustery. The wind blew the bare trees, snapping them back and forth at its whim. The sky was a steel-gray, clouds roiling along the path of the wind.

Cath gazed out the kitchen window. There were white-caps on the river. It looked cold and miserable. She didn't want to go out at all, much less to search for a tree. She set the coffee to brew and pulled down a box of her favorite cereal. She wasn't cooking breakfast this morning.

She filled her bowl and got the milk. A movement outside caught her eye and she leaned over the sink to see better. Jake was walking along the bank of the river, hands in his pockets, head bent against the wind. He stopped opposite the window and gazed out across the river for a long moment. She wondered what he was doing out there. Then she wondered if he were freezing. His jacket didn't seem heavy enough for the wind that was gusting.

For a long moment Cath watched Jake. He seemed frozen

in place. What was he thinking? Any regrets about their marriage? Or was he miles away at some newsworthy site, wondering how long before he'd be back in the field again?

When he turned and began walking toward the house, she darted away from the window. Pouring the milk on her cereal, she sat down just as he came in the back door. It would weaken her stance if he knew how much she longed to be with him. If he'd only agree to stay home, they could make the best future in the world. But that would mean changing almost everything about him, and Cath didn't see that happening.

"Morning," he said, closing the door behind him. It slammed when the wind snapped it from his hand.

"Good morning," Cath replied. "Coffee's ready and there's cereal for breakfast. What were you doing outside so early?" *Especially after your late night*, she wanted to add, but prudently didn't voice the thought.

"I wanted to see some of the river. Could you have a dock here? Maybe a small boat to take out on the water?"

"I guess. I never asked Aunt Sally. She was in her sixties when I first started coming during the summers. She had a neighbor a few doors down who had a boat, which they tied to a small dock. I used to go out in it a lot. We'd even swim from the dock in the hot weather. The river current isn't that strong."

"Nice house and yard. You have a lot of land around it."

"An acre, I think it is."

He poured himself a cup of coffee. Cath watched him as she ate. He didn't seem any the worse for wear after last night.

She was still a bit shaken from her nightmare, and from the poignant words from Tansy. Which reminded her.

"What do you know about a battle at Kings Mountain?" she asked.

"We won it," he said, getting a bowl and spoon. He snagged the box of cereal and filled his bowl. Sitting near Cath, he reached for the milk.

"When was it?"

He looked at her in puzzlement. "It was during the Revolutionary War. One of the battles that began changing the tide for the colonists. Can't remember exactly when it was, but I think it wasn't too long afterward that Washington met Cornwallis at Yorktown, maybe a year or so. So maybe 1780, around there."

"Imagine that," Cath said softly, amazed she had a journal from the 1700s.

"Why do you want to know about Kings Mountain?" he asked.

"It's mentioned in that diary I found yesterday. I want to see if I can find others. I didn't realize it was so old. The leather is still in good condition, the writing a bit faded, but it's not deteriorating like I'd think a book that old would."

"Probably not made like paper was later. If it's from the 1700s rags were the primary component, lasted much longer than the later wood-pulp paper. Are you still going with me to get that tree?"

"I don't know. It looks cold outside." She was having second thoughts, and thirds. Being with him and not hoping for a future was almost more than she could bear. She wanted him to storm in and say he loved her more than anything—even his job—and would never leave.

"It's cold and blustery and threatening to storm. We might have snow before night. But it feels good after the heat of the Middle East. Bundle up, you won't freeze," he said.

So much for a promise never to leave.

They ate in silence. Cath was afraid to disturb the quiet. She hadn't a clue what Jake was thinking. At the end of the holiday, would he quietly go back to work and let her get the divorce uncontested? Or would he argue against it for whatever reason, and then take off? The only thing she knew for certain, he would not be remaining long in Washington.

Glancing at the kitchen clock, she saw it was too early to go for the tree, yet she didn't want to get started on another room until after they got back. She knew how dirty she'd get.

"I sorted through some of the decorations last night," Jake said, rising to take his bowl to the sink. "I even tested the lights. Most work. We can get replacements at a store. You'll like the ornaments…your aunt had some unusual ones."

Cath looked out the window at the signs of the wind. She wasn't sure she wanted to go tree hunting in the best of times, and today's weather didn't qualify for best. Why had she agreed to go?

Promptly at ten they arrived at the tree farm. Despite it being so close to Christmas, they were not the only ones there, but the other two families had a half dozen children between them running around, exclaiming which tree was the biggest and begging their parents to buy it quick before someone else got it.

"Cut it yourself or we'll do it," the man by the gate said. He gestured to saws and small hatchets.

Jake looked at them and then at Cath.

"At the risk of proving totally inept, I say we try cutting it ourselves," he said.

"Don't look at me, I know nothing about being a lumberjack."

The man on the stool laughed. "Nothing to it, ma'am. Just cut near the ground, level so it'll set right in your stand. No need to be a lumberjack."

Jake laughed and took a small saw. He started down one row.

Cath followed slowly, watching the children. If they had had children earlier, their kids would be running around now, excited about getting a tree. What an exciting time holidays were with children. The boys and girls were having such fun running up and down the rows. She could just imagine that fun continuing after they chose their tree. They'd go home and each mother and father would encourage them to decorate it. Ornaments that were family heirlooms would be lovingly placed on the branches. Maybe each child would get a special ornament commemorating this Christmas. Tinsel would be hung—carefully by the mother, and thrown on by children. Laughter, hot chocolate, dreams would be shared. She wanted those happy days for herself. She wanted a family.

Jake was way ahead of her when she looked for him. She hurried down the aisle, thinking how bland the outing was with just the two of them.

When she caught up with him, she was startled by the happiness in his eyes.

"I measured the space in the living room and we can have a seven-foot tree. This starts the seven footers," he said, pointing to a tree a few inches taller than he was.

Cath hadn't even thought about that aspect.

"Did you see those kids?" she asked, looking back down where they were.

"Yeah, noisy, weren't they?"

"Jake! They're so excited about getting a tree. I can't wait until I have children to share days like this with them."

He looked away. When she glanced at him, the happiness had faded. Was that sadness she saw in his gaze? A reminder that if she had children, it would be with another man. She'd start a family without Jake.

The thought pierced like a knife. She couldn't imagine another man filling her heart like Jake had. Would there be anyone else for her? Or was she risking a long and lonely future by saying goodbye?

He didn't like the idea of her with someone else, yet he refused to do anything about them. He had his job, she wished him joy in it. Surely he could see there was no future for the two of them.

"This is a nice tree," she said, trying to get the expedition over with. It was safer back at the house. She wasn't trying to make things any more difficult than they were. But if he thought taking her to buy a tree would repair six years of neglect, he had to have rocks in his head.

"If that's the one you like, I'll cut it down."

She could be imagining the disappointment in his tone, but she wasn't sure. It wouldn't hurt to extend the expedition a little longer. "Oh, wait. Let's look at a couple more. Just to be sure."

They spent more than a few minutes looking at different trees. While the conifers had been trimmed to conform to a perfect shape, there were slight imperfections in each one.

Jake commented on some, Cath on others until they had been there almost an hour, and not settled on a tree.

"I'm freezing," she said. The earlier families had left. Another group had shown up. The tree farm seemed to be doing a good business for three days prior to Christmas.

"I wanted that last tree. Agree with me so we can cut it down and head for home," she said. "My fingers may have frostbite."

"It's not that cold. If that's the one you want, I'll settle for it."

"Settle? It's a gorgeous tree!"

"It has a gap near the bottom."

"Put that side next to the wall. I want that tree!"

"Fine, we'll take that one. We also need to stop at the store on the way home, to get the bulbs for the burned out lights. Do we need tinsel?" he reminded her.

Cath walked around her chosen tree slowly, examining it from top to bottom. There was one bare spot, but not a large one, it could be right next to the wall where no one would see it. The fragrance filled the air. It would be wonderful in Aunt Sally's old house.

Not that anyone would see the tree except Jake and her. They had no friends here, had not invited anyone to share the day with them. Still, she wanted it to look nice—in honor of using Aunt Sally's ornaments, she told herself. But mostly she wanted to get out of the cold.

"Glad that's settled," she said in mock frustration. She laughed, feeling joy rising at the thought of decorating it. Christmas had always been her favorite holiday. "Can you cut it?" she asked.

"I can try. Hold it steady as I cut through the trunk."

Jake knelt down and applied the saw. When the tree began to wobble, Cath grabbed hold and held on, trying to keep it upright. With a final swipe of the saw, the tree tumbled onto her, engulfing her completely in fragrant branches.

"Ohh, get it off me before we both fall," Cath called, giggling at the unexpected fun.

Jake pulled it away, and gently tipped it into the pathway. "Grab the top, I'll get the trunk and we'll carry it to the car."

"Will it fit on the car? It's huge!"

"We'll tie it on top. Hope it won't cover the windshield."

With the help of the lot owner, they tied the tree on the car. After paying him, Jake opened the passenger door for Cath.

"Next stop, that store we passed when we turned on Winston, then home," he said.

"I'll stay in the car to make sure no one steals our tree. It's a pretty one, isn't it?" she asked.

"Lovely," he said, but his eyes weren't on the tree, they were on her.

Cath caught her breath, almost swept away by the light in Jake's eyes.

She looked ahead, motioning him to close the door. "I'm cold, shut the door." She was not getting caught up in some romantic notion that getting a tree together changed anything. It was another memory to cherish. But it also signified the end of a relationship. Her heart ached with the thought of no more Christmases with Jake.

As he rounded the car, she saw another family walking to their car, all four children struggling to hold on to the large tree. The mother and father exchanged loving smiles.

Cath caught her breath and looked away. She needed to hold on to her dream, and ignore the temptation that called to her. She wanted her own family, not a man who spent most of his life halfway round the world!

It was early afternoon by the time they turned into the road that Aunt Sally's house was on. Jake was satisfied their outing had been a step in the right direction. Cath had been distant at the beginning, but warmed up to the fun of finding a tree as the morning went on. She'd been laughing at the end. He knew she'd mentioned clearing and cleaning another bedroom this afternoon, but he had a feeling she'd rather decorate their tree.

He'd bought some cider in the store and some Christmas cookies. They weren't homemade, but would do in a pinch.

As they pulled into the long driveway the cell phone in Cath's purse rang.

"Expecting someone?" he asked.

"No," she said, rummaging around in the purse and pulled out her phone.

"Hello?" Cath listened a moment, then gave him an odd look.

"I know, Abby. He's here now."

So her friend was calling to warn her. Interesting.

"The phone was in my purse, which I left on the kitchen counter. Unless I was in that room when you called, I wouldn't have heard it ring."

She was silent another moment.

"It's okay," she said slowly.

Jake would bet Abby asked how things were going between them. Jake squelched the urge to reach for the phone and tell Abby to mind her own business. He and Cath would work things out. But Cath was acting more emotional than usual and he had to walk warily around her. Alienating her by being rude wouldn't help.

Jake slowly got out of the car. He could stay and listen to one half of the conversation, or get going on unloading the tree and enticing Cath to forget cleaning the old house and concentrate on decorating it instead.

Though if she insisted on cleaning this afternoon, he'd suggest the room he was using. She had done nothing to make him feel welcomed. His room wasn't dusted or aired. He'd just collapsed on the bed both last night and the first night and made do with the covers that were there. He'd slept in worse, so hadn't complained, but a bit of the welcome he had hoped to find upon returning home would have helped.

"Want to help me take the tree inside?" he asked, peering back into the car.

Cath turned, frowning when she saw him. "Oh. Sure. I'm going to have to go, Abby. I'll call you later." He could almost feel the dismay when she realized he was still there. Tough.

Angrily he turned and began to untie the tree. Cath had enjoyed the morning. He knew she had. Now the phone call brought back her intent with a vengeance. Time was fleeting. It was already three days until Christmas. If he didn't make some progress soon, she'd be returning to Washington before he knew it and to the divorce she wanted so passionately.

He had to find a way to turn that passion toward their marriage.

Dragging the tree off the car, he waited for her to get the light end and they carried it to the front of the house.

"Lean it against the railing. I'll get something to make a stand," he said.

"Try the carriage house. Aunt Sally had tools and other things there. Maybe some scrap wood," she said. "I'll get the things from the car." Gone was the excitement she'd displayed when finding the tree. Now it was back to the business of ending a marriage.

Jake headed for the carriage house in the rear, wishing Abby hadn't called. A man could only stand so much. He needed time to get his emotions under control. It wouldn't pay to make himself look like a fool by railing at Cath. He had time and a hope from the response she'd given when he kissed her. She wasn't immune to him, or out of love, despite what she was saying. She couldn't be.

The carriage house hadn't been used for horses in decades. It had served as Aunt Sally's garage and catch-all—what the cellar didn't hold looked like it was out here. There was a workbench of sorts along one wall. In the back was an old carriage, rotten wheels and all. The cleared space on the right had held Sally's car until she'd given up driving several years prior to her death.

Jake rummaged around the area and found some loose wooden boards. Taking the hammer and some nails from the workbench, he banged together a makeshift stand and headed back to the tree.

His optimism restored, Jake set to work. He liked challenges. He had to get through to Cath. One way or another, he would do it or die trying.

Cath was feeling oddly flustered. She hadn't expected to enjoy getting the tree, but the outing had ended up being fun. And she loved the tree they'd selected. Her arms were full of the packages from the store, more lights, tinsel and a star for the top. The tree itself was thick and full, and smelled so divine it would keep the house fragrant for days.

They could use Aunt Sally's decorations and make it beautiful. But for a moment, she wanted to flee to a dirty bedroom and plunge into cleaning. It was safer than making Christmas memories with Jake.

She looked at the old house. How many Christmases had it known? Had Aunt Sally decorated it each year, or being alone, had only the minimum ornaments displayed to mark the occasion?

She couldn't believe she never inquired after her aunt's practices. She'd invited her to spend the holidays with them more than once, but Aunt Sally had always said she liked to be in her own home at Christmas.

For a moment, Cath wondered if she should decorate. She loved classroom decorations with all the children participating, chaotic, frenzied though it was. She looked forward to it every year. And to helping Abby decorate her home with her two children. Cath loved decorating their condo, too, though it was only seen by herself and a few friends. Always, every year, she hoped Jake would make it home for the holiday. If she moved here, she'd want all the trappings of family and home. Maybe she should make this year a practice run. Next Christmas she'd know what else to plan on. Maybe outlining the old house in outside lights.

Jake came around the side of the house, boards and hammer in hand.

"Do you know what you're doing?" she asked. She didn't believe she'd ever seen Jake with a hammer in hand.

"I did this as a kid," he said.

She was surprised. Jake rarely talked about his past. His father had died when he'd been nine and his mother had remarried to a man who hadn't liked Jake. She knew he'd been an unhappy teenager who had had to live in a family with new babies and happiness all around—except for him.

"I think this will hold," he said a few moments later. He righted the tree and stepped back. It remained standing, tall and straight.

He looked over at the front door. "Open that and we'll take the tree in that way. I need your help to keep the branches from dragging."

Cath went through the kitchen, dropping her packages, and continued on to the front door. She flung it wide and went to help Jake with the tree.

In only a few moments they had it situated between the

two front windows. The fragrance of pine filled the room. Cath thought the place felt warmer just by having the tree. Maybe they could find some logs and have a fire. She'd love an old-fashioned Christmas. Maybe it would even snow as Jake had predicted.

She watched Jake as he turned the tree slightly, hiding the bare spot. What was she going to do with him for the next few days? Surely he'd get bored and head for more exciting places before Christmas. She fully expected him to leave at the first sign of any breaking news.

"I'm going to fix lunch," Cath said. She was torn with the desire to decorate and the need to put distance between herself and Jake.

As she walked down the hall, she heard Jake's cell phone ring. So it happened earlier than she thought.

She took her time making sandwiches. There was nothing she wanted to prepare for dinner. Maybe she'd go out. She could head for Williamsburg, find a place to eat and then wander around the shops that were decorated for the holidays.

Jake came in just as she began to eat. His plate with a sandwich and some chips was at his place.

"Thanks," he said, taking the chair. He ate two bites before looking at her.

"We can put on the lights and ornaments this afternoon."

She shrugged. "I need to get the rooms cleaned, if I want to stay on schedule."

"Hire a service," he said. "It's a holiday, take some time off."

"It's not just the cleaning, I'm trying to assess what to do with everything—the furniture and knickknacks."

He ate in silence for a few minutes.

"Was that your office that called?" she asked, unable to resist.

He nodded.

"A new assignment?"

"No."

If he thought she was going to play twenty questions, he didn't know her. But curiosity burned. Who had called?

"Tell you what," Jake said. "Let's clean Aunt Sally's old room, then after dinner, we'll build a fire in the fireplace and decorate the tree. Tomorrow we'll decorate the rest of the house if you like."

She looked at him suspiciously. How had he known she wanted a fire in the fireplace?

"Maybe."

"For heaven's sake, Cath. Stop blowing hot and cold. Let's agree to spend this Christmas together in harmony. We can make decisions about the future before the New Year, but let's take the next few days for ourselves."

She grudgingly admitted to herself she would have been shocked if Jake had just up and told her out of the clear blue that he wanted to end their marriage. Maybe she needed to give him time to get used to the idea without sniping at each other. It wasn't as if she no longer cared about the man. That was the problem. She was beginning to think she would never get over Jake Morgan.

"I'm not blowing hot and cold. I'll agree to spend the few days until Christmas in harmony. But no talking about the future, one way or the other. And no trying to get me to change my mind," she said, wondering what she'd do if she never did find someone else to love. She'd end up an old lady living in a big house all alone like her great-aunt.

"Fine. Tell me about your work," he said.

"What?"

"You pointed out I don't know a lot about where you work, or your co-workers, except for Abby. So tell me."

Cath thought about it for a moment, then nodded and began to tell him about a typical day, mentioning her children—the sweet ones and the troublemakers. She talked about how excited she was each year to be encouraging a new group of students to do their best, to learn what they could and to establish good study habits.

He listened without interruption, watching her as she talked, his eyes narrowed as if assessing all she said.

She didn't care, she loved sharing that part of her life with him. She had all along but he had never seemed interested before. She loved working as a teacher, and was happy she got to see her students for another few years after her class before they went on to other schools.

"What about the other teachers?" he asked at one point. She had refilled their beverage glasses, the sandwiches long gone.

"Except for Abby, I don't interact all that much with the other teachers—not away from school. I do share yard duty with Brent Mulphy and Stella Hawkins. We keep an eye on the students when they take recess. Of course, Abby and I have been friends for years."

"No trouble with parents?"

"One or two each term, but nothing I can't handle."

He shook his head. "A room full of eight-year-olds, sounds more intimidating than front-line firing to me."

She smiled. "I love children. And that's the best age, in my opinion. They can read, they've started doing more complicated math than just addition and subtraction, and they aren't in their snotty stage of life."

"Ever think of moving into administration?"

She shook her head. "I love teaching. And I'm good at

it. That's why I think I could get a job down here without too much trouble."

He pushed his plate away. "You're serious about moving here?"

"I'm seriously thinking about it," she said carefully.

His cell rang again. He fished it out of his jeans pocket, checked the caller and frowned. "I need to take this."

Cath rose and gathered their dishes as Jake headed for the front of the house. She rinsed, dried and put away the plates, and headed upstairs. She wanted to keep to her timetable on clearing the house, but when she stood in Aunt Sally's old bedroom, she paused. Jake's duffel was on the floor, opened, a few items of clothing spilling out. His laptop was closed, sitting on top of the dresser. She never understood how the thing stood up to the casual abuse he gave it. Stuffing it in a duffel, under his arm, or in a backpack didn't seem her idea of ways to handle a sensitive piece of equipment like that. But it seemed to work fine instead of being totally wrecked with his usage.

Looking at the old furnishings in the large room, including the tall secretary with books behind the glass doors, Cath thought about the journal she found. Would there be others in Aunt Sally's bookcase? Or in other boxes in the cellar? She hadn't read but one entry and was anxious to know more about Tansy and Jonathan. Maybe Jake would let her use his laptop to research historical sites so she could see what she could find out about the battle at Kings Mountain.

"Ready to work?" he asked, joining her before she knew it. She had been woolgathering if she missed hearing him climb the stairs.

"This is the largest of the bedrooms. Maybe I should wait and do it last," she said, feeling daunted by the task.

"I wouldn't mind a clean room to sleep in."

Another pang of guilt with the cavalier way she'd treated him. He deserved better.

"You're right. There are clean sheets in the cupboard. They might be a bit musty, but that's all there is. Let's get going."

The afternoon went fast as they developed a working relationship that melded their different abilities. Jake brought down the old curtains and hauled them away. He moved the furniture for Cath to clean behind and beneath, then pushed them back.

Since she'd already donated all of Aunt Sally's clothing last summer, there was little in the room beyond the furnishings. All knickknacks were confined to the large secretary desk, along with several shelves of books.

"You'll need to check to see if any of these are worth anything," he said, opening the double glass doors and reaching for a couple of books, leafing through the volumes.

"The lawyers did an appraisal for inheritance taxes. No first editions or anything," she murmured, scanning the spines of the books. One looked like a journal. She pulled it from the second shelf and opened it. It was, but written by Aunt Sally herself, many years previously. Cath would like to read it, but right now her focus was on finding out more about the lonely woman whose writings she'd found yesterday.

It was dark outside by the time they finished the room. They made the bed, and Cath tried not to think about their large king-size bed at home. It had seemed too large for one person whenever Jake was gone from home. Cath had even thought about using their guest room, but she felt close to him in their bed, so never moved out of the room.

Jake put his duffel on a chair when she mopped the hardwood floor. A good coat of wax would go a long way to making the floor look good. She surveyed the room when finished. Almost all traces of Aunt Sally had disappeared. Jake's things now dominated. She turned, not liking the yearning that seemed to rise every time she looked at Jake.

Cath was tired, and not in the mood to get dressed enough to go out once she showered. Soup and sandwiches again, it looked like. Jake might count himself lucky to be getting out of a marriage if that's all she fed him.

"How about we order pizza?" Jake suggested as he prepared to haul the last of the rags and trash downstairs. "Saves us going out, or either of us cooking. Go take your shower and I'll call in the order. It'll probably be here by the time you're through and I grab a quick shower."

If she let herself think about it, it would seem just like being married. Which of course they were, but they had so little experience in acting like a married couple. They ate out a lot when Jake was home. He claimed he didn't want her to have to spend time in the kitchen when she could be with him. But he sometimes joined her in preparing meals. He had on several occasions, and she almost smiled at the memories. So much of their marriage had been spent apart. But there was nothing to complain about when they'd been together.

"That sounds good," she said, glad not to even have to heat soup.

Cath quickly showered and changed into comfortable slacks, a warm sweater and house slippers. She passed Jake on the stairs when she headed down. He held out his wallet.

"Pay the guy if he shows up before I get out."

She took it, still warm from his body. The leather was soft and supple. It was stuffed with money, credit cards and his driver's license. She flipped it open. Facing her was an annual school photo teachers got each year. She'd given him this one several years ago. She hadn't known he kept it in his wallet. It made her feel funny. Hadn't he said thinking of her kept him going sometimes? Did he pull out the wallet and look at the photo often?

She felt sad at the thought of him thousands of miles away and as lonely as she was. Where had they gone wrong? Could anything be fixed?

unusual place to raise one, especially here in this chilly
climate. Several pieces of the pie were gone from the plate.
He smiled drowsily, as if well fed. Claim the ace, Red King,
Queen Lady, Jack, in center. He picked up the entire
and laid it on the plate quietly, as if gathering the cards.
She had no idea of much of him, no notion of what
comment to suggest she was, or that his new task would
make her think in bad?

Chapter 5

As soon as they finished the pizza, Cath pleaded tired-
ness and escaped to her room. She wasn't as tired as she
said, just unable to face an evening with Jake, trying to
keep her distance when half the time she yearned to feel
his strong arms around her, wanted to hear the steady beat
of his heart beneath her ear. She wasn't in the mood to decorate a tree. Being with him was an exercise in trying to
ignore her rising awareness. She wished she knew more
about what he'd been doing since she'd seen him last. How
much danger he'd been in, did he get enough to eat? What
did he do for recreation?

But to ask would give rise to his thinking she was mel-
lowing and maybe even reconsidering her decision. She
didn't plan to give any false or overly optimistic messages.
Her decision had been hard fought, and she couldn't allow
emotions to cloud the issue.

She took the journal and pulled the afghan from the bed,

going to the chair near the window. It was a bit drafty, but the wool afghan would keep her warm. The light on the small table gave a softness to the room that enabled Cath to imagine how it had looked in the days before electricity, when candles and oil lamps had been the means of illumination.

The entry began:

Three days until Christmas. It began to snow today. I worry about Jonathan getting through the drifts. His horse is old, if still alive. He talked about fighting on foot in the last letter I received from him. If it snows, do they cease fighting? He made no mention of the warm muffler I sent in that hastily scribbled missive. Had he not received it? I sent it with Master Jerome who was riding to rejoin the regiment. I fear Jonathan will get a chill and pray he doesn't get sick. I wish he would come home for Christmas. He said he would try.

I'm so lonely with him gone. I miss him so. Maybe if I had babes to care for my mind would not dwell on my husband. But our marriage is young and I don't like the days slipping away without him here.

I worry about him. Would that I could go where he goes, keeping some kind of accommodation for him to make sure he eats properly and stays warm and dry. It is probably very shocking of me, but I miss lying in his arms at night. I felt so safe and cherished with him holding me close. It's this horrible war that is making things so difficult. When will it end?

Cath gazed off into space, feeling warm and safe in the room, despite the slight draft. She could empathize with the

longing and worry of the long-ago Tansy. Hadn't she lain in
bed at night worrying about Jake, wondering if he were all
right? How long after he was injured or killed would it have
been before she heard anything? Unlike the Revolutionary
War days, communications were much faster now. Still, in
war zones, or disaster areas, difficulties cropped up making
communications impossible. She'd been kept awake long
into the night many times, worrying about hearing from
him. Imagining him dying far from home, and far from her.

She shivered. He was safe. Maybe he was one of those in-
dividuals blessed through danger. He thrived on it. It scared
her to death when she learned of some of the situations he'd
come through unscathed. How long could his luck hold?

Maybe she should have thoughts like Tansy, going with
Jake, to make sure he ate right. He was too thin, she'd noticed that on the first night. And she wasn't doing much to
help him gain back that weight. Soup and sandwiches and
pizza weren't a substitute for good nutrition.

Feeling restless, Cath laid down the journal and pushed
aside the afghan. She rose and went to the stairs. The light
was on in the living room. Slowly she descended and
walked quietly to the door of the front room.

Jake was winding lights around the tree. The bottom
third of the tree had been encircled, he was now working on
the upper branches. He had all the lights on, and the sparkling spots of color shimmered in the tears that filled her
eyes.

Alone. It seemed so sad to decorate a Christmas tree
alone. She had not done it in recent years, preferring to
spend the day with her friend Abby and her family. At the
condo, she'd had lots of other decorations, but not a tree.

Watching Jake, her heart felt a tug of sadness. He'd
come home expecting to celebrate the holidays with her

and she'd been gone. According to him, he'd done extraordinary things to get this time and she had shoved it back in his face. He had nowhere else to go, except back to the dangerous places that made news. He and his family had been estranged for years. He'd never returned home after leaving for college.

She blamed his mother for her total switch of allegiance when she remarried. How sad for her son. She would never understand how the woman could ignore her firstborn child. Granted her other children needed her love as well, but to turn from her first was inconceivable to Cath.

Maybe their own marriage wasn't going to last. But she could be kind enough, generous enough to offer him one happy last holiday together.

"Jake?"

He looked over at her. "I thought you went to bed."

"No, I wanted to rest for a little while. I was reading. Why didn't you wait until tomorrow? We could have done this together."

"Really? I got the feeling you didn't want anything to do with me," he said, turning back to the tree. "If I wanted to see it decorated, I had to do it myself."

She stepped into the room.

"I haven't had a tree since the one we got together on our second Christmas," she said slowly. The ornaments they'd brought up from the cellar had been put on the coffee table, the lids of the boxes off so each one could easily be seen. There were globes and spirals, fancy ones and plain. Each held a memory for her great-aunt, lost now to the ages.

"I can help," she said lowly.

He glanced over and shook his head. "Not if it's a chore, Cath. I don't know a lot about holidays, usually working right through them as if they were any other day, but I do know they should be celebrated. Doing it as an obligation doesn't work."

"Christmas used to be my favorite holiday," she said, lifting a shiny ornament and studying it. She remembered the days her parents had made so special for her. Lots of presents, big ham dinner with biscuits, sweet potatoes and of course plum pudding. Her mouth watered for some of that dessert, usually made months before the holidays and brought out as a special treat.

"As I said, usually just another day for me," Jake said.

"What about when you were a child? It had to be special then."

She watched as his expression turned bleak. She wished she hadn't brought it up.

"Maybe when I was young. But it all changed after my dad died."

She knew some of the story, how his mother's new family became more important than her first child. How her step-father and he had never gotten along, and his mother always sided with the man. Jake had earned a scholarship for college and left home, never to return.

Cath had wished for brothers and sisters as she'd grown up, but when she'd learned of Jake's family life, she'd been glad to be spared that. How awful not to feel loved and cherished, as her family made her feel.

As Jake had made her feel in the early days of their marriage.

As he still could.

"What?" he said, catching her gaze.

"I was remembering," she said softly. "We started out so great, why did it go wrong?"

"I don't think anything went wrong," he said.

She snapped out of her mood. "Well, it did." She turned

and searched the box for a hook for the ornament. "When you get the lights on, I'll start with the ornaments," she said, looking for the box of hooks they'd bought earlier. She'd get the ornaments ready to hang. It would give her something to do, besides being melancholy about Tansy and her Jonathan being separated so long, or her and Jake's situation.

For several awkward moments they continued working. Cath's nerves stretched thin. She moved around the boxes until Jake was behind her and she couldn't see him, hoping it would calm the rampaging awareness that had her as antsy as a cat in a room full of rocking chairs. She could still hear him moving, hear the soft swish of the branches as he fastened the lights.

"We need Christmas carols," she said at last, almost about to explode. She looked around the room, but saw nothing that looked like a radio or CD player.

"I think there're some records in the room off the dining room," Jake said.

"Records?"

"I take it your aunt was a bit old-fashioned," he said. "Though I wouldn't have expected it."

Jake had met Aunt Sally at their wedding where she and he had hit it off. Cath and Jake had spent a long weekend with Aunt Sally that first year. He hadn't been able to come to visit after that—work.

She left the room, not wanting to think about the past. Or the present. What she should focus on was the future. The glorious future when she'd have lots of family around her at holidays and not feel sad and lonely.

She found the record player and a cabinet full of albums. Skimming through them quickly, she found several Christmas carol albums bunched together. In less than ten minutes, she had the record player hooked up in the living room and the sound of carols filled the room.

"I thought everyone had CDs now," she commented, resuming her task of putting hooks on ornaments. She had worked through two boxes and was starting on the third.

"What else goes on before the ornaments?" Jake asked, looking at the tree.

"The garland. That silvery thing."

"I know what a garland is," he said, lifting it from one box.

When the record player changed, the song "Silver Bells" began. Jake looked at her, and then stepped over, sweeping her into his arms.

"What are you doing?" she asked, startled.

"Dancing," he said, moving them around the large living room.

Cath laughed. "It's hardly dance music."

"Sure it is, we're dancing, aren't we?" He danced with an ease that belied his years in rough places. It was as if he did it all the time.

Cath started to protest, the words dying on her lips. This was fun. She loved to dance and had done so little over the length of their marriage. Giving herself up to the moment, she swayed with the music, following Jake's lead, imagining them at a huge Christmas ball. She'd be wearing a sexy red dress—for the season, and for sex appeal. Jake would be in a dark suit, or even a tux. She knew he looked fabulous in a tux; he'd worn one to their wedding.

They'd dance the night away.

When the song ended, the next one was definitely not one to dance to. Slowly they came to a halt.

She looked up into his face, still caught up by the magic of the moment. "Thank you," she said.

"Thank you," he replied, and kissed her.

Still held in his arms, Cath didn't have to move an inch. She let herself continue in the magic, kissing him back, reveling in the sensations so long missing from her life. His body was strong against hers, his muscles a complement to her softer curves. She'd always felt special with Jake—that hadn't changed. The old memories and affection swelled and she let the future fade for a moment. Capturing the present was as good as it got.

Jake ended the kiss slowly. He wanted to carry his wife up the stairs and make love to her all night long. But he hesitated. She'd been as much a participant in the kiss as he had been. Her breathing attested to the fact. He didn't want to spook her. He wasn't going to settle for one night. And if he pushed the issue, he knew she could kick him out and refuse to see him again.

She opened her eyes and looked at him. The temptation to sweep her up was almost more than he could resist. She looked beautiful.

"I bought cider and Christmas cookies today. Want some?" he asked, hoping she wouldn't comment on the fact they shouldn't be kissing if they were getting a divorce. He wasn't sure he could handle that discussion tonight.

"Sure. Want the cider warmed?"

"Of course."

They went into the kitchen, just like old married folks, he thought wryly. Which in a way they were. But this was only their second Christmas together. How had he let work keep him away?

He opened the package of cookies while Cath heated the cider. Sitting at the table, he watched her, wishing so many things had been different. Knowing the future wasn't going to go like he wanted and helpless to change anything.

He should be used to it. Life had not gone the way he'd expected since his father died so long ago.

"Tomorrow I have to get back to my schedule," she said.

"Cleaning another room?"

"Yes. One way or another, I want this place ready for whatever I decide by the time I leave at New Year's."

"Are you serious about moving here?" he asked. Another drawback. He couldn't see living in this old house, surrounded by old families who'd lived here for generations, several miles from Williamsburg. It would take an hour or longer to get to Richmond or Norfolk, and neither city was exactly the hub of the world.

"I'm still thinking about it. It's a great place to live and would be wonderful for children."

He bit a savage bite from the cookie. "There's a lot more in life than children," he said.

She looked at him and shrugged. "Jake, let's not fight over anything. Let's enjoy this Christmas. For all the things that might have been, let's give ourselves a terrific memory to last all our lives."

"Why?"

"Why not?"

He studied her for a moment. "Why the change of heart? Yesterday you ordered me out."

She licked her lips. "I was thinking we don't have a lot of memories since we haven't spent a lot of time together. Don't you think one day you'll regret not having a family, not spending time with that family? Careers are fine but are not supposed to be so consuming people don't have time for other things."

He didn't look ahead that far. One day he'd be too old to investigate the news in foreign locales. Maybe too old to work at all. What would he do then? Thinking back to the past didn't figure in his plans. But if he was alone, wouldn't it be something to have one special memory of the girl he'd loved enough to marry six years ago? He'd failed her, he knew. But that was something else he couldn't change. Maybe Cath was right, take the gift of a perfect Christmas and treasure the memory all the rest of his life.

He wasn't willing to concede he'd be alone. There had to be some way he could reach her, show her they belonged together. Convince her to stay with him.

If they had the best Christmas ever, wouldn't that sway Cath they were good together? Make her see they shouldn't throw away what they had on a nebulous future which might not include that huge family she was always talking about.

"We can give it a try," he said, already coming up with ideas to change his wife's mind and keep their marriage intact. Wasn't Christmas the time of miracles? He'd need one to keep Cath, and he was way overdue to receive a miracle.

She poured the cider into mugs and went to sit at the table, handing Jake one.

"I forgot to ask you earlier if you'd check on the battle of Kings Mountain for me. I saw mention of it in the journal I'm reading."

"Know who wrote it?"

"Tansy. Her husband was Jonathan. I'm guessing Williamson, since Aunt Sally said that her family had owned the house since it was built. She never married. I guess it came down through the sons, but don't really know. You'd think I'd know more about my family history."

"Most people don't know much beyond the relatives they actually knew. We can look it up on the internet if you like. I brought my laptop."

"Naturally," she said dryly. Then wrinkled her nose.

"That was tacky. Of course you'd have your laptop. Thanks for the offer. Aunt Sally didn't have a computer and I'd hate to wait until I return home. I want to know about the war. And if Jonathan came home."

"Doesn't the journal say?" he asked.

"I'm reading a day at a time. She wrote several pages each day." Cath toyed with her mug for a moment, darting another glance at Jake.

"In a way, I'm seeing some of myself in her journal. She's home alone—here I guess—and missing her husband. It must have been hard to be a woman back then with her husband gone. She mentions neighbors helping out with some of the farm chores. I think Jonathan had been gone for months."

"Some men were gone years. Some went to fight except when they had to return home for harvest. It was a rag-tag army at best."

"She was so lonely. I wish I knew how old she was. Sounds like she and Jonathan hadn't been married that long."

"Maybe there're other journals."

"I hope so. I wanted to look in the trunk again. Maybe I missed another one. It was mostly full of clothes, so another journal could have slid down."

"We can look tomorrow."

"What about cleaning?"

"How long will it take to look through a few boxes to see if there are other journals? You remember where the trunk was?"

She nodded. Right by that old cradle. Had it been Tansy and Jonathan's?

"Then look in nearby boxes. Chances are stuff is stored

by age. There sure doesn't seem to be any other method to the storage."

"Mmm." Cath sipped her cider, wondering about Tansy and the past and how closely she felt tied to the woman. Was history repeating itself with a slight twist? Jake wasn't going to war to fight, but he was away for long periods of time, and usually reporting on armed conflicts.

"I'm tired. I'm going up to bed for good now," she said, rising a little later.

He followed her to the foot of the stairs.

"I'm glad you came back down to decorate the tree," he said.

"Me, too. It's pretty, isn't it?" she asked, looking at it through the archway. It sparkled and shimmered with lights and ornaments.

"We didn't get any tinsel on it," she said.

"It doesn't need it. Good night, Cath."

He kissed her briefly and headed to the living room. He'd clean up the boxes and other clutter and then head for bed. Tomorrow he'd begin his campaign.

Cath awoke with a feeling of anticipation. She and Jake had reached a truce last night. They'd enjoy each other's company for the next couple of days, and then separate. It would be nice to have someone to share the holidays with. And with this new truce, there'd be no pushing to change her decision.

She frowned. At least she hoped so. The kisses he'd given her last night didn't seem as platonic as they could be. But he'd been away for a long time. What was a kiss or two between friends?

Could they be friends? She tried to picture them meeting

for dinner or something each time he returned to the States. She could not picture them reminiscing together.

There was too much between them, including that flare of attraction and awareness that rose every time he came near her. Just lying in her bed she felt fluttery merely thinking about Jake. God she wished things were different and that he'd be home for her every night!

Pushing aside her confused thoughts, she rose and quickly dressed. Despite the heater, it was still cold in the bedrooms. One glance out the window showed a storm was brewing. The intermittent sunshine of yesterday was gone. Gray skies made the day seem dreary. There would probably be rain by afternoon, she thought.

Wearing old jeans and a sweatshirt, she went downstairs. The house was silent. The Christmas tree lights had been turned on, sparkling in the pale morning light. Jake was already up.

But when she went into the kitchen, he wasn't there. The coffee was warm on the stove. The box of Christmas cookies was on the table. Had that been his breakfast? She looked out the window to see if he was on one of his walks and spotted him near the river. He seemed to like walking along the bank. It must be so peaceful and serene after the places he'd visited.

Still, wasn't he cold? The branches on the trees swayed in the wind. She looked at the sky again, ominous in its grayness. Would it snow? She wished she had a radio to keep up with the weather forecasts. Aunt Sally hadn't had a radio, only an old television set that was on its last legs the last time Cath visited. She hadn't seen a new one since she'd been here. The old one was in Aunt Sally's bedroom—not a place she was going with Jake ensconced there.

Pouring herself a cup of coffee, she watched Jake. He stood near the edge of the bank, a short drop to the river. She almost called out to be careful. What if he slipped or tripped and fell into the icy river?

Then she almost laughed. How foolish. The man practically lived in danger zones. What was a riverbank?

He turned and walked with his head bent, pausing and then stooping down. She could not see what he was doing, but watched until he stood. He glanced at the house. Could he see her at the window?

Cath turned quickly and went to the refrigerator to pull out some eggs. She'd prepare a big breakfast, mainly for him, and then get ready to plunge into the cleaning she had scheduled.

By midmorning, Jake had received two calls, each pulling him away from the tasks at hand. They'd started on the room across from the one he was using as soon as breakfast was finished. They worked well together and the task went quickly, despite the interruptions.

"Another room?" Jake asked as they left that one, cleaning supplies in hand.

"Not today. After I shower and fix lunch, I want to use the laptop to see what I can find out about the war. Maybe even find mention of Jonathan. I suppose his last name was Williamson. But it could have been a different one that many generations ago."

"I have a couple of calls to make this afternoon, so you can be searching for your long-lost kin while I work."

She bit her lip. Was this when he'd get a new assignment and be off? Would he leave before Christmas? It was two days away. Even if something was happening that needed reporting, surely Jake could stay for two more days. Let someone else cover the news.

When had she gone from wishing him not there to hoping he'd stay another two days?

Chapter 6

Cath settled in the living room with Jake's laptop. The lights still shone from the tree. Looking out the window, she was surprised to see light snowflakes drifting down. She'd known a storm was brewing, but hadn't expected snow. So it might be a white Christmas, she mused.

She spent the next couple of hours researching the War for Independence, noting major Southern battles, searching for Jonathan Williamson. There was no record of a soldier by that name that she found, but she was fascinated about the accounts of the different skirmishes.

"Find anything?" Jake asked, standing in the doorway. He'd been on the phone the entire time. She'd heard the murmur of his voice coming from the kitchen.

"Lots of information, nothing on a Jonathan Williamson from Virginia. Are you finished your calls?"

"For the time being."

"No major story needing your reporting?" she asked,

stretching out her legs. She was feeling a bit stiff from sitting for two hours in front of the computer after all the bending she'd done while cleaning.

"No." He walked over to one of the front windows and looked out. "It's snowing heavier now than before," he said.

She put the computer on the table and rose to join him. Several inches of snow blanketed the yard and trees. She shivered, not really cold, but feeling the chill from the air near the glass.

"You have the only television in your room," she said. "Check the news to see what to expect."

"Or look it up on the internet," he said.

She complied and found the forecast more severe than she'd expected. "It says we could have more than a foot of snow. And the cold weather is due to continue through the week, so it's not going to melt anytime soon."

"Do we need to go anywhere?"

Cath shook her head, staring at the five-day forecast on the computer. She'd bought enough food to last a week or longer. She had made sure she bought all she needed for a nice Christmas dinner. It wouldn't be a hardship to remain inside.

"I wish we had some wood for a fire," she said wistfully, shutting down the computer.

"There's some stacked beside the barn."

"Carriage house," she corrected absently. "Is there? Do you suppose it'll burn?"

"It's been there at least since last summer, probably longer. It'll be nice and dry. I'll bring some in."

"I'll help."

They bundled up and went out into the snow. Cath lifted her head to the falling flakes, delighting in the feel of them landing on her cheeks. She laughed and spun around.

"This is so much fun. Usually I hate having it snow, because I have to go to work and know the streets are going to be treacherous. But this is different. No responsibilities until January. It can snow all week!"

He watched her with a brooding gaze. "If it snowed all week, we'd have ten feet of snow to plow through at the end."

"You know what I mean. Isn't this fun?"

"It beats the dry heat of the Middle East," he said. "Come on, the wood is on the far side."

They brought in several armfuls of split logs, stacking them near the large fireplace. Then Jake found a tarp in the carriage house and covered the rest of the pile so it wouldn't get wet with the snow.

"Isn't that a little late?" Cath asked, watching him. "There's already snow sticking."

"But it's not much and we may end up needing this for heat if something happens to the power. This will keep any more snow from accumulating directly on the wood."

"Want to walk along the river?" Cath asked, not ready to go back inside. She'd seen him several times along the bank of the river. What was the appeal? In the muted light, the water looked gray and cold as it silently flowed on its way to the sea.

"Until our feet get cold," he said.

"We should have brought boots."

"I wasn't expecting to come at all," he reminded her. Taking her hand in his, he gestured upstream. "Let's go this way, I haven't explored this direction."

The snow made walking treacherous. They stayed well away from the riverbank, slipping and skidding from time to time as they trudged along in the quiet of the afternoon. Soon they passed another house, lights blazing from the downstairs windows, necessary with the storm darkening the sky.

"Do you know who lives there?" Jake asked.

"Mrs. Watson. She was one of Aunt Sally's favorite friends, though she was younger by a decade or more. When I visited, she'd often have us over for dinner. Other than Mrs. Watson and the McDonalds, Aunt Sally devoted herself to me and didn't visit with her friends or neighbors while I was staying with her. The McDonalds were the family on the other side who had the boat I used."

The next house they walked behind was dark. No one home, obviously. "The Carstairs live here. Wonder if they've gone off for the holidays."

Some time later Cath stopped. "My feet are freezing." She was getting cold all over, except for her hand held by Jake. Her hair was covered with snow, as was Jake's. She shook her head, dislodging a shower of flakes. Shivering in the cold air, she noticed the wind seemed to have picked up.

"Time to return anyway," Jake said. "Can you feel the wind?"

She nodded.

They hurried back to the house. Entering the kitchen, Cath toed off her shoes, wiggling her toes against the linoleum floor. "It feels so much warmer in here."

"Want to get that fire going now, or later?" Jake asked, shrugging out of his jacket.

Once again Cath wondered if it were warm enough for him. She should have thought of that before suggesting the walk.

"Now's fine, I guess. What are we going to do the rest of the afternoon?" It was too early to start supper, but Cath wasn't sure she just wanted to sit in the living room together and talk.

"We could explore the cellar a bit more," he said, hanging both their jackets across the back of two chairs to let them drip on the floor as the snow melted. "Look for those journals you want to find."

"Okay." Cath wasn't as excited about exploring the cellar as Jake seemed, but she knew she'd much rather have him with her than do it on her own. Maybe in addition to searching for the journals, she could make a hasty inventory and get some idea of what would be involved in clearing the place.

On the other hand, if she did decide to remain, she would have years ahead of her in which to go through the items in the cellar and determine what to keep and what to discard.

She grabbed a tablet and pencil and headed down the steps after Jake. He seemed to relish the idea of wandering through the spooky place. Halfway down the door slammed behind her.

"Did you leave a window open?" Jake asked from the bottom of the stairs.

"No, but that door slams shut a lot. I forgot to prop it open. I think the house slants or something," she said, descending the remaining stairs. "When you think about it, a house that's two hundred years old and still standing is pretty remarkable."

"There speaks a child of modern America. I've been places where dwellings are several hundred years old, not just two."

"Mmm." She looked around. The dim lighting faintly illuminated the clutter. "Where do we start?"

"It's your cellar, where did you find the journal?"

"Over here." She retraced her steps from earlier and soon

stopped by the old cradle. Nudging it, she watched it rock gently for a couple of moments. "I wonder how old this is? It's probably been in the family for generations."

Jake looked at the cradle, the tightness in his chest returning. Did all roads lead to children? A sadness swept through him. He wished he could see Cath when she was pregnant. See her holding a newborn, her head bent over him, her blond hair shielding her face. Then she'd look up and he'd see the love shining in her eyes.

Like he used to see it shining for him. Couldn't Cath see what they had was good? How could she throw it all away?

"Probably has dry rot," he said. He looked over the area. Other furniture was haphazardly stacked out of the narrow aisle. There were trunks and crates and boxes stacked two and three high.

"It does not have dry rot and with a little cleaning and polish it'll be beautiful. Carry it upstairs for me, would you?"

"Whatever for?" He looked at her.

"I can clean it up while I'm here."

"Cath—" He had nothing to say. It had all been said. "Fine." He pulled it away from the other furniture and lifted it. It was heavier than he expected and awkward, but he maneuvered it through the narrow space and to the bottom of the stairs. "Get the door," he said, motioning her to go ahead of him.

She passed him and ran up the steps.

"It's stuck," she said, pushing against it.

"Great." He set down the cradle and, skipping every other step, joined Cath at the top. He tried the door. It didn't budge.

"It didn't lock, did it?" he asked, twisting the knob.

"No. It sticks sometimes."

He pushed it with his shoulder. There wasn't enough room on the top step to get much leverage. Jake tried again. The solid door held firm.

He looked around the frame. "The hinges are on the other side, but maybe I can pry off the board on this side and get to them."

Just then the electricity failed and they were plunged into darkness.

"Jake?" Cath reached out and clutched his arm.

He turned and drew her closer. "It's all right. Just be careful and don't fall down the stairs. I guess the storm got worse."

"This place gives me the creeps," she said.

"It's only the underside of the house. Come on, take the stairs slowly and we'll get to the bottom. Do you know if your aunt had any flashlights or candles down here?"

"I haven't a clue. I never came here much when I was a kid. I know there are candles in the drawer in the kitchen."

"Fat lot of good they do us right now."

"Can't you pry off the frame and get the door open?"

"Sure. It may take a little longer in the dark, but we'll manage." He wasn't sure how, but she sounded nervous. He said what he could to ease her mind.

They reached the bottom, as Jake found out when his shins connected with the cradle. "Dammit," he muttered. If Cath had let the fool thing stay where she found it...

"So how can you work on the door when you can't see anything?" she asked, still holding tightly to his arm. "And where are you going to find any tools? I bet Aunt Sally had them all in the carriage house."

"If we can find a screwdriver or some kind of metal wedge to pry off the board surrounding the door, we'll be all set. There has to be something around here."

"I don't know where anything is in this place," she said. "How can you find anything in the dark?"

"Then we'll just sit down and wait for the power outage to end. It might not be long. Probably not as long as some of the places I've been."

"Or it could last a day or two," Cath said.

"Don't borrow trouble."

They sat on the bottom step. Jake looked off into the darkness. His eyes would have adjusted by now to any light. There was none. He could try to find some device that would work, but not knowing the layout, or what was even available, it sounded like a fool's errand. Plus, if Cath didn't turn loose his arm, he wasn't going anywhere.

He pried her fingers off, then laced them with his. "There's nothing to be scared about," he said. "It's just old furniture and boxes of stuff."

"Maybe ghosts."

He laughed. "I doubt it. Your aunt Sally lived here all her life, she'd have told you if there were any ghosts."

"Maybe."

"Tell me about Tansy. Isn't that the name of the woman who wrote that journal you're captivated by?" he said, hoping to get her mind off her fear. "She may have been in this cellar herself."

"I wonder who she was. And what happened to them."

"How far have you read?"

"Just a couple of entries. They're lengthy, as if she had lots of time on her hands and poured her feelings out on the page. She talks about neighbors, and the cold, and trying to get the farm chores done on her own. I sometimes feel—"

Jake could tell she was holding something back. "What? There's more to it, surely," he said.

"She was lonely and afraid for her husband," Cath said

in a soft voice. "It's uncanny how her words reflect my own feelings."

"What?" That startled him.

"Did you think I never worried about you when you were gone? You don't exactly have a routine, boring job, Jake. You put yourself in danger all the time and never give a thought to how those of us back home feel."

"Who else would care?" he asked.

"I bet your mother does," she said.

"Don't go there, Cath," he warned. He rarely thought about his mother. That was in the past and he planned for it to stay there. Cath knew he had nothing to do with his family, and why. Cath was all he needed.

For a moment he wondered what would happen if she went through with her plan of divorce. He couldn't imagine finding another woman to spend his life with.

"Okay, then we'll leave your mother out of it and talk about me. Us. You wanted to know why I want a divorce. Imagine the roles were reversed and I went to Bosnia in the midst of fighting, or to an earthquake area where the building codes are so laughable that the mildest aftershock topples whole buildings. No guarantees of safety. You wouldn't worry?"

Jake nodded, then remembered she couldn't see in the dark. "Of course I'd worry, especially about someone like you."

"Leave that aside. I understand you think you're invincible, but you're not. Terrible things happen to journalists. So that's one part. The other is the loneliness. Jake, I don't like living alone. I don't like having no one to share my day with, or make plans for the weekend, or to just talk about friends and co-workers with. I miss having someone there to talk over situations that are new and different, to get some ideas for dealing with problem children, or gifted ones. I'm tired of sandwiches for dinner, but don't want to cook for one."

"I'm not a teacher," he said. "I can't stay in one place and do my job, Cath. You know that."

"That was an example. Honestly, you're not trying to see my side of it."

"I'm lonely, too, Cath," he confessed.

"Then why, for heaven's sake, aren't you home living with me?"

"You know my job—"

"No! Stop! I do not want to hear a word about your job. I want to hear about you. Why aren't we sharing a home, making a family, building a life together?"

"How do you propose I support this family if I don't report the news?" He was starting to get mad. Why was he the one at fault? She could travel with him. Granted, not to a war zone or disaster area. But she could move to London or Rome and be closer to where he usually worked. It would be easier for him to get to London than Washington.

"I don't have a suggestion, but I do think that's the crux of the matter. You like your job and it isn't in Washington. Or here. I'm growing to love this house. I don't know the neighbors, but maybe I'll make an effort to meet them and see if I could fit in. I think a complete break and change would be good," she said.

He hoped he wasn't hearing things that weren't there, he could swear he heard an undertone of sadness in her voice. Was there a chance she really didn't want to end their marriage? If so, she had a funny way of showing it.

"What changed?" he asked. "We've been married six years. What changed, Cath?"

"Aunt Sally's death made me look at things differently,

I think. I only saw her a few times a year even though Washington isn't that far away. I should have visited more often. Having flying visits from you isn't enough. I see friends and co-workers going home to families each night, and I go home to an empty condo. I'm not getting any younger. If I want to find another man, to have a family, I need to do something now. I don't want to be old like my parents were when I have a child. I want to enjoy each stage of development from baby to toddler to teenager."

"You're around children all day," he said.

"Other people's children. And only a few hours a day. I don't hear the stories at the dinner table about what they learned in school, or what their best friend said. I don't make cookies or Halloween costumes, or Christmas decorations. It was hard being the only child of older parents. I want what I have never had."

"It's overrated," he grumbled.

"You should want what you never had, Jake. You said your mother turned to her new children by her second husband, virtually ignoring you. You missed as much as I did growing up. Maybe it was even worse since you witnessed it but couldn't participate."

"Don't psychoanalyze me, Cath. I did fine, got out as soon as I was eighteen. My mother is welcome to her second family."

"You know she was wrong to ignore you, or let your stepfather have the influence he had. You would make a great father—if you were home. You'd remember what your real father did and follow his example. But it's never going to happen, is it, Jake? We've been through this a dozen times before. You have your job and I have my dreams and they don't mesh."

He turned to her, finding her head in the darkness and

covering her lips with his. This part of their marriage had always worked. She responded as she always did. Her kiss was warm and welcoming and so at odds with the words she spoke. This wasn't a woman who wanted to leave her marriage; he couldn't believe that. Yet if something didn't change, and soon, she'd follow through with her plan.

Could he show her how much they meant to each other?

His hands skimmed over her shoulders down to her back, pulling her into his lap and deeper into the embrace. She was like liquid silk, warm and pliant and sweet. He murmured words of wanting in her ear, brushing kisses against her cheeks, trailing them to her throat, feeling the rapid pulse at the base.

Her arms tightened around him, and he felt her breasts press against his chest. If the cellar wasn't cold and dusty, he'd make love to her here and now. He'd been gone too long. And it looked as if his strategy was backfiring on him. He didn't know if Cath was softening, but he wanted her more than ever. He couldn't bear the thought of her walking away forever. Yet the ending seemed inevitable. Why hadn't he seen that from the beginning?

"Hello, anyone home?" a faint voice called.

Jake and Cath sprang apart, turning as one to the door at the top of the stairs.

"Wait here," he said, standing and setting her on her feet. He climbed the stairs and pounded on the door. "We're trapped in the cellar. Are you in the house?"

"Dear me, I came to use your phone." The voice came from an elderly woman.

"I'll run home and get my nephew, maybe he can help."

Less than five minutes later Jake heard footsteps in the kitchen. Someone rattled the handle of the door.

"Is it locked?" a man asked.

"No, stuck only. I've tried pushing from this side," Jake said.

"Hold on. I've got hold of the handle. You push and I'll pull."

For several seconds they tried but the door wouldn't budge.

"Can you see the hinges?" Jake called.

"Sure. They look old as can be. Let me find something to pry them off," the man answered.

"There're tools in the carriage house," Cath called.

Within ten minutes the man had the hinges off and together he and Jake were able to pry open the door. The stranger lifted it out of the way as Cath scrambled up the steps, glad to escape the cellar. She'd never again complain about the dim lighting—it was much better than total darkness.

"Thank you!" she exclaimed when she stepped into the kitchen.

An elderly woman and a handsome young man stood looking at her.

"You're welcome, Cath dear. I thought you'd come to visit me before now. How have you been?" the woman asked.

"I've been fine, Mrs. Watson. And we've been so busy cleaning and clearing out things I haven't had a chance to do any visiting. I'm glad to see you." Cath gave her a quick hug and then smiled at the young man beside her.

"This is my nephew, staying with me for Christmas. Bart Butler."

"Jake Morgan." Jake extended his hand and they shook. "And my wife, Cath."

"Sally and I were neighbors for more than forty years. I sure do miss her. I remember how very fond of you she was. Calling you the granddaughter she never had," Mrs. Watson told Cath.

She nodded, remembering her aunt telling her that. She considered Cath's father the child she never had, and had doted on him as well.

"My goodness, I came to see if you had a phone that worked. Mine is dead and I need to call to refill a prescription before Christmas," Pearl said. "I told Bart I could manage on my own in the snow, but didn't expect to find that door stuck. Sally used to say she was going to get it fixed. I guess she never got around to it."

"My cell works," Jake said, nodding to the kitchen counter where he'd left it. From now on, he'd keep it with him.

"I appreciate that," Bart said. "I don't mind driving into town, but if they can't fill it or there's a problem, I'd hate to drive all the way in this weather for nothing."

"Glad you needed the phone. We couldn't see a thing in the dark and I was wondering how we'd get out," Jake said, handing his phone to Mrs. Watson.

"We could have been stuck there all night," Cath said with a shiver. "I should have come over when I first arrived to tell you I was staying for Christmas."

"We saw the lights, so we knew you were here," Bart said as his aunt spoke on the phone. "I saw you out walking earlier. Too cold for me."

"You're not from here?" Cath asked.

"I live in Richmond. But I'm spending the holidays with my aunt this year. She didn't want to come to Richmond."

"No other family?" Jake asked.

"A boatload. My folks are taking a cruise this year, however. And two of my sisters are taking their families skiing. My brother and his wife are spending Christmas with her folks this year, so I was on my own. Aunt Pearl thought it better for me to come visit her than for her to visit me. I think she had some concern on the ability of a bachelor to fix a suitable Christmas meal."

Jake didn't like the smile Cath gave the man. Was she already sizing up Bart Butler as a candidate for her next husband? How convenient that would be, living right next door to Sally's house.

"There, it's all taken care of, dear," Mrs. Watson said to her nephew. "They'll even deliver tomorrow, even though it's Christmas Eve. So you don't have to drive in the snow."

"Good." He smiled at his aunt. "Not that I wouldn't have gone for you."

"I know, dear. We'd best be going back. It is colder than I thought it would be."

"Thanks for rescuing us," Cath said.

"Anytime," Bart said, turning his smile in Cath's direction.

"Do you have any idea how long the power will be out?" she asked.

"Not a clue. If our phone worked, we could have called the power company. They usually can estimate when it'll be restored. You can call, if you want to get an estimate," Bart said.

"Wait while I check." Cath retrieved Jake's phone and looked for the phone book. She remembered Jake's finding the Christmas Tree Farm in the book, and leaving it on the dining room table.

The power company estimated electricity would be restored within two hours. It would be full dark by then, as it was already after four.

"Will you two be all right?" Pearl asked.

"Of course," Jake said, putting a proprietary arm across Cath's shoulders. He didn't need any more attention from the neighbors, especially Bart.

"Aunt Sally had oil lamps and we'll light them if we need light," Cath said.

"There's a gas stove, so you'll be able to cook," Pearl said, glancing around the kitchen. "Or you are both welcome to come over to our house for supper."

"We'll manage," Jake said.

"We'll be fine. Thank you for inviting us. I hope to see you again before I return to Washington," Cath said graciously, nudging Jake surreptitiously in the ribs.

"Oh, dear, you're leaving after the holidays? We were hoping you were going to stay. This house seems so lonely when no one is here," Pearl said.

"We live in Washington," Jake said firmly.

"Actually, I'm thinking of moving here next summer," Cath said, slipping from under his arm and moving closer to Pearl. "I'm a teacher. Do you think I'd have a chance of finding a job around here?"

"Sure thing," Bart said with a broad smile. "The area is growing and new schools need teachers. Aunt Pearl knows a couple of people on the school board, maybe she could put in a good word. It'd be nice for her to have a close neighbor again. The family on the other side of her house only visits on weekends."

Jake could imagine how nice Pearl would find it. Or was Bart more concerned about when *he* visited?

"No decisions have been made," he said, glaring at Cath. For every step forward, she seemed determined to take one back.

Chapter 7

When Mrs. Watson and her nephew left, Jake turned to study the door. The old house had settled over the years, and the door frame was no longer square. He had enough basic skills to plane the door so it would fit better, and shaving a bit of wood from it would insure it wouldn't stick shut again. Bart had offered to help, but he didn't need the young neighbor's assistance.

Jake planned to fix it right away if he could find the proper tools. He didn't like thinking what might have happened to Cath if she'd been caught down there alone with no neighbors needing the phone.

"If you're going to fix that now, could you bring up the cradle first?" Cath asked.

Jake nodded and brought it up. He placed it gently down in the center of the kitchen. It was old, yet had obviously been cared for through the years. How many babies had slept in its shelter? Cath's eyes were shining as she gazed at it. He felt a pang. Once she'd looked at him that way. Would she ever do so again?

"I'm going to the garage to see if there're any tools I can use to fix the door. It's too cold to let the cellar air come up into this level if we don't have to," he said.

Maybe he couldn't bring that shine to her eyes again, but he could keep her safe.

Cath nodded, already reaching for the rags she'd used for cleaning. She'd wipe down the cradle, give it a good polish to see what it looked like. Maybe there was even a small mattress for it somewhere and some bedding, though she couldn't imagine who had been the last baby to use it. Had it been her father? She didn't believe she herself had ever been put in it as her parents hadn't visited often, preferring Sally to come to their house.

The simple carving on the headboard was of flowers. She worked to get all the dust out of the crevices and corners, wondering who had made it, who had done the carving. A proud father-to-be, she was sure. Maybe even Jonathan?

Jake returned with a handful of tools. He moved the door, placing it half on the table, half on the back of two chairs and started shaving curlicues of wood from the edge. Working on their respective projects kept both from feeling chilled in the cooling air. They'd really need the fire in a while if the electricity didn't come back on. While the heater was oil fueled, it needed electricity to work.

Cath brought out the wood wax she'd seen beneath the sink and began to work it into the old wood. Once finished, she sat back on her heels and smiled. The cradle was a beautiful piece of furniture. It was worn a bit on the sides, as if by many arms reaching in to pick up an infant, but that made it all the more special. The carving was as sharp and clear as if it had been done yesterday.

She pushed it to set it rocking. It continued on its own for several moments. How safe and secure it would hold a baby. Would one of her children sleep in it? She looked over to where Jake worked on the door. Together they'd make the world's most perfect baby. If he'd only be there for her.

Cath rose, cleaned up and pulled some milk from the refrigerator. "Want some hot chocolate?" she asked as Jake patiently shaved another thin sliver of wood from the door. "It's getting cold in here."

"Sure. I'm almost done. Then we can go into the living room and build that fire."

She put the pan on the gas stove and slowly heated it. She glanced from time to time at Jake, feeling odd. It was so domestic, wife in the kitchen fixing something for them both, husband working on a project. How many times had they'd done something like this? Too few. Looking around the old kitchen she could imagine Tansy preparing something for her Jonathan. Instead of the gas range Cath used, Tansy might have had a woodstove, or even an open hearth. Had Jonathan sat in the warm kitchen, lovingly carving the cradle with flowers and designs for a baby's arrival? The modern kitchen faded and for a moment Cath could imagine how it might have looked two hundred years ago.

"Is it still snowing?" Jake asked.

Cath started, then looked out the window. "Yes." She had better pay attention so the milk didn't boil over. In only a couple of minutes, she had two large mugs of chocolate topped with whipped cream. She carried Jake's to him. He brushed her fingers when he took the mug and looked deep into her eyes.

"Thanks," he said. Taking a sip, he never let his gaze waiver.

Cath felt the touch almost like a shock. She returned his regard, lost in the dark brown of his eyes, the message clear. He wanted her. With effort she tore her gaze away.

"It'll be dark before long. Do you think I should get the oil lamps out and make sure they have fuel?" she asked, feeling flustered. She could almost grasp the tangible desire that flooded through her. She had loved Jake so much when they first married. In many ways, nothing had changed.

"It wouldn't hurt. Even if the power comes back, there's nothing saying it won't go out again later," he said, sipping the hot beverage.

"Better have candles in each room, then, with matches so we'd have light to get to the lamps," Cath said, glad for something to do. The spell was broken. She needed to re-member to keep her distance.

The lamps were right where she remembered. Opening the cupboard she took stock of everything stored in them. She planned to leave the cleaning of the kitchen until last, able to make better inroads into the bedrooms and other rooms of the house first. If this cabinet was any indication, the room would take days to sort through and organize. Cath mentally revised her schedule. With both the cellar and kitchen ahead, not to mention the carriage house, there was truly no way she could complete everything this holiday.

Maybe she'd come down for the next few weekends and keep plugging away at the tasks. That way she'd be finished before summer.

It wouldn't be the same with Jake gone, she thought, taking down the lamps and setting them on the counter. She had planned to work alone, but his arrival had changed that. Now she couldn't imagine doing all this on her own.

What if she'd been caught in the cellar alone? What if Mrs. Watson had not needed to use the phone?

Taking down three lamps, she washed the globes. Then she raised the wick on each. Still plenty of oil in the base and the wicks looked trimmed. Lighting them, she soon had a bright, steady glow from each lamp.

"They work," she said just as the heater gave an *umph* and the lights came on in the cellar.

"Your timing is perfect. Maybe you should have lit them earlier," Jake teased.

"Maybe." She blew them out and put them on one side of the counter, just in case.

She glanced at the clock. It wasn't yet six o'clock.

"Do you think I have time to bake some cookies?"

"Why not, we're not on any schedule. And a warm oven will help bring up the temperature in this room."

Cath wasn't sure why she had a sudden desire to bake, must be the housework, nesting. Or maybe it was she wanted to do something for Jake, fatten him up while he was with her, so she felt she was doing something. She began to mix the ingredients for shortbread cookies. They were his favorite.

"There, I think that'll work," Jake said, sanding the edge of the door lightly, then wiping off the dust. "Help me put it back in place."

They rehung the door and it swung closed. She turned the knob and the door opened easily. Letting it go, it once again slammed shut. Again she opened it with no effort.

"That's perfect. Thanks," she said.

He gathered the tools and started for the carriage house. "I'll sweep up the mess when I get back."

"I can manage that," Cath said, "you did all the work." She quickly swept up the wood chips and sawdust and moved the cradle to the back wall, out of the way. The first batch of cookies was ready to come from the oven. She put in another batch.

Some time later Cath realized Jake hadn't come back from the carriage house. What was he doing out there? She glanced out the window, but the angle was wrong. All she could see was the river and the edge of the old building. He wasn't standing on the banks like she'd seen him before. Was he still in the carriage house?

Jake leaned against the back door of the carriage house and stared at the slow-moving river. He didn't see the silvery water as it drifted by, nor the snow that softly drifted from the sky. He was miles away in thought. It felt as if he was trying to hold a slippery eel or something. The tighter he held on, the more Cath seemed to slip away.

He wasn't ready to go back inside. Yet it was too cold and wet to walk along the river. So his choice was to stand here and freeze. He turned back into the carriage house. Another place needing to be cleaned. Had Cath allowed for that in her schedule? He walked around the old structure. It had gaps in the walls, but the roof looked sound. Obviously a catch-all place, it was stacked with boxes and old furniture. Either there'd been no more room in the cellar, or this furniture wasn't as treasured.

He spied an old carriage in one corner, too dilapidated to use. Once horses had pulled that carriage, maybe taking the Williamsons into Williamsburg or even as far as Richmond.

Walking over, he noticed how the barrel springs sagged, and how the spokes to the high wheels were broken in spots, making the carriage sag at an odd angle. Everything was covered in a thick layer of dust. The conveyance looked to be from the late 1800s, not that he was an expert on old carriages. He tried moving it, but feared the wheels would collapse after budging it only a little and having them creak in protest.

He kicked the dirt. Dry as dust. At least the weather was kept from the place. Glancing around, he saw signs of deterioration of the old building. It was not as in good a shape as the house. The gaps in the walls let the elements in if the wind blew in the right direction. He turned to head to the house when he spotted a small sliver of metal jutting up near the carriage wheel. The small movement of the carriage must have dislodged the dirt to reveal it. He looked closer, then scraped away some of the dirt and uncovered a small metal box. Had it deliberately been hidden, or had it fallen and been covered by dirt over the years?

Taking it to the workbench on the far side, he brushed off the accumulated dirt. The fastener was rusted. He tried to pry it open, then broke the latch to lift the lid. Inside were several coins and a gold pendant on a chain. Lifting it, he saw it was a locket, letters entwined on one side. How long had it been buried? To whom had it belonged, and why had it never been recovered?

"More mysteries for Cath to unravel," he murmured. He examined the coins, gold with an eagle on one side. Jake was startled to find the dates stamped on them from the 1850s. There were also two Confederate coins. Someone's treasure hidden from marauding Yankee troops?

He put them in his pocket, knowing they'd make the perfect Christmas surprise for Cath. She loved old things, and to get such a treasure from her own property would be special. He still lived with the fantasy of seeing her in that sexy nightie he'd bought. Maybe wearing this gold locket in the firelight.

Cath took out the last batch of cookies, setting them on a rack to cool. Where was Jake? She peered out the kitchen window again, but didn't see him. She was starting to get concerned. His jacket wasn't thick and it was cold enough inside to give her an idea of how cold it was outside. Should she go look for him?

She opened the back door. From there she could see into the carriage house. Jake was at the workbench, bending over something. She hoped he had enough sense to come in out of the cold before he caught a chill or something.

Reassured he was fine, she went into the living room. It still felt cool, despite the efforts of the heater. The fire they'd started earlier had died down. She added logs and stirred it to get it going again.

Feeling restless, she considered what to do. Maybe she'd read some more of Tansy's journal. Their expedition to search for more books had been aborted and she wasn't anxious to go back down in the cellar again. Next time, she'd make sure they carried flashlights. Of course the door wouldn't jam again, but she didn't want to be caught in the far corner if the power failed.

Or she could use Jake's computer to try to find out more about Jonathan Williamson. Had he fought in other battles leading up to Yorktown?

She watched as the logs flared and began to give off some heat. Satisfied the fire would warm things up, she turned on the laptop and began to search for more about the war Jonathan fought in. Knowing she had a great-great-grandfather fight changed how she viewed history.

A short time later she gave up on the war and began to look for websites describing life in the 1700s in America. Some were geared for elementary school level and she loved the sketches of clothes, houses, cooking utensils and early carriages. Maybe she'd make a special project for her kids when school started again.

The more she read, the more she appreciated the fine work that had gone into building the house, built before modern equipment. Two hundred years later it was still housing a member of the Williamson family.

Impatient to find out what happened to Tansy and Jonathan, she turned off the computer and went to find the journal.

The next entry began:

Tomorrow is Christmas. It has begun to snow in earnest. Everything is covered and I hope my chickens survive. It is unusually cold. If I don't get the eggs right when they are laid, they could be frozen. It's hard to walk to the chicken coop, but I have a rope to use as a guide. Still no word from my husband. I hope he is planning a wonderful surprise and will show up tonight before I retire. I would so welcome another night in his arms. And Christmas won't be a special day without him here.

I miss my family. Maybe I should have gone to stay with my parents, but I could not bear the thought of Jonathan making his way home and not finding me here.

Cath gave a start. That was what she'd done, left home when Jake said he'd made a monumental effort to get home for the holidays. She bit her lip in remorse. She should have at least let him know where she was.

Jake had figured it out. Jonathan would surely have known if his wife wasn't home that she'd be with her parents. How sweet of Tansy to wait alone and lonely in hopes of her husband's arrival.

Everything in the house is ready. I have boughs of holly decorating the rooms, and a yule log ready for the fireplace. I have mulled the cider, which fills the house with a delicious fragrance. I do hope I don't have to drink it all by myself. I'm sure several neighbors will stop by to wish me a happy Christmas in the afternoon. Last year Jonathan and I drove to friends and neighbors to raise a glass of cheer. It was so festive. I never suspected we wouldn't do it this year as well. Maybe we shall, if only he gets home soon.

The entry ended abruptly.

Cath felt a frisson of dread as she turned the page. In stark letters the words—

Jonathan is dead. How will I go on?

The paper was smudged, as if by tears.

Cath's heart dropped. Slowly she ran her fingers over the long-dried tears. What happened? The entry contained only those blunt words, no date, no details, nothing.

Quickly she fanned through the remaining pages, but they were blank. That was all? She couldn't let it end there, she had to know! Were there other journals? Had Tansy thrown this one away after writing the horrible truth only to start another one when she could?

Cath jumped up and almost ran to the kitchen. Wenching open the door Jake had fixed, she flicked on the dim lights and hurried down the stairs, the door slamming behind her. She remembered where she'd found the first diary. Would there be more? Poor Tansy. Cath was almost as heartsick as Tansy must have been. She'd become involved with them, felt as if she knew Tansy and almost knew Jonathan. She'd so hoped he'd made it home for Christmas; instead, he had died. When? Where?

How had Tansy found out? How had she stood it?

Cath found the trunk and flung it open, rummaging around, but there were no journals.

She shut the lid and pulled down the box next to the trunk. Ripping off the tape holding it closed, she rummaged inside. Clothing. She felt through the stack to see if there were any books. None.

Tossing the box to one side she pulled down another. It almost fell from her hands it weighed so much. Opening it, Cath found the carton full of books. But a quick look and she knew there was no journal.

"Cath?" Jake called.

"I'm in the cellar," she yelled back, almost manic in her quest to find another journal. Tansy's story couldn't end with those brief words. What happened to her? Was she pregnant with Jonathan's child and didn't know it? Had she remarried, or remained a widow the rest of her life? Wasn't she a great-grandmother—therefore she had to have had a baby.

She pushed the heavy box aside, reaching for another.

"What are you doing?" Jake asked as he rounded the corner and saw her ripping into yet another carton.

"I'm searching for the blasted journal, what does it look like I'm doing?"

"Going through things like your life depended upon it."

She sat back on her heels and looked at him. "Jonathan died," she said sadly.

"Who— Oh, the guy from Kings Mountain?"

She nodded, rubbing her chest. "I know it happened more than two hundred years ago, but honestly, I felt I got to know Tansy, she and I had a lot in common. Both our husbands gone on dangerous missions. Both of us lonely and alone. But I thought he'd come home. You came home. Instead the journal ended with 'Jonathan is dead.' I need to know what happened to Tansy."

Unexpectedly tears filled her eyes. She tried to blink them away, but the parallel was too strong. Tansy's husband had left never to return. That was the fear Cath had lived with for years. What if Jake had been killed at one of the skirmishes he covered? Or at the earthquake center when another trembler shook?

Yet she was planning to send Jake away, never to return. How could she stand to have him out of her life forever? Was she certain that was the way she wanted things?

"Hey, honey, it's okay," Jake said, stepping over one of the boxes and squatting down beside her. He brushed away the tears that ran down her cheek. "Sad to know he died, but it's so long ago. You knew he was dead."

"But not like that. Not leaving Tansy behind. What happened to her? Oh, Jake, it's so unfair. People should fall in love and get married and live happily ever after. Not have one leave the other. I think she was only about twenty. They hadn't been married that long. What did she do for the rest of her life without Jonathan? Her love for him shone in every page she wrote." Cath couldn't help the tears, her heart ached for the couple of long ago. And for the couple of today. How had they come to this pass? She ached for love and family and a normal life with a husband safe at home each night.

Jake sat on the hard ground and pulled her into his lap, cuddling her as she cried. "We'll look and see what we can find. And if there's no other journal, we'll try the local historical society, or churchyard. We'll find out what happened to them."

"They're like us in a way," she said, burrowing closer, trying to feel safe, to have him wrap her in his arms tightly and never let her go. Her tears wet his shirt. Jake's heartbeat sounded beneath her ear, giving her comfort. His arms held her tightly, making her feel safe. The sadness was overwhelming. For Tansy and for herself. How had Tansy made it through? Cath didn't think she herself would want to go on if she knew Jake was no longer in the world.

Yet she was sending him out of her life.

Confused, hurt, sad, she didn't move. If she could stop time forever, it would be this very moment. Only, she wanted the ache in her heart to go away.

"It's getting cold, Cath. Let's go upstairs and sit by the fire," Jake said a little later when her sobs eased. "We'll have dinner and discuss how we can go about finding out about Tansy and her husband."

Cath didn't want to move, but she wasn't the one sitting on the hard-packed dirt floor. She pushed away and wiped her cheeks. Reluctantly standing, she surveyed the boxes and trunks stacked everywhere.

"I thought maybe Tansy started a fresh journal, one that didn't hold the bad memories the one I was reading did. She may never have written another word. I don't know. It was pure chance that I found that one."

Jake rose and looked around. "It could take a month to go

through every box in this space. And, as you say, she may not have started another one. Let's try other means first."

Cath nodded. "If we can't find anything, I'll come back this summer and go through every single container in the cellar. I need to know what happened."

She needed to know that Tansy had moved on, found happiness and lived to be a grandmother who loved her family. That was the ending Cath wanted for Tansy—and for herself. She wanted some assurance that when Jake left, she'd be able to go on and find the family she so yearned for. She didn't want regrets or second thoughts. She didn't want to spend the rest of her life alone.

"Did your aunt do a family tree?" Jake asked when they went upstairs. "Maybe Tansy and Jonathan were on it and you'd have some indication of what happened."

"I don't know if she did or not. She talked about the family a lot when I visited as a young child. But not so much after I was grown. I think she felt she had told me all there was. I wish I had paid better attention. I don't remember hearing about a Tansy, though. It's an unusual name, I think I'd remember."

When they reached the living room, Jake added logs to the fire. The wood they'd brought in was dry and caught quickly. The room was noticeably warmer than the cellar. The lights on the tree seemed to grow brighter as the daylight faded into night. The snow continued, but the wind had died down.

"This beats the Middle East," he said, sitting on the sofa, and reaching for Cath's hand, lacing their fingers, resting their linked hands on his leg.

Slowly she leaned toward him, resting against his arm, her head on his shoulder. She still looked sad. He wished she'd smile, or laugh, or even get angry with him. He hated seeing her so unhappy.

Slowly she turned to look at him. "I should have made you welcome when you arrived. I'm sorry, Jake. I was just so set on ending our marriage, I didn't think about how you must have pulled some strings or something to get the time off. I'd much rather you be here than the Middle East. You could have been killed and never come home—just like Jonathan." Tears shimmered in her eyes again.

"No, Cath. I'd always come home to you." He had a sudden urge to give her the necklace, but held back. It would wait until tomorrow. Maybe it would cheer her up. Once he cleaned it, maybe the letters would reveal to whom it belonged. Wouldn't it be serendipity if it had once been Tansy's. Unlikely, however. The box was not from the 1700s. Probably someone had used it as a treasure box, hid it and forgot about it.

"This is a house made for a family, with lots of children," Cath said, gazing into the fire. "I hope Tansy found someone else to love, to share the farm with. Do you think she did?"

Jake couldn't get too worked up over a couple who had been dead for almost two hundred years, but he could see Cath was truly upset by her discovery. What could he do to take her mind away from it?

"I'm sure we'll find out. It may take a bit of time, but we'll find the answer. We can't do anything until after Christmas."

"I know. And it's probably silly, but I thought for sure I was going to read that Jonathan showed up in time for Christmas. I was counting on it," Cath said sadly.

His wife liked happy endings. He only wished she saw one for them.

Dinner was easily prepared and quickly eaten. Cath had little to say. Jake didn't push her. But he did watch her, conscious of the comments she'd made earlier about them not knowing each other well. They'd been married for six years, but he would never have expected this reaction to reading a two-hundred-year-old diary. He'd picked it up and scanned the last few pages. The death announcement was stark. Maybe seeing it written down had been the final straw for the young widow.

Or maybe she'd gone on to write a dozen more journals and they'd been lost or scattered over the years. He hoped they'd be able to find something out at the local historical society. Williamsburg prided itself on its history, surely the society would have information.

When they'd finished, Cath put a small plate of cookies on the table. "I should take some to Mrs. Watson, don't you think? If they hadn't come over today, who knows how long we'd have been stuck in the cellar."

"Take them tomorrow. It's pitch-black outside and treacherous to boot with the snow."

"Actually that'd be better. Tansy mentioned in her journal how they visited neighbors and friends on Christmas day. We'll be following an old tradition."

Jake could think of a new tradition he'd like to start. He rose and began to clear the dishes. Washing up took very little time. When they were finished, Cath looked at a loss.

Suggesting they go back to the living room, Jake found the Christmas records and put them on.

"Dance with me, sweetheart," he said, drawing her into his arms.

For a long time they danced to Christmas carols. She was sweet and soft in his arms. She made no move to end their closeness. Feeling bold, Jake began to give her soft kisses—first on her hair, then her forehead, moving down to her cheeks, and then capturing her mouth.

Cath sighed softly and encircled his neck, kissing him back.

"Come spend the night with me, Cath," he said softly.

She pulled back and gazed up into his eyes, hers soft and dreamy.

"I love you, Jake," she said.

Taking time to bank the fire, turn off the Christmas lights and shut off the record player, Jake leashed his impatience. He wanted to make love to her right then and there, but he wasn't some teenager unable to control himself. In bed, all night long, was better.

Hoping she wouldn't have second thoughts, he raced through the tasks and then walked with her up the stairs, fearing every step she'd change her mind.

"We only have the present," Cath said. "No one can see into the future. Would Jonathan not have gone to fight if he'd known he'd be killed? Would Tansy have married him if she'd known they'd have such a short life together?"

"Hush, Cath. It's in the past. Didn't the journal say they were happy?"

"Tansy missed him so much. I knew how she felt."

"I'm home now, sweetheart." Jake drew her into his arms and kissed her again. She responded almost feverishly. He started to ask where, but decided for the bed he knew was large enough for both of them. The door to his bedroom stood open. It was cooler inside without the warmth of the fire from the living room. But he had no doubt they'd warm up quickly.

Slowly they moved toward the bed, hands touching, lips kissing, the soft sighs and rustling of clothing being shed the only sound in the silent night.

The sheets were cool but momentarily. He eased her down and followed quickly.

"Oh, Jake, I love you," Cath said, reaching eagerly for him.

Chapter 8

Had last night been a mistake? Slowly coming awake in the still-dark morning, Cath took stock. She was wrapped in her husband's arms. She felt cherished and well loved, but confused. She'd clung to Jake during the night, afraid of losing him as Tansy had lost Jonathan. Yet hadn't she considered all the changes she needed to make?

Being with Jake clouded the issue. She had tried to turn him away that first night. If he'd gone, things would be different. But he'd refused. Now they'd made love again and she had to admit how much she loved her husband. Together she felt whole, as if some missing part had been restored.

Frowning, she wished last night had never happened. It would be doubly hard to bid him goodbye now. She'd psyched herself up and all her arguments had fled like the wind when he kissed her. Would this change the dynamics of their marriage? Would he finally realize how much being together meant to her? She could counter all his objections, if he'd only give them a chance. They'd make a wonderful family, she knew it.

Cath slowly slipped out of bed, snatching up her clothes and heading for the bathroom. Time to get up and dressed and start breakfast. And think about a different future than she'd planned when she arrived at the old house a few days ago.

When she left the bathroom a little while later, Jake was leaning against the wall of the hall, wearing jeans and a loose shirt. He smiled when he saw her, leaning over to kiss her.

"Good morning. Why did you get up so early?"

"I wanted to start breakfast," she said. It sounded like a poor excuse. She wasn't brave enough to tell him how confused she was. He'd pounce on her uncertainty and get concessions from her before she knew what she was saying. She needed to be careful, and make sure she knew what she was doing with her future.

"Make a big one, I've worked up an appetite." He kissed her again, then stepped around her and entered the bathroom.

Cath stood still for a few moments, relishing the embrace, fleeting though it had been. Her heart raced, her skin felt warm. For two cents, she'd turn and join Jake in the shower.

"Which would be totally dumb," she told herself. Putting yesterday's clothes in the laundry basket in her room, she headed downstairs. She went into the living room and turned on the lights. The sky was lightening, but remained overcast. It had stopped snowing with more than eight inches on the ground.

When she leaned over to plug in the tree lights, Cath saw two wrapped boxes, one larger than the other. She realized with a pang it was Christmas morning and she had not gotten Jake a Christmas gift! As his work could take him anywhere around the world at any time, she had not bought anything due to the difficulty insuring the packages would reach him.

Yet there was the proof he hadn't forgotten her.

She tried to think of something she'd have that she could wrap and give him, but nothing came to mind. She'd have to confess she hadn't bought him anything. How sad would that be for Christmas?

Would he see her turning away similar to his mother? He'd lived with his mother's second family for nine years, but each year was more unhappy than the one before. He'd told Cath once how he'd felt like an outsider always looking in. And now she was going to make him feel like an outsider again. She'd bought presents for Abby and her family, even some of her friends. But nothing for her own husband.

What kind of woman was she?

Not that she would have minded yesterday or the day before. It would help cement her decision. But after last night, dare she hope things would be different? Maybe they could find common ground, start a family, find a way to have Jake work closer to home, or at least come home more frequently.

There was nothing she could do about it. She'd have to make it up to him in other ways.

Cath prepared a large breakfast of eggs, sausage, grits and toast, with orange juice and coffee for beverages. The last piece of toast popped up as Jake entered.

"My mouth is watering," he said, coming over to her and kissing her neck. "And not for the food."

She smiled and leaned against him for a moment, savoring the intimacy. She'd missed him when he was gone. She'd never get enough. "Eat, then we need to talk."

"Do you know how much I hate that phrase—we need to talk? It's never good," he said.

"What do you mean?" she asked as she served their plates and carried them to the table.

"It usually means a time to bring up bad news."

"Not this time. At least I don't think so. Sit down and eat."

"And then we'll talk, I know. So we remain silent during breakfast?"

She giggled and shook her head. "No." She sat and looked at him, biting her lip. "I'm sorry I need to tell you I didn't get you anything for Christmas. I didn't know you would be home."

"No problem. Actually the present I got you can be for both of us," he said easily.

"Oh." She gave a soft sigh of relief he didn't seem hurt. "Well, then, if you're not upset."

"No, Cath. After last night, I'm not at all upset."

She smiled in shy delight remembering.

"I have a ham I want to bake for dinner. I thought we could eat around one o'clock, if that suits you. Then later in the day we can take the cookies to Mrs. Watson."

Jake nodded.

His cell phone rang.

Cath groaned. "Not on Christmas!"

"It won't take long." He rose and left the room.

Despite last night, the scenario was familiar. Nothing had changed. Cath finished her meal alone, watching as his grew cold.

She cleared her dish and ran water over it, setting it aside until he finished and she would wash all the dishes at one time. Taking her coffee, she headed for the living room, passing Jake who paced in front of the window in the dining room.

"Not what I want to hear, Sam," he said as she walked through.

She started a fire, settling back on the sofa and sipping her coffee. Even though it was Christmas, she could still look through other boxes in the cellar for another journal. Or even for the family history her aunt had accumulated. If the historical society was open in the morning, she'd try there as well. She hoped they weren't closed until after New Year's.

Jake came in sometime later.

"Sorry about the call, Cath. It was important."

"Your breakfast got cold."

"Still delicious." He stood near the tree, hesitating.

That was unlike him. Cath always thought of him as charging right in. Was he about to tell her he was leaving?

Stooping, he swept up the two boxes and joined her on the sofa. "Two for you. Merry Christmas, Cath." He leaned over and kissed her gently.

Offering the larger box, Jake sat back to watch her open it. He hoped after last night she'd be glad to get the filmy nightie. He hadn't been able to resist when he'd seen it in the window of a shop in the London airport.

"Oh, my goodness." Cath held up the sheer gown—it was pale eggshell-blue, with lace at the top and bottom, and lace shoulders. "It's beautiful."

"You'll be beautiful in it."

She looked at him with a hint of mischief in her eyes. "Let me guess, this is the one we'll both like."

He nodded, watching warily for any hint she was changing back into the freezing woman he'd found when he arrived. But she was as warm and close as she'd been last night.

"Thank you, Jake." She leaned over and gave him a sweet kiss.

"Want to model it now?" he suggested.

She laughed. "No. I know what will happen and I have to get dinner started before too long. The ham will take a while to bake."

"Later then, for sure."

She nodded, gently folding it and replacing it in the box.

"This isn't really from me," he said slowly, offering the smaller box. "I found these in the carriage house but thought they'd make a nice surprise."

She took the box, feeling something slide inside. Opening the paper, she lifted the lid.

"Oh." A gleaming gold locket lay on some tissue paper. Gently she lifted the necklace and held it in her hand. It was oval, about an inch in length. Initials had been engraved on the front with fancy curlicues.

"It's Tansy?" she asked, tracing a J and T. "Is this a locket from Tansy?"

"I thought of her when I found it. Jonathan and Tansy. It could be their initials, the engraving is so fancy it's hard to tell. Anyway, the locket looks old. Check out the fastener."

"It was in the carriage house?" Cath asked, lifting it gently, letting the delicate chain slip through her fingers as she gazed at the locket itself.

"In a metal box with some gold coin from the 1850s and a couple of Confederate coins. My guess is someone hid their treasure to keep it out of enemy hands and forgot it was there. Or maybe something happened to the person and no one ever knew what happened to the box. It wasn't buried very deep. I dislodged some dirt when I tried to move that carriage and found it."

"It couldn't have been Tansy, then. She would have died long before the Confederacy," Cath said. Slowly she opened the locket. A small curl of brown and black hair was tied in a faded ribbon, nestled in the tiny center of the locket.

"Or it was hers and passed down in your family," Jake suggested.

Cath touched the hair. "Whose, do you think?"

Jake looked at it for a moment. "Maybe both of them. There are two different colors there. Try it on."

Cath closed the locket, undid the fastener and presented her back to Jake, holding the ends in her hands.

"Fasten, please."

He brushed away her hair, fumbled with the unfamiliar connector, feeling her warmth radiating to his fingers. When it was hooked, he kissed the soft skin of her neck, moving around to her cheek as she turned to face him, ending at her mouth. It was a long time before Cath rose to check out the locket in the mirror.

Jake sat in the kitchen as Cath began preparing their dinner. She said she could manage everything when he offered to help, but would like the company. They still hadn't had that talk she'd mentioned earlier. Maybe he should open it up with his news.

"My call this morning was from Sam Miller, head of programming for the network," he began.

"And he wants you in some hot spot ASAP," she said without looking up.

"Actually I was getting feedback on my request for a stateside assignment."

She turned at that, staring at him in disbelief. "What?"

"I don't know if they can accommodate me. But I put in the request."

"You love your job."

"I'm not letting a job come between us. If it comes to the choice of my marriage or my job, I choose you."

Her face lit up. Jake felt his reaction like a kick. His desire flared. It was all he could do to keep from getting up and dragging her over to the table to make love with her again right then and there.

"That's wonderful. What would you do? Oh, Jake, this is the best present I could get." She wiped her hands on the towel and came over to give him a kiss. "You're really going to stay where it's safe? You'll be home a lot more, right?"

"Nothing's settled yet. But if they don't come through, I'll look for another network. I'm damn good at what I do. There have been other offers over the years. I'm sure I'll get something."

"There have?" She hadn't expected that, he could tell. Maybe he shouldn't be so forthcoming. But the comment she'd made about their not knowing each other rankled. He wanted to change that.

He'd never entertained moving from foreign reporting, so hadn't bothered to tell her when the offers had come before. Another mark against him. Cath was right, they weren't functioning as a married couple. That was going to change. If she'd forget her damn-fool idea of divorce, he'd do what he could to be the husband she wanted.

"One or two," he said casually.

She looked at him for a moment, then pushed away and went back to the food preparation.

Jake knew he'd blown it. He should have kept quiet about other offers. He spotted the cradle over to one side. Another topic he'd have to address sooner or later. Why had she fallen in love with that cradle? Maybe if he stayed home from now on, they could do enough together she'd forget having a baby.

"While the ham is baking, we could look again in the cellar for more journals," Cath suggested.

"If you want. This time we'll take flashlights," he said.

They spent most of the morning going through boxes near where Cath had found Tansy's journal. Nothing turned up. They moved deeper into the cellar, finding clothing from long ago. There were old shoes, the leather hardened and cracked. Another box had paper from early in the twentieth century.

"No sense in saving all this…it's all totally ruined," Cath murmured, as she rummaged through the mildewed pages.

"Clearing out this space is going to take longer than we have now," Jake said. It looked to him as if the job would take a month of steady work.

"When you asked for a stateside assignment, does it mean as much travel as you've been doing?" she asked.

"There won't be as much, depending on the job."

"Any chance you could work from here? I still think this would be a great house to raise a family in. I could look this spring for a teaching job to start in the fall, give my notice where I am now at the end of the school year. That would give us the summer to sell the condo. Or we could keep it as a place to stay when we go to Washington. Or if you need to work there."

"Early yet to know what a new job would entail. Let's leave that up in the air for the present," he suggested. He didn't have a firm choice yet. But had been very clear when talking to Sam about what he wanted.

"I hate for this place to sit empty for so long."

"It's been empty for four months, another few won't hurt it. We can come down every month for at least one weekend, to check on things."

"We could start fixing it up the way we want it," Cath chatted happily.

Jake felt impending doom at the direction of her thoughts. Just because he changed jobs didn't mean everything was changing.

She ripped the tape off another box and opened the flaps.

"I found them!" she called excitedly. "This box has several journals and I recognize her handwriting."

Jake joined Cath. She was fanning through different books, putting one down to pick up another. "I don't know the sequence, I wish she'd dated every first page just so I could put them in order. There are other journals here as well, different handwriting. Oh, this is so cool!"

"Let's take them upstairs and see if we can put them in some kind of order," he suggested. It was cramped in the narrow space between furniture and boxes.

"I hope she started writing after Jonathan died. The last one ended so abruptly."

"If not, maybe someone else wrote about her."

Jake carried the box upstairs and put it on the kitchen table. It was dusty and had cobwebs trailing from the base.

Cath wiped off the box, then opened it again and began to pull out the different books that housed thoughts of her ancestors.

The phone rang.

"Not again!" she exclaimed.

"It's yours, not mine," Jake said, pointing to the cell phone on the kitchen counter.

Cath dashed across to answer it.

"Hi, Abby. Merry Christmas!"

Jake continued to take out the books, opening each one to see if there were any dates. Some writers had dated each entry, but not the ones Tansy wrote. The dated ones he put in order. They were from the 1800s. The others had no dates. Maybe reading them would enable him to determine approximate time frames.

"Things have changed for the best," Cath was saying. "I'll have lots to tell you when I get back. Are you having a good day? Yes, I want to talk to the kids. Was Jimmy thrilled with the bike?"

Jake turned slowly to watch his wife as she talked with Abby's children. She looked so happy. She loved being a teacher. She'd talked about it early in their marriage. She had that same glow now.

Jake turned back to the task at hand. Time enough to discuss a family later. For now, she was happy to find the journals.

Cath hung up and went to stand beside Jake. He explained the two piles, one with dates, one without. She skimmed the first few pages of each book in the undated pile. She'd gone through almost all of them, not finding one she thought was a continuation of Tansy's journal.

"Maybe she didn't write again," she said, setting yet another one aside and picking up a new one from the diminishing pile.

Jake was logging them into a file, with opening sentences for those that had no dates.

"Wait, this is it. I recognize her handwriting. Listen to this," Cath said. *"I saw a robin today. It is the first sign of spring. And I was pleased to notice him. The winter was long and I still feel dark and chilled in my soul. I go to*

Jonathan's grave every day, but there is no comfort there. I've planted a rosebush and hope it grows. He loved roses.

"'The farm is too much for me to handle alone now that planting season is upon us. I've hired a man to work the farm and invited my cousin Timothy and his wife to join me. I do not wish to live alone and they are young and full of life. I'm hoping to find some joy in living and maybe they will give me that.'" Cath looked up. "I wonder if this was written a few months after she learned of Jonathan's death. Sounds like it, doesn't it?"

Jake nodded. "Where is Jonathan buried?"

"I have no idea, maybe in the churchyard of that old church out on the Williamsburg road. We could go look."

He glanced out the window. "When the weather improves."

"Sissy," she teased, going back to the journal.

He continued his task while she read silently.

"Jake," her voice sounded odd.

"What?" He looked up.

"She's writing about the gold locket Jonathan had given a neighbor to give to her on Christmas morning, one with their initials entwined. It was her most cherished possession. You were right, Jonathan had entwined a lock from both their heads to show they were joined forever," Cath said, rubbing the necklace. "Do you suppose he had a premonition he wouldn't be coming back?"

"He could have just thought he wouldn't be home in time for Christmas," Jake suggested.

Cath shivered with the knowledge the locket she was wearing was Tansy's. She'd suspected as much that morning, but this added to her belief.

As she read the words of the woman who had died so long ago, she didn't find any mention of children. Tansy had not been pregnant with Jonathan's baby. Had she later remarried?

It was too soon after Jonathan's death for Tansy to be thinking along those lines. Yet Cath was impatient to find out what happened. She so hoped Tansy had found happiness—especially now when Cath found her own happiness. She couldn't believe Jake would change his career for her. For them. It showed how much he loved her. She'd be hard-pressed to give up her own job for him. Not that he'd asked her to—except to suggest she travel with him.

Did that mean he loved her more than she loved him? She felt odd with the idea. Why wouldn't she give up her career for the man she loved if he asked? Or even without being asked? Marriage was a two-way street. One partner couldn't make all the sacrifices. Had she been selfish in demanding he change? She wanted her husband home every night, but maybe it didn't have to mean in Washington.

The thought was almost too overwhelming. Had she expected more than she should have?

She'd been so sure this fall that leaving Jake was the right choice. Now that they'd spent some time together, she couldn't imagine not spending the rest of her life with him. And if he found a job in the U.S., it would mean they'd have a normal family life.

A lingering sadness filled her. Was it for Tansy? Cath was getting the happy ending denied Tansy.

She tried to shake off the melancholia. Her own life did not parallel Tansy's. Granted both husbands had been gone for an extended period of time, and both she and Tansy had missed them terribly and feared for their lives. But unlike Jonathan, Jake was home and safe. She didn't wish to delve beyond that right now.

After their early-afternoon dinner, Cath wrapped the cookies to take to the neighbor. She dressed warmly and was ready before Jake.

"I don't see why we need to do this," he grumbled. "They probably have a ton of food and won't even eat the cookies."

"It's tradition," Cath said. "Tansy mentioned visiting friends and neighbors at Christmas. I want to start some new traditions as well. And if we move here, we'll want to be on good terms with our neighbors."

"A friendly hello as we drive out of the driveway would work," he said, donning his own light jacket.

"Aren't you cold in that?" she asked.

"If I stay out too long, yeah, I get cold. But the weather feels good after the heat I've lived in for the last few months. I have a heavier jacket at home, but didn't think to get it before starting out."

Cath should feel guilty her letter had sent him hurrying after her without the rest he needed, or the chance to get appropriate clothing. She should, but she didn't. His decisive move in following her showed her how much he cared. It meant all the more to her after last night. She was buoyed with hope for their future.

The walk to Pearl Watson's house was difficult. There was no sidewalk, so they walked across the yards. The snow hid any obstacles and made it difficult. Twice Cath slipped and would have fallen had Jake not caught her. She didn't know how Pearl had made it the other day. Of course, the snow hadn't been as deep then.

The clouds parted and the sun shone, giving the snow a sparkling look as if a thousand diamonds glittered. It was almost too bright to see.

The visit was all Cath had hoped. Pearl had welcomed them warmly and thanked them for the cookies, which, luckily, Cath hadn't dropped when she'd slipped. A fire burned merrily in the fireplace and the living room was decorated to the nth degree with fresh pine and holly and many ornaments and figurines that Cath guessed Pearl had collected over the years. Jake gave every indication he enjoyed the visit, talking football and sports with Bart and complimenting Pearl on her delicious mulled wine and fruit cake.

Cath knew he was being overly polite—he didn't like fruit cake. Still, she appreciated his efforts.

They didn't stay long, but Cath enjoyed the visit. It was fun, however, to return to their home together, closing out the cold. They'd eat dinner, she'd model the fancy new nightie and knew exactly where they'd end up. She could hardly wait.

Chapter 9

As if deliberately building the tension, when they entered the house, Jake suggested they watch a movie on television. Christmas favorites were playing all week, and he thought one was starting in a few minutes.

"The only television is in your room," Cath pointed out.

He shrugged. "So we watch it there." His eyes gleamed, belying the casual tone of his voice.

Her heart skipped a beat.

"Want to take up some snacks?" she asked.

"Sure. Make it a light supper and later we can come down for dessert, if we want."

She sliced some ham, added an assortment of cheeses, heated the biscuits and cut a couple of apples. The warm cider would round off the makeshift meal, she decided.

She wasn't sure where Jake was while she was preparing their evening meal. She didn't hear any murmured conversation, so at least he wasn't on the phone. She spotted hers still on the counter and went to turn it off. Not that anyone was likely to call her, but just in case. She just wished she knew where his was, she'd turn it off as well.

And maybe chuck it out into the snow. Let him find it come spring!

Carrying the meal upstairs, she was surprised to find Jake had brought in a bunch of pillows, building a seating area for them on the double bed. A chenille afghan lay at the foot of the bed, to cover legs if they got cool watching the movie.

Soft lighting completed the ambiance. Cath smiled, feeling her anticipation rise another notch. Was he planning to watch TV or seduce his wife?

Jake switched on the set. The Christmas movie was just beginning. They watched the opening scenes of the familiar story while eating the light supper. Once they finished eating, Jake put his arm around her shoulder and pulled her close, snuggling her next to him as the action unfolded. Cath tried to concentrate on the characters of the old black-and-white movie, but she was too conscious of Jake pressed along the length of her. His scent filled the air. His warmth kept the coolness at bay. She glanced over but he seemed absorbed in the film. She reached out to take his hand and threaded her fingers through his, feeling his palm against hers. This was a moment she'd remember forever. The two of them together in perfect harmony.

"If we decide to move here, I think we should put a fireplace in this room," she said at one of the commercial breaks.

He looked at the outside wall where the chimney ran. "I suppose it could be fairly easily done, tapping into the existing chimney."

"And we'd build the dock you wanted. Get a small boat."

"Build a gazebo near the water, where we could sit on summer evenings," Jake said.

Cath took it as a very positive sign that Jake was participating in her daydreams of what she'd have her ideal house be. Maybe they would move here and make it reality.

To Cath's amazement, they made it through to the end of the movie. It was getting late. After making a big push to get her in bed since he arrived, she was a bit surprised he hadn't rushed her tonight.

"Ready for bed?" he asked.

"I guess."

"Try on the gown I brought," he suggested.

She nodded, rising. Away from him, she felt the coolness of the air. At least the bed would be warmed from their bodies when they got in again.

"Let me get the dishes done first." Was she deliberately tantalizing him by delaying? She smiled mischievously and gathered the plates.

Together they went downstairs. Cath put the dishes in the sink and rinsed them off while Jake turned off the Christmas tree lights and made sure the fire was contained.

He offered the box with the gown when she met him at the foot of the stairs.

"I'll change in the bathroom," she said breathlessly. She felt as shy as a new bride.

The gown fit perfectly, if a floating froth of sheer silk that flowed from her shoulders had any fit to it. The pale eggshell-blue was almost virginal. Excitement brought color to her cheeks. She brushed her hair until it gleamed, studying herself in the mirror. She looked like a bride.

Her heart tripping double-time, she wished she had a wrap or something to cover her from the bathroom to the bedroom. Head held high, feeling feminine and sexy, she almost floated to the room they'd share tonight.

Jake had turned back the sheets and shed most of his clothes. He wore only the dark trousers. One bedside light gave soft illumination.

He looked at her when she entered and Cath heard his breath catch.

"You are so beautiful," he said, coming around the bed to meet her.

She was glad he thought so. Forgotten was the pain of the past, the long, lonely times. She had tonight, and their future. Cath was sublimely happy as she walked toward the man she loved.

"You're beautiful," he repeated as he reached out to touch her soft shoulders, slipping the lacy strap down a bit and bending to kiss her warm skin. "Gold and lace, you should always wear gold and lace," he said as he drew her into his arms.

The light had been extinguished, the covers drawn over them. Cath lay in blissful afterglow, reveling in being in Jake's arms. Her breathing had returned to normal and she felt safe and happy. This was how their marriage should have been all along. How it had been every time he'd returned home. She had lived in fear of his safety each time he left. His staying would make a world of difference. The one thing to make their lives complete would be a baby.

She suddenly realized they hadn't used any birth control, and Jake knew she wasn't on the Pill. It was surely a sign he was ready to start their family, despite his words to the contrary. She smiled in secret glee. Maybe they'd make a baby that very night.

"Tell me about the job possibilities," she said, feeling

warm and sleepy. She wanted to know more. How did he feel about making the change?

"I'm not sure what they'll have for me. Ideally I'd like a position that allows some analysis and then on-air reporting. On the other hand, it's the analysis part I like. I can do that without being the one to report it."

"Won't you miss the travel, seeing all those exotic places?"

"Exotic only if that's considered foreign. War zones and disaster areas aren't exactly the place of vacations. I've been doing this for twelve years, Cath. I might have done it for another twelve, but you're too important to me. Time to let others get the fame, and for me to settle down and come home each night to my wife."

She smiled, rubbing her fingertips against his strong chest.

Her decision had brought this about. She hoped he'd never regret giving up his way of life for hers. She'd do all she could to make him happy and glad he'd made this change.

"It could be that by next Christmas, we'll have someone else to share the holidays with," she said dreamily.

"Hmm?"

"A baby."

She felt him tense. Her euphoric mood vanished in a heartbeat. She realized they really hadn't discussed anything of significance. He said he'd look for a stateside job. But there'd been no mention of how soon. And what if he couldn't find the one he liked? Suddenly Cath felt vulnerable and uncertain. They had not talked about starting a family. She'd told him she was ready. When would he be?

"What?" she asked, feeling constrained by his embrace instead of warmed by it. "If you get a job in the U.S., there's no reason we can't start our family. We're not getting any younger and I don't want to be old parents like mine were."

"Getting a job in the States is a long way from having a family. We need time to ourselves. Get to know each other all over again. I'm not sure I can live here. I might have to be in Atlanta or Washington or even New York. Too early to make firm plans until I know what I'll be doing."

"We've had time to ourselves. Six years' worth. And we will still have time for each other. It takes nine months to have a baby. And even after it's born, we'll make time for the two of us. I love you, Jake. I want to share in my life, share in yours. We'll always make time for us. But if you're home all the time, any arguments about having a baby disappear. It's time. Past time if you ask me."

"No."

"Hey, this is a two-way street. Are you telling me you don't want kids? Ever?" Just when she thought things had turned for the best, he was throwing her a curve. What if Jake never wanted children? Her decision made this fall would have to stand. But after the past two nights, she wasn't sure she was strong enough to walk away from love.

"We can't have children, Cath," he said a long moment later.

"Just because your dad died young and you got a rotten deal with your stepfather doesn't mean you won't be a terrific father. I know you will be."

He brushed back her hair and kissed her. The darkness wasn't the cozy place it once had been. Cath wanted to see his expression. She wanted to rail against his stubborn stance. Why was he so adamant against having children? She knew he'd be a great father.

"Listen to what I'm saying, Cath. We can't have children."

"I don't see why you are so against it—"

"Dammit, *listen!* Cannot have children. Not won't, not delay. Can not."

She didn't understand. "Why not?"

He released her and sat up in the bed, drawing the sheets down with him. The sudden cool air against her skin didn't chill her as much as Jake's words.

She sat up, straining to see him in the dark.

"Dammit, what we have is good, Cath. We love each other. I'll stay with you, be with you. We'll do things like all married couples. We'll have a good life."

"As we would with children."

"I can't have children," he said heavily.

"What do you mean you can't have children?" she asked.

He sighed and got out of bed. She heard the sound of his jeans being pulled on. Afraid of what he would say next, she clutched the covers to her, trying to recapture the warmth.

"I cannot father a child," he said from the darkness.

"What?"

"I'm sterile. I had mumps when I was a teenager. There's no way I can ever father a child."

She stared at the place from which his voice came, picturing him in her mind, wishing the lights were on. The words echoed in her mind. *Sterile.*

Licking dry lips, she carefully asked, "How long have you known that?"

"Since I was seventeen and my younger sister gave me the mumps. The doctor had me tested afterward."

The words hit like a hammer. He'd wooed her and courted her and married her all the time knowing he could never have children. All these years she'd thought he was scarred by the experiences with his stepfather. That when they were ready, that when he was secure in her love, they'd start a family and he could finally experience how loving one could be. Instead she'd been kept in the dark. He'd always known they would never have a family.

"How could you not tell me, Jake? How could you marry me and not share this important fact? What were you thinking?" Her eyes were dry, the pain in her heart threatened to rip it apart. She was hurt beyond tears. He had to have known she would one day want children. All couples who married had children. At least all the ones she knew did. Yet he'd never given her a hint that they would never have a child together. Until tonight. Just when everything looked perfect, he'd hit her with this.

"There are lots of couples out there who have very happy lives without children," Jake said stiffly.

"Maybe if we'd built a solid marriage over the last six years, we'd have a chance. But this is more than I can deal with." Cath felt a part of herself die. "We've been married six years! You couldn't find a minute in all that time to tell me?"

"And have you say, sorry Charlie, I'm out of here? I've already had one woman turn on me, I didn't want another. We didn't discuss children at the onset. And over the years, we never talked about it. It was Sally's death that gave you the idea. Admit it. What we have is good, Cath. Don't turn your back on that!"

To her, having a family was fundamentally important. She was alone in the world except for friends, and for Jake. She wanted children and grandchildren and large family gatherings at holidays. She wanted love and quiet sharing times. Laughter and funny sayings of children to treasure. She yearned to share her life with offspring. Tell them about her parents and Aunt Sally, and even Tansy. To have continuity down through the ages.

But it was never going to happen. Jake had known that and not told her. In six years, he'd never shared that crucial fact.

She tried to absorb the magnitude of his revelation, but she was numb. She pushed aside the covers and rose. The nightie was somewhere on the floor, but she didn't even try to find it. It scarcely provided any covering. She went to the door and out into the hall and to her room. Closing the door, she locked it. Turning on the light, she quickly dressed in warm sweats and crawled into her bed. Her thoughts were in a jumble, but overriding them all was the knowledge that if she stayed with Jake Morgan, she would never become a mother. And he had known that all along.

Jake stood by the empty bed, listening to her walk down the hall, the closing of her door, the snick of the lock. He stared into the darkness, knowing his last hope had died.

It was only after several minutes, when he began to feel the cold, that he roused himself enough to get dressed. No point in getting back into that bed they'd shared. The memories would be more than he could deal with. He flipped on the light and found a sweatshirt. Dressing quickly, he pulled on socks and his shoes. Maybe a walk would help.

Hell, nothing was ever going to help.

He'd suspected this day might come. From the first moment she'd begun to talk about having children, he'd known he'd have to tell her. It had not seemed important before. She had children at school, he was gone a lot. But all fall she'd talked about it on the phone calls and in their e-mails.

Why couldn't she have been some woman all caught up in her career who didn't want to have children? Or the favorite aunt of dozens of kids, so having her own wouldn't be as important.

Why couldn't he be enough?

He'd deliberately stayed away these past few months, hoping to delay the inevitable. It had worked, sort of. He'd squeezed a few more weeks out of his marriage. It would end for certain now. Getting a job in the States had nothing to do with it. Even if he were home every night, she'd never stay.

How ironic that he was finally willing to change and it would do no good.

He went downstairs. The outline of the Christmas tree reminded him of the gift he'd given her. It had hurt a little that she had nothing for him. But she'd been coming from an entirely different direction. He'd not dwelt on it, but maybe he should have.

Yet, all he could remember was how beautiful she had been in the nightgown. At least he'd been given that.

Heading for the kitchen, Jake looked for the bottle of whiskey he'd had the other night. The way things were going, he was going to become good friends with alcohol.

He stopped and shook his head. He didn't need that crutch. The only thing it had accomplished the other night was to give him a headache in the morning.

He turned on the lights. It was two o'clock in the morning. Too dark to go for a walk, too early to be up, but he didn't feel a bit sleepy.

Mostly he felt lost.

Astonished, he sat down and gazed out of the dark window. He was a highly respected journalist. He had friends and acquaintances on three continents. He could write his own ticket for his career.

Yet without Cath, without their marriage, he felt adrift.

Like he'd felt when his father died. And when his mother had transferred her allegiance to her new husband virtually deserting her only son.

Anger took hold. If Cath only wanted a sperm donor, let her find one. If the bond they'd built over the years wasn't enough, so be it. He couldn't change that. He'd tried to rebuild their ties, to keep his marriage strong, but against this he had no defense.

Cath awoke late. She had been a long time going to sleep. The sun was shining, its glare reflecting off the snow, almost blinding in its brilliant light. Feeling groggy and out of sorts, she lay in bed wondering if she ever had to get up. Maybe she could just stay beneath the covers and not deal with life.

But she had things to do. Now more than ever she needed to decide if she was moving here, getting a divorce and moving on with her life.

Slow tears welled in her eyes. How could Jake have not told her? It spoke more to the flimsy strength of their marriage than anything. Granted, they had not discussed children before they married. Actually never discussed it at all. She'd said she wanted a baby this fall and he'd brushed it aside.

But she'd always thought they'd have children eventually. He had to know that.

Even if they didn't want children, wouldn't a husband have shared that major item of information with his wife?

Only if they had a strong marriage.

Which, obviously, they didn't.

The tears ran down the side of her face, wetting her pillow. It had been cruel of Jake to insist he stay for Christmas, for him to tell her he was returning to the States for good and then when her hopes were at their highest, to tell her the truth.

Her heart felt as if it were breaking. There would be no little boy with his daddy's dark hair. No little girl wanting to know the facts about everything. No children at all with Jake. Ever.

By the time Cath rose, she had a headache and was mildly hungry. She took a quick shower. Going downstairs, she was prepared to ask Jake to leave. If he refused, she'd leave. Abby would let her stay with her family until Cath could make other arrangements.

The house was silent. The Christmas tree wasn't lit, though its fragrance still filled the room. Cath barely glanced in. She went to the kitchen, gearing up to confront Jake. It, too, was empty.

Where was he? She looked out the window. There were prints in the snow, but nothing to tell her where he had gone. To the carriage house? On one of his walks? She didn't care.

She prepared a sandwich and ate it standing. Geared up to confront him, she felt let down he wasn't around.

Once she'd eaten, she went back upstairs, carrying her cleaning supplies. There was one more bedroom to clean and the second floor would be taken care of. The work gave her something to do, and the exercise would burn off some of the anguish, she hoped.

The afternoon passed slowly. As she worked she made mental lists of things needed such as curtains for all bedrooms. The rugs in the rooms had been taken out and would require a thorough cleaning. She wanted a nightstand for the room she was working on, there wasn't one. Maybe she should paint the bedrooms. She could use a different color for each one.

For the time being, she'd keep the furniture. It was functional.

And she didn't need baby furniture.

She blinked back the tears. Nothing had changed from the day she left Washington. Granted, for a short time she'd thought her world had changed. She'd thought she and Jake would have it all.

Instead she was back to square one—end the marriage and find a man who'd love her, stay with her and give her children.

When she finished the last bedroom, she vacuumed the hallway, and wiped down the bath.

Tomorrow, if she was still here, she'd begin on the ground floor.

Cath carried all the supplies downstairs. Leaving them in the dining room, she glanced at the stack of journals. She wasn't in the mood to read about Tansy and her life. It had an unhappy ending, just like Cath's.

She frowned. Not like hers. Jake was still alive and well. Tansy had lost her husband to death.

Cath swallowed. In comparison, she had so much. Tansy would have given anything to see her Jonathan again. Cath and Jake had spent several wonderful days together.

Going into the kitchen, Cath realized it was after four and she still hadn't seen or heard Jake today. Had he left? She raced back upstairs to check his room.

The bed was tumbled as it had been last night. Her new nightgown was in a pile on the floor. Jake's duffel bag was opened on a chair. Some of his things were strewn about. He hadn't left.

So where was he? she wondered as she went back to the kitchen. The cradle seemed to mock her, gleaming in the light. She should never have had Jake bring it up. Never cleaned it up and dreamed dreams as she envisioned a baby lying asleep in it. Their baby.

Chapter 10

Cath put the ham in the oven to warm again and began to heat some vegetables. It was growing dark and she still hadn't seen or heard from Jake. Where was he? Despite her heartache, she was growing concerned. She'd checked the carriage house and found an excuse to go next door to see if he was there. On her way back from Mrs. Watson's, she realized Jake's car was not in the driveway. Had he left without taking his things?

She stayed in the kitchen, not wanting to be reminded of decorating the tree by using the living room. Christmas was over.

She heard the car in the driveway. Anger flared again. She wanted to rail against him for keeping her in the dark for so long. Why hadn't he told her long ago?

Though she couldn't think when the appropriate time would be. Had she told him about her appendectomy? She thought so, but maybe not. Still, it wasn't the same thing.

He'd known she wanted a baby this fall. The first time she'd brought up the subject would have been an appropriate time to tell her.

He hadn't because she would have left. He explained that.

Tears welled again. She dashed them away and began to calmly slice the ham when he entered the kitchen.

She heard the slap of papers on the table and turned.

"Your aunt did write a family history and turned a copy in to the local library. They had a genealogy section with lots of information. All you want to know about Tansy and Jonathan is in there."

"You went to research Tansy and Jonathan?" she asked in disbelief. He'd turned her world upside down and then gone off to do research?

"Wrapping up loose ends, Cath. I'll be leaving in the morning." He walked through to the dining room. A moment later she heard his step on the stairs.

No apology, no sign of regret. She stared at the thick stack of paper. He had flung them down and walked away. Tying up loose ends. She crossed to the table. Picking up the stack, she noticed several paper-clipped sections. One was a family history, another was the history of the house and a third looked like official documents from the county clerk's office. Jake had obviously spent all day locating this material. He knew she'd wished to know more, and had found what she wanted.

She sat at the table and began to read what her aunt Sally had written more than twenty years ago. When the buzzer sounded, it jarred her. She got up and turned off the stove and oven. Serving her plate, she went back to the table and picked up the pages. She'd read in her room.

Passing Jake's room, she hesitated by the closed door. What was there to say?

"Dinner's on the stove," she called, and turned for her room. She closed that door and sat in the chair near the window. Reading as she ate, and then continuing when she was finished, Cath was fascinated by the history her aunt had unearthed.

Saddened, too, to learn that Tansy had never remarried. She'd mourned her Jonathan all her life. And it had been a long one. She had died in the 1830s, at the age of ninety-two. She'd lived in the house Jonathan had built—the large house built for a family to grow in—until her death. It had been filled with love and laughter and children. Her cousin Timothy Williamson and his wife had had eleven children. And Tansy had helped raise every one.

Cath looked away from the history, wondering how much of what Tansy felt would be in the later journals. For a moment a shiver of apprehension coursed through her. What if she were more like Tansy than she wanted to admit? What if she never found another man to love as she loved Jake? What if she mourned him all her life and lived to be in her nineties? She yearned for children, but not every woman who wanted a baby had one. Tansy had loved her cousin's children. How much must she have missed having her own with Jonathan?

The house had been in her family for years, but came down through Tansy's cousin, not Jonathan. Their last name had been White. It was Tansy's cousin Timothy who had been the first Williamson to live in the house.

Aunt Sally even wrote about the necklace, saying it had been lost during the Civil War, just as Jake had guessed.

Sally lamented the fact her nephew, Cath's father, had not wanted the old house. It should stay in the family. She hoped her grandniece would bring it back to life, and so she ended the history.

Cath could never sell it. Not after all this.

She might never fill it with children, but it was her heritage and she would hold on to it.

She didn't feel herself falling asleep, but woke with a stiff neck sometime later. It was almost 4:00 a.m.! She quickly dressed for bed and crawled into the cold sheets, going back to sleep. This time she dreamed she was an old woman, alone in a big house, with Tansy's necklace. She sat in front of a fireplace in the kitchen and lamented war.

When Cath awoke again, it was midmorning. She needed to talk to Jake before he left. She couldn't let things end like this.

He sat at the kitchen table, his duffel near the back door, when she entered a short time later. A hot cup of coffee held in his hand. He was reading one of the journals.

"Good morning," he said without looking up.

"Good morning. Ready to leave, I see," she said. Her heart raced. Sadness overwhelmed her. Six years of love and worry and loneliness and sparks of sheer joy crowded the memories of her mind. She saw a fabulously handsome, virile man sitting at her table, and her heart skipped a beat.

"It may be that I'm more like Tansy than I expected, though her blood doesn't run through my veins," she said, pulling out a chair and sitting before her knees gave way.

"No?" he asked.

"She never had children. She lived with her cousin and his wife and was auntie to their children. They were the ones to inherit when she died. She was Tansy White, not even a Williamson."

"You'll go on to have that family, Cath. Some smart guy will snap you up in no time and make sure you have a dozen kids, if that's how many you want."

"Why didn't you tell me, Jake?" she asked.

"I figured you'd leave once you knew. I hoped against it, hoped you'd get enough of children at the school. I figured that's the way it'd play out if I ever had to tell you." He swallowed hard, studying her as if memorizing every feature. "Look at my mother. One child wasn't enough for her. She had to remarry and have three more. Then her life was complete. Only, somewhere along the way she forgot about that first child. Her second family became her focus. Things would have been different if my father had lived. But he didn't. And children became the overruling passion of my mother. When you first brought it up, I was stunned. For once in my life, I thought I was wanted for myself. Not for some genetic donation to create a baby. Never once in five years did you mention having children. Then suddenly, wham, it's the most important thing you can think of."

Cath blinked. She had never thought about his feeling that way. She knew about his family. He had shared that, and it had been hard for such a proud man to admit how left out he'd been as a child. He'd overcome a great deal to achieve all he had. She wouldn't for one second want to diminish that. Or consider him only a means to an end. She'd loved him, wanted his children as a part of that love.

She'd never considered this point of view. If someone thought that of her, it would hurt. After all that Jake had gone through, she regretted his feeling that way. She'd never wanted to hurt him.

For a long moment all she heard was the sound of water dripping from the roof as the sun melted the snow. The fragrance of coffee would forever be tied to this conversation. She stared at him, not knowing what to say.

Jake broke eye contact first. He lifted his cup and drained it. "I'll be on my way in a little while. Thought I'd take one more walk along the river. I called Sam last night and canceled the request to stay stateside. I'll be heading for London in the morning. Have your attorney send the papers to the office and they'll be forwarded to me."

He rose, shrugged on his jacket and headed out.

Cath sat as still as a statue, fearing if she moved an inch, she'd shatter into a thousand pieces. How cruel her actions must seem. His announcement had caught her unaware, but that didn't mean she didn't love him. She didn't only want him as a sperm donor. She wanted her husband!

I thought I was wanted for myself. His words echoed in her mind.

All she could picture was the bewilderment a young boy must have felt when his father died. And again when his mother remarried and started a new family. Always on the outside, never feeling truly wanted.

Cath loved Jake. She had from the first time she'd met him. She hadn't been thinking about children back then, but about the most wonderful man in the world. A man who seemed equally taken with her. Would she have left him if he'd told her at the very beginning? She began to think she wouldn't have. In the beginning it had been just Cath and Jake. It was only lately that she yearned for more. Aunt Sally's death had changed things for her and she had only looked at her own selfish desire. Was it a woman thing, wanting a baby? She frowned. She did not want to be labeled a woman like his mother. She'd harbored uncharitable thoughts about the woman since she'd first heard about her. Today's revelation made her even more angry at his mother. She should have cherished and loved her first child. Had her goal been to have children just to have them, or to love and raise them?

What was hers?

She feared she was more like Tansy than she expected.

The truth was Cath had never looked at another man after she fell in love with Jake. Even thinking she was ending her marriage, she couldn't summon up a spark of interest in finding another man. Everyone would be compared with Jake. And found lacking.

But could she give up her dream of a family?

Two was a family.

She wanted more.

Sometimes in life people didn't get what they wanted. Aunt Sally hadn't. Her fiancé had been killed at Normandy and she'd never found another to love. Cath shivered.

Were there other women in her family who were one-man women? What if she never found another man to love? Could she throw away what she had in the nebulous hope of finding love again?

She'd debated that in her mind all fall long. She thought she'd settled it. But seeing Jake changed everything.

"Cath!" A voice yelled from the yard.

She went to the door and opened it, stepping onto the back stoop.

Bart was running along the river, heading downstream, toward the McDonald yard.

"Bart?"

"Cath, get blankets and come a running. Jake fell into the river. I'm hoping to get him out at the dock."

She stood in shock for a moment—Jake had fallen into the river? He could freeze to death! She saw Pearl running from her house, two blankets in her arms.

"Cath, call for an ambulance. We couldn't get him out, the banks are too steep and it's so slippery with this slush," Pearl called, sliding as she ran after Bart.

Cath didn't hesitate, though she longed to cry out against the injustice of it all. He couldn't die! He'd been in wars and natural disasters, he couldn't die in her backyard. She whirled and went into action. As a teacher she'd been trained in emergency procedures. She called 9-1-1 and reported an accidental plunge into the James River. An ambulance was promised immediately. Cath flung on her jacket and scooped up the afghan from the sofa and dashed out the back door, running as fast as she could after Pearl and Bart. She could see them on the dock in the distance.

Over and over in her mind chanted the words, *wanted for myself.* She did want Jake for himself. For herself. *She loved Jake.* With a soul-searing depth that frightened her. And gave meaning to her life. That would never change. How had she ever thought it would?

The slushy ground was slippery and sloppy. The sunshine belied the danger beneath her feet. Melting snow made it almost impossible to keep from falling. Cath slipped and fell twice, soaking her jeans and scraping one palm. Keeping the afghan as dry as possible, each time she scrambled to her feet and kept going. Her heart raced, time seemed to drag by, each second an eternity. She had to get to Jake. Had to tell him he was all she wanted. He would be enough for her the rest of her days, if he only didn't die! God, don't let her end up like Tansy, losing the only man she loved!

The river water would be barely above freezing. How long would someone last in such cold water? Could he catch hold of the landing platform at the McDonald's dock? Was it still there? She hadn't used that since she was a teenager. Who knew what changes might have been made over the past ten years?

"Jake," she screamed, running as fast as the terrain permitted.

As she drew closer she could see Pearl on the dock that jutted twenty feet into the river. Bart had jumped down to the landing platform. She caught her breath. Jake had been stopped by the platform, but she couldn't tell if he'd caught it or slammed into it by the river current. Bart was struggling to pull Jake from the water. In only a moment both men were lying on the landing. Jake was streaming water, soaking Bart.

Cath reached the dock and jumped down beside the two men. Bart sat up.

"You okay?" he asked, and gently pushed Jake to lie on his back.

His eyes were closed, his lips blue, but, thank God, he was breathing very faintly. A scrape near his hairline bled sluggishly.

Cath unfolded the afghan and wrapped it around him, snuggling closer to share her own body heat. He was soaking wet and freezing cold.

"Jake, say something. Are you all right?" she asked frantically.

"Here, take these blankets, too. He needs to get warm. That water is freezing," Pearl said, dropping down the blankets she held. "Are you dry enough, Bart, or do you need to wrap up, too?" she asked.

"I'm fine. My slacks are wet, but I'll be okay for a little while. Get Jake warm first," he said.

Cath was trying. She rubbed his face gently, feeling the chill of his skin against her palms. She feared her hands were getting too cold to help.

"Why doesn't he say something?" she asked, rubbing his hands, they felt like ice.

"I think he hit his head when he was trying to catch hold of the landing platform," Bart said. "He was doing okay until then. Good thing we saw him slip in. He could freeze to death in that water in just a few minutes."

They wrapped the blankets around him, but Jake made no move to help himself. Cath pressed herself against him. "He will be all right, won't he?" she asked. He was still breathing but was so still, and his lips remained blue.

The ambulance siren could be heard.

"I'll go tell them where we are," Pearl said, hurrying toward Cath's house.

"What happened?" Cath asked as she and Bart chafed his limbs, trying to warm Jake.

"He was walking along the bank, too close to the edge, hit a patch of slush and over the side he went. I ran out—he was holding on to a clump of grass at the water's edge, but we couldn't get him out. It's only about a three-foot drop, but the ground is so slippery with the slush. I couldn't get too near the edge, for fear of joining him."

Cath shuddered to think of both men in the water. Who would have fished them both out?

"He told me you spoke of a dock downstream, he said he'd try for that. Then he let go and drifted along the shore. I ran to tell Aunt Pearl and then headed for the dock. He was still lucid when he reached here, but whacked his head a moment later."

Cath held Jake tightly, saying everything she could to make him hold on.

"I love you, Jake. It doesn't matter about anything else. We're a family, you and me. And that's enough. Hold on, love. Help is on the way."

Cath had never felt so helpless. Jake was her rock, her anchor. What if he didn't recover? What if he did but had changed his mind and wanted nothing to do with a woman like his mother who put so much emphasis on kids to the detriment of everything else?

"I'm sorry, Jake. So sorry. Come back to me. Don't be like Jonathan and leave forever. Stay with me. Grow old with me. Jake, please wake up!"

The paramedics hurried to the dock. In less time than Cath could imagine, they had Jake on a stretcher and were heading for the ambulance.

"We'll come to the hospital with you, dear," Pearl said, when Bart and Cath climbed up on the dock.

"Can't I go in the ambulance with him?" Cath asked.

One of the paramedics looked at Bart and shook his head. Cath saw the sign and almost collapsed.

"I'm going!" she said. "And you're going to make sure my husband is fine!"

The ride to the hospital was a nightmare. Jake was so cold they broke out warming bags and packed them around him. He never regained consciousness. Once at the hospital, he was wheeled away and Cath was left to answer the questions of the admitting clerk.

Pearl and Bart arrived a short time later.

"How is he?" Pearl asked when they found Cath in the small waiting room.

"I haven't heard. He has to be all right!" She couldn't voice her fear that she'd left things too late. She would not become another Tansy. This family story would have a happy ending! At least she hoped so. She prayed for Jake's recovery, glad Pearl and Bart had come to be with her. She felt alone and afraid. What if Jake didn't recover?

She knew Tansy's anguish. How would she go on?

A half hour later a young intern came into the waiting room.

"Mrs. Morgan?" he called.

"Yes?" Cath jumped up and almost ran over to where he stood.

"It looks as if your husband's going to be fine. He's being taken to a room now. We want to keep him over night. He has a concussion and his body temperature is still well below normal. We're warming him up slowly and will monitor the concussion. You can see him in about fifteen minutes, room 307. But just for a moment. Rest and warmth are the best things for him now."

"Thank you." Cath burst into tears, feeling as if the weight of the world had been lifted. She had to see him, to make things right.

"We'll wait here for you, dear," Pearl said, settling back down in the uncomfortable seat.

"Take your time. We'll drive you home when you're ready to leave," Bart said, sitting beside his aunt.

Cath almost told them she'd never be ready to leave, but knew the hospital probably wouldn't let her stay.

She found the room on the third floor. It was a semiprivate room, but only one bed was occupied. Jake was bundled in blankets, one hand lying on the sheet, the rest of him covered from neck to toes. He had his eyes closed, and a white bandage on his head.

She entered. Had he regained consciousness?

"Jake?"

He opened his eyes and looked at her. Then he deliberately turned his head and closed his eyes, shutting her out completely.

"Oh, Jake, I'm so sorry," she said. Reaching out to take his hand, Cath was startled when he snatched it away, slipping it beneath the blanket, out of reach.

"You're going to be fine, the doctor said." She moved around the bed, but he merely turned his head the other way.

"Go home, Cath. There's nothing more to be said."

"Yes, there is. I was wrong. I'm sorry. I want our marriage to flourish."

"Get out."

"Jake, didn't you hear me?"

He looked at her then, his eyes bloodshot, his lips still faintly blue. "Did you hear me? Get out!"

"Not until you listen to me."

"Sorry, time for me to check vitals again," a nurse said in the doorway. "And I have some more warm blankets and a warm drink for you, Mr. Morgan."

"She was just leaving," Jake murmured, turning from Cath.

"I'll check on you later," Cath said tentatively.

"Don't bother. I'm only in here for observation. I'll be out in the morning."

"Then I'll come pick you up."

She left before he could say anything else. The nurse was already talking about seeing how much warmer he was.

Cath felt shell-shocked. He hadn't wanted to see her. She had apologized and he'd brushed it off.

She had to make him see she'd had a change of heart.

"How is he?" Pearl asked when Cath entered the waiting room.

"Cranky," she said, hoping it was the near-death experience making him that way, not that she'd lost her last chance.

"Men do not make the best patients," Pearl said.

"I resent that," Bart said, rising. "Ready to go home?"

Cath nodded, feeling drained and tired. And immensely

sad. Had she lost what she just realized was worth more than anything to her? How would she go on if Jake truly left?

When Bart dropped her off at the old house, he asked if she needed anything.

"Actually you could help me move something, if you would." She'd had enough time to think between the hospital and home. She knew what she was going to do. She was betting her future on it.

"Sure thing."

They moved the cradle back to the spot in the cellar where Cath had first found it. Without a second glance at it, she left it behind and followed Bart back to the kitchen.

"I appreciate your saving Jake, if I didn't say so before, I'm sorry. He's all I have."

"He might have saved himself if he hadn't hit his head. Glad I saw him slip, or he'd have been in a real mess."

Or dead. Cath shuddered.

"Let us know how he does," Pearl said, giving Cath a hug. "Want to come over to our place for supper tonight?"

"Thank you, but no. I have a lot to do before Jake gets home tomorrow. And if he calls, I want to be home." Cath thanked them both for their help and watched as they drove the short distance to Pearl's house.

Cath went to the living room and sank on the sofa, gazing at the ashes in the fireplace. She hoped they didn't reflect the state of her marriage.

For a long time she sat in thought. All the arguments she'd had during the fall rose, but were dismissed in light of the knowledge she now had. Finally she rose and went to find Jake's computer. With only a small search, she found what she was looking for. Using her cell phone, she called Sam Miller.

It took her a few minutes to get through to the man himself, but she patiently used Jake's name at every stage and refused to tell anyone else why she was calling.

When they were finished, she brought up the boxes for the ornaments and began to disassemble the Christmas tree.

Chapter 11

Jake walked up the driveway. He'd had the cab drop him at the curb. The snow continued to melt. Some of the asphalt was visible now. His car needed to be cleared. He'd load his duffel and head out. He'd missed his flight, but once he got to a phone, he'd square things with Sam.

His head still ached. The doctor had told him it might for several weeks. He'd given him some pain pills, but Jake hadn't taken any. He was driving up to D.C. as soon as he got his things, no sense risking that by getting dopey on drugs.

When he reached the back door, he noticed the Christmas tree leaning against the house. It still looked fresh and vibrant. In only a few more days, however, the needles would begin to drop until it was merely brittle branches.

Sort of like he felt, he thought wryly.

Opening the door, he stepped into the kitchen. His duffel was still by the door, where he'd left it yesterday. Beside it sat two suitcases—Cath's.

He should grab his bag and leave. But he couldn't resist telling her goodbye. He'd acted like an idiot at the hospital. He hated her seeing him down and out. Things had been bad enough without that. He'd rather her remember him standing on his own two feet than helplessly shivering while trying to get warm.

Just then she breezed into the kitchen, carrying a heavy box.

"Jake! I was coming at ten to pick you up," she said, putting the box on the kitchen table. She ran over to him and hugged him. Involuntarily his arms came up around her and he buried his face in her sweet hair. Closing his eyes he focused on every impression, burning each into his memory. Her hair was soft and sweet and smelled like apple blossoms. Her body was feminine and curvy, molding with his. Her arms were tight around him, clinging like they'd never let go. Her voice was melodic, the prettiest he'd ever heard.

"I was so worried about you. I stopped back at the hospital last night, but you were asleep and the doctor said that was the best thing. They were checking you every couple of hours for the concussion, but it wasn't getting worse." She pulled back a little and looked up at him, her eyes full of concern.

"Should you be up and about so soon? How's your head?" she asked.

"It aches, but I was released with a clean bill of health. Just have to be careful and not bang it into anything."

She smiled, hugging him again.

"I came for my bag, Cath."

"Sure. Mine are ready. I did want to take the journals, though," she said, stepping away and moving back to the carton on the table. "Hold the door, will you?"

"What are you talking about?"

"Taking the journals?"

"No, that your bags are ready."

"I have to stop at the condo for my passport. And see about another set of clothes. Mostly I brought old things down here to do cleaning in."

"Where are you going?"

"Damascus," she said.

His eyes narrowed. Had the blow to the head addled his brains? What was she talking about?

"Damascus?"

She nodded. Picking up the carton, she carried it toward him. "Open the door for me, will you?"

He didn't budge.

"I'm going to Damascus," he said.

"I know, that's why I'm going," she said, standing in front of him with the heavy box.

"What are you talking about?"

"Get the door, this is heavy!"

He opened the door and followed her to her car, opening the back door so she could slide the carton on the seat.

"I just need to put my suitcases in and get the lunch I fixed for us and I'm ready. I would have had this all done before ten, when I planned to go to the hospital to get you."

"Damascus," he repeated, closing the car door and studying her.

"I talked to Sam Miller yesterday and asked for the safest place closest to where you were going. He said Damascus. I can stay there and you can come home whenever you get a break."

Cath watched him close his eyes and shake his head, then heard him groan softly.

Anxious, she reached out to grab his arm.

"Are you sure you should be up?"

He opened his eyes and nodded slowly. "I just shouldn't be making sudden moves. Cath, you are not going to Damascus."

"I am. I'm going wherever you go."

"You're a teacher in Washington, not a nomad like me."

"I'm changing that. I love you, Jake. I knew it before I almost lost you yesterday, but that was a scare I never want to live through again. It showed me how precious our love is. And how fleeting it could be. I don't want to end up like Tansy, mourning you the rest of my life. Or even Aunt Sally."

"Aunt Sally?"

"She lost her love in the Second World War. She never found another. I can't take that risk when I already love the world's most fantastic man."

"I thought you wanted children."

"I thought I did, too. But what I wanted was *your children.* Since that isn't going to happen, then I'll drop the subject."

"Just like that?"

She hesitated only a moment, feeling the pang at losing the dream. But compared with what she'd learned yesterday when she thought she might lose him, it was a minor price to pay, the loss of a dream. She smiled at him with all the love in her heart.

"Just like that. I love you, Jake. You, and only you, are who I want to be my family." She held her breath. She'd put everything on the line, faxing in her resignation, leaving her friends, to go with this man. What if he turned away like he had yesterday? It would be no more than she deserved, but more than she could bear.

He didn't move for a moment. Just when Cath thought

she'd explode he reached for her, pulling her into a tight embrace. His mouth found hers and he kissed her long and hard.

"You don't have to go with me," he said a minute later. "I can still ask for a stateside assignment."

"I want to be with you. I'm tired of being alone. And I want you to know beyond anything how much I love you. You were willing to give up your career for me. I want to show you I'm willing to give up my job for you. I don't want anything to keep us apart."

"You love teaching."

"I do. I love you more. Besides, I can find a job teaching English in Damascus, I bet. I want you to know beyond a shadow of a doubt that you are all I need to make my life perfect."

He kissed her again, holding her like she was fragile crystal. Cath reveled in being in his arms, longing to remain there all her life. She'd readjust her plans for the future. Nothing was as important as being with this special man.

"You don't have to leave everything to show me you love me."

"I want to. I've never been to Damascus."

"I'll ask for a stateside assignment."

"After this one, but only if you want."

"I want. Maybe even something close enough we can stay in this house. It's your legacy from the past. Don't sell it, Cath. It's got a great history behind it."

For a fleeting moment Cath regretted there would be no children to leave it to when she and Jake no longer lived in it. But life was what it was. She'd already glimpsed what it would be like without Jake and what it could be with him. There was no hardship in that choice. She'd been fooling herself all autumn that she could leave. She could no more give him up than she could give up breathing.

"Whenever we're ready, we'll come back," she said. The future wasn't the one she'd thought to have, but with Jake it would always be more than enough.

Epilogue

Jake paced the small room, stopping at the window, then turning to pace back to where Cath was sitting. The utilitarian furnishings were uncomfortable, how could she sit so calmly?

"How can you be so patient?" he asked. "Aren't you scared to death?"

She smiled and shook her head. "You've been shot at, almost drowned in the James River and had bricks fall on you from the earthquake last fall. What are you afraid of?"

"Messing up."

"You won't," she said with conviction.

"It's more than I can handle."

"It's not."

"You're sure?"

"Oh, yes. We'll make it—together." Laughter filled her eyes. He frowned and turned to pace back to the window, staring over the bleak landscape. Snow had turned dirty along the side of the street. The black tree branches looked stark against the gray sky. More snow was predicted that night. He hoped the storm would hold off until they were gone.

They'd signed the last of the papers earlier that afternoon. Everything was set for their flight home. It was the waiting that was getting to him. And the uncertainty.

Jake turned and looked at his wife. She smiled at him, obviously amused at his behavior. For a moment he felt silly. He was a grown man, had faced dangers most men rarely even thought about. He couldn't believe Cath had given up everything to follow him. The past couple of years had been fantastic. They were closer than ever. They'd visited every capital in Europe, stopped in exotic locales around the Mediterranean. Theirs was a strong love that would sustain him through anything. Even this.

He hoped.

The door opened. Cath jumped to her feet. Slowly Jake turned, his heart pounding.

"Here they are," the woman said in heavily accented English. "Anna and Alexander. We call him Sasha as a baby name." Her uniform was gray, the apron she wore was white. Her eyes were kind.

The two-year-old girl stared at them, her blue eyes bright with wonder. Cath knelt near her and held out a dolly.

"Hello, Anna. I'm your new mommy," she said softly. Then carefully she reached out and pulled the child into her arms. "I'm so happy to see you today," she said, her voice breaking slightly. She closed her eyes for a moment, but not before Jake saw the tears.

Jake took a deep breath and stepped forward.

"Here you go," the woman said, handing the baby to Jake. He hesitated a moment, then took the seven-month-old boy.

The baby's blue eyes stared up into Jake's. For a moment panic took hold, then sanity returned. He'd wanted to do this. For Cath, and for himself.

Now he was a father of two children, orphaned by the fighting in their home country, alone in the world except for him and Cath.

The baby's fist waved and Jake caught it, feeling the tiny fingers wrap around his thumb. He said the words he'd never expected to say.

"Hello, Sasha, I'm your daddy."

Already he felt the tendrils of love wrap around his heart. He looked at Cath and smiled. They had discussed the option of adoption shortly after they arrived in Damascus. Cath had a heart full of love to share, and he wanted to be right there with her. She was right, together they could do this.

They were flying home tonight—to spend Christmas at the house beside the James River. He had a yard to fence, a dock to build and two precious children to love and raise. Their legacy to the future.

"Ready, Daddy?" Cath asked, picking up Anna and carrying her over to Jake.

He leaned over and gave the little toddler a kiss on the cheek, then one for Cath.

"We're ready, Mommy, let's get our kids home."

* * * * *

CHRISTMAS GIFT: A FAMILY

Barbara Hannay

Chapter 1

Christmas Eve. Oh, joy! For Jo Berry it meant sitting behind a shop counter in Bindi Creek, staring out through the dusty front window at the heat haze shimmering on the almost empty main street, and trying not to think about all the fabulous parties she was missing back in the city.

She was especially trying not to think about the office party tonight. Mind you, she had a feeling things might get out of hand. Her friend Renee was determined to nail a big career boost by impressing the boss but, apart from buying something clingy and skimpy to wear, her idea of pitching for a promotion usually involved clearing her desk of sharp objects.

Jo still clung to the belief that a girl could smash her way through the glass ceiling via non-stop slog and professionalism, without the aid of deep cleavage, or tying the boss up with tinsel.

Still, she would have liked to be in Brisbane tonight. She

enjoyed her friends' company and it was great fun to be on the fringes of an occasional outrageous party.

It wasn't her friends' wild antics that had stopped her from partying in the city. Every Christmas she took her annual leave and travelled home to help out in her family's shop.

And no, she wasn't a goody two-shoes, but honestly, what else could a girl do when she had a dad on an invalid pension and a mum who was run off her feet trying to play Santa Claus to half a dozen children while preparing Christmas dinner, *plus* running Bindi Creek's only general store during the pre-Christmas rush?

Not that anyone actually rushed in Bindi Creek.

At least…no one usually rushed.

Nothing exciting happened.

And yet…right now there was someone in a very great hurry.

From her perch on a stool behind the counter, Jo watched with interest as a black four-wheel drive scorched down the street, screeched to an abrupt and noisy halt in the middle of the road and then veered sharply to park on the wrong side of the road—directly outside the shop.

A lanky, dark-haired stranger jumped out.

A very handsome, lanky, dark-haired stranger.

Oh, wow!

He was quite possibly the most gorgeous man Jo had ever seen, not counting movie stars, Olympic athletes or European princes in her favourite celebrity magazines.

In spite of the layer of dust that covered his vehicle and the intense, sweltering December heat, he was dressed in city clothes—tailored camel-coloured trousers and a white business shirt, although as a concession to the heat his shirt was open at the neck and his long sleeves were rolled back to his elbows to reveal lightly tanned, muscular forearms.

Jo slid from her stool and tucked a wing of brown hair behind one ear as she stood waiting for the ping of the bell over the shop door. *Please, please come in, you gorgeous thing.*

But the newcomer lingered on the footpath, studying her mum's window display.

Jo couldn't help staring at him.

As he stood with his wide shoulders relaxed and his hands resting lightly on his lean hips, she decided there was a certain elegant charm in the way his soft dark hair had been ruffled and messed into spikes. And there was definite appeal in the very masculine way he rubbed his lightly stubbled jaw as he studied her mother's dreadful tinsel-draped arrangement of tinned plum puddings, boxes of shortbread and packets of chocolate-covered sultanas.

He lifted his gaze and peered inside the shop and, before Jo could duck, his eyes—light blue or green, she couldn't be sure—met hers. Darn, he'd caught her staring.

She felt her cheeks grow hot as he stared back. Then he smiled. But it was rather a stiff smile and she sensed instantly that he was searching for something. By the time he entered the shop her curiosity was fully aroused.

"Good afternoon," she said warmly. He was close enough now for her to see that his eyes were green rather than blue and fringed by the blackest of lashes. "Can I help you?"

This time his smile was of the slightly crooked variety, the kind that should come with a health warning about dangers to women.

"I'll just look around for a moment," he said, casting a doubtful glance at the bags of sugar and flour and the shelves of tinned food that filled the store.

As soon as he spoke Jo realised he was English. His voice was deep and rich—refined and mellow—reminding her of actors in Jane Austen movies and men who lived in stately homes surrounded by green acres of parkland and edged by forest.

"Look around as much as you like," she said, trying to sound casual, as if divine Englishmen were a regular part of life in Bindi Creek. And then, because he wasn't a local, she added, "Just sing out if I can be of any help."

At times like this, when the shop wasn't busy, she usually amused herself by trying to guess what a customer might buy. What was this guy after? Engine oil? Shaving cream? *Condoms?*

From the far side of the shop he called, "Do you have any dolls? Perhaps a baby doll?"

Good grief.

"I want the best possible gift for a little girl." It was a command rather than a request. "Little girls still play with dolls, don't they?"

"Some of them do. But I'm sorry, we don't have any dolls here."

He frowned. "You must have little tea sets? Or perhaps a music box?"

In a general store in the middle of the outback? Where did he think he was? A toy shop? "Sorry, we don't have anything like that."

"Nothing suitable at all?"

Think, Jo, think... She walked towards him along the aisles, checking the shelves as critically as he had. Food, household items and pet supplies, a few basic hardware products, a tiny collection of paperback novels... "I assume you're looking for a Christmas present?"

"Yes, for a little girl. She's five years old."

It was the same age as her little sister, Tilly. Jo shook her head. "I'm afraid you're not going to have much luck here."

She pointed to the old-fashioned glass jars on the counter. "We have some fancy sweets and chocolates especially for Christmas."

"I guess they might do." He groaned and ran long fingers through his ruffled hair. Jo caught the glint of gold.

"I'd better get something as a fallback." He began to pick up items at random—throw-away pens, Christmas decorations, a wooden ruler and a school notebook.

Thinking of the beautiful baby doll with a complete change of clothes that she'd bought in Brisbane for Tilly, Jo decided he definitely needed help. But given their limited stock it wasn't going to be easy.

How intriguing… What was this man doing out here in the middle of nowhere?

"How far are you travelling?" she asked.

"To Agate Downs."

"Oh, I know that property. The Martens' place. It's not far. So you're looking for a present for the little girl they're caring for, are you?"

He looked startled. "You know her?" He moved closer, his expression more intense.

"Ivy? This is a small town. Sure, I've met her. Do you know what she likes?"

His throat worked. "No, I've never met her."

"She's a lovely little thing." Jo was being totally honest. She'd been quite smitten by the little girl. She had the most exquisite face Jo had ever seen on a child and her prettiness was all the more striking because it contrasted so strongly with the ugly scars on her arm. The poor little mite had been terribly burned in an accident a few years ago. "Ivy's been in here to shop with Ellen Marten a couple of times this week."

"Really?"

The eagerness in his voice and his eyes was perplexing. Jo looked at him sharply. Was she getting carried away or was there a resemblance between this man and the child? Ivy's hair was dark and her eyes were clear green like his.

What was going on? Could he be Ivy's father? Jo didn't like to be too nosy, so she hadn't asked the Martens about Ivy's parents, but she'd heard rumours about a tragedy and there'd actually been talk about an estranged father coming to claim her.

Her customer sighed and gave a little shake of his head. "I'd completely forgotten that a little girl at Christmas needs a present."

She felt a rush of sympathy. *Come on, Jo, do something to help.*

"Would you like some of these?" she asked, lifting the lid on a huge jar of chocolates wrapped in red, silver and gold foil. "Ivy's quite partial to them." Just yesterday she'd slipped the little girl a chocolate when Ellen Marten wasn't looking and she'd been rewarded by a beaming smile.

"I'll take the lot," he said, looking exceptionally pleased. "And I'll have a couple of tins of the shortbread and a bag of those nuts."

Jo lifted the metal scoop and said, "Perhaps I could gift wrap these things to make them look a little more festive?"

She was rewarded by another of his dangerous smiles. "That would be wonderful."

Leaning one hip against the counter, he folded his arms across his chest and watched her as she began to wrap his purchases in red sparkly paper. She felt self-conscious as his green eyes watched her hands at work, cutting and folding paper, reaching for sticky tape and then measuring lengths of shiny silver and gold ribbon.

If it had been any other customer she would have chattered away, but she was too absorbed by the mystery of his connection with Ivy.

He didn't seem in a hurry so she took her time making the gifts as pretty as she could, adding a sprinkle of glitter and a tiny white fluffy snowman on the chocolates.

"Thank you so much, that's terrific." He reached into his back pocket for his wallet, extracted several notes and held them out.

She noticed the glint of gold again. He was wearing a signet ring, engraved with a crest and worn on his little finger.

"You will charge extra for all the trouble you've gone to, won't you?" he said.

"Not when it's Christmas." She sent him a quick smile as she handed him his change.

She expected him to leave then, but he continued to stand there, looking at the bright parcels on the counter with a long distance look in his eyes, as if he were lost in thought.

"Was there something else?" she asked tentatively. She wouldn't mind at all if he wanted to stay longer. Nothing else like him was likely to happen to her this Christmas.

"If only I could take something more exciting, something Ivy would really love," he said, and he glanced behind him to the slightly dusty row of reading material and reached for a comic book. "What about this?"

An Action Man comic? Jo did her best not to look shocked. "I don't think Ivy's started school yet," she suggested gently. "I'd be surprised if she could read."

He closed his eyes for a moment. "It would have been so

simple to pick up a toy in Sydney. There isn't time to ring a city toy shop and fly something out, is there?"

"Well…no. I shouldn't think so…" Goodness, if he was prepared to hire an aircraft, this must be important. He *must* be Ivy's father—and he must also be a man who made sure he got what he wanted. No wonder a box of chocolates seemed unsatisfactory, even with the pretty wrapping.

"There are no other shops around here?"

"No toy shops, I'm afraid. Not unless you want to backtrack about two hundred kilometres."

With an air of resignation he began to gather up his parcels, but he moved without haste.

"You really want to make a big impression on Ivy, don't you?" Jo suggested.

He nodded. "It's vitally important."

There was an intensity in his voice and a sadness in his eyes that sent an unexpected tiny pain sweeping through her. How awful for him if he was Ivy's father, but had never met his daughter. And where was Ivy's mother? What tragedy had occurred? Jo's own family were very close and her soft heart ached for him.

"Well…thank you very much for all your help," he said, turning to go.

Oh, crumbs. She felt rotten about sending him away with such inappropriate presents. "Look," she said to his back. "If this present is really important, I might be able to help you."

He turned and looked at her, his green eyes intense. Fuzzy heat flashed through her.

"I have a mountain of toys that I've bought for my brothers and sisters," she said. "Probably more than I'll need. If—if you'd like to take a look at them, you're welcome. We should be able to find some little toy to add to the chocolates."

His green eyes studied her and she tried to look calm and unaffected, but then he did the crooked smile thing and her insides went crazy.

"That's incredibly kind of you."

"I'll just call one of my brothers to come and mind the shop," she said. "Wait here." And, before he could protest, she hurried away through a door at the back of the shop.

It led directly into their house.

Down the central hallway she rushed, heading straight for the backyard where she knew from the boys' shouts that they were playing cricket. And with every hasty step she fought off doubts.

She knew it was impulsive, but somehow this was something she had to do. Poor little Ivy deserved a proper Christmas present. And of course spending more time with Ivy's gorgeous father was simply a chore to be endured…

She managed to convince her brother Bill that he was needed and then she almost ran back through the house. She was a touch breathless as she re-entered the shop.

The Englishman was still there, looking strangely out of place beside a mountain of dried dog food. He seemed to be making polite conversation with old Hilda Bligh, the town gossip.

"There you are, Jo," said Hilda. "I was just telling Mr Strickland that if the shop's empty we usually holler until someone comes."

Goodness, Hilda already knew the man's name. No doubt the old girl had been treated to one of his dangerously attractive smiles.

"Sorry, Mrs Bligh, you know what Christmas Eve can be like. Here's Bill. He'll look after you."

Jo glanced towards the Englishman, feeling rather foolish because she was about to invite him into her home and she didn't know the first thing about him. "Can you come this way?" she asked him.

"It was very nice to meet you, Mr Strickland," called Hilda Bligh, smiling after him coyly.

Jo led the man through the doorway and into the shabby central passage that ran the full length of their house.

"So you're Mr Strickland?" she said once they were clear of the shop.

"Yes, my name's Hugh—Hugh Strickland. And I believe you're Jo."

Jo nodded.

"Short for Josephine?"

"Joanna." She held out her hand. "Joanna Berry." Somehow it seemed important to shake hands—to make this exchange businesslike. But it wasn't exactly businesslike to have her hand clasped warmly by Hugh Strickland.

"I take it Hilda Bligh filled you in?" she asked.

"Indeed, and with astonishing attention to detail."

She groaned. "I hate to think what she's told you."

Hugh smiled. "I don't think she told me what you scored on your spelling test in the second grade, but I believe I know just about everything else."

"I'm sorry. Outback towns are so—"

"Exposing?"

Jo nodded her head and sighed. This really was the weirdest situation.

"Yes, well…" She took a deep breath. "We'd better take a look at these toys. I'm afraid I'm going to have to take you into my bedroom."

"Really?"

He didn't look shocked—he was too smooth for that—but

Jo knew he was surprised. She made a joke of it. "Of course I don't usually invite strange men into my room within minutes of meeting them."

Amusement sparkled in his eyes. "Mrs Bligh didn't mention it."

Thank heavens he had a sense of humour.

"I've hidden the presents in there, you see, and I can't bring them out or one of the children might find them." She turned and led him down the passage.

But, despite her matter-of-fact air, she was suddenly nervous. It didn't seem possible that she was actually doing this. She, ordinary, average Jo Berry, was taking a man who was a mixture of every gorgeous British actor she'd ever swooned over into her dreadful bedroom.

It was more than dreadful. She'd taken all her favourite bits and pieces to decorate her flat in Brisbane, so her room was as bare and as ugly as a prison cell.

It held nothing more than a simple iron bed with a worn and faded cover, bare timber floorboards, a scratched, unvarnished nightstand and an ancient wardrobe, once polished silky oak, but painted creamy-orange by her father during one of Mum's decorating drives. The old Holland blind that covered her window was faded with age and had a watermark stain where rain had got in during a storm several summers ago.

"Perhaps this isn't a good idea," Hugh said. "I can't take gifts from your family."

"But isn't it vitally important to have a present for little Ivy?"

"Well…"

Without further hesitation, Jo dragged her suitcase out from under the bed. "Luckily I haven't wrapped these yet," she said, looking up at him over her shoulder.

And he was smiling again—that dangerous smile—with his eyes fixed directly on the expanding gap between her T-shirt and her jeans.

Heaving the suitcase on to her bed, she began hauling gifts out to pile on her bedspread.

What she was looking for were the stocking fillers she'd bought to help her mother out—small fluffy toys, plastic spiders, dress-up jewellery, fishing lures, puzzles…

But she more or less had to get everything out because these things were mixed in with the main presents—the action figures and video games for Bill and Eric; the books and CDs for the older boys; the "magic' magnetic drawing board and hair accessories for Grace and the baby doll for Tilly.

She glanced up at Hugh and felt a pang of dismay when she saw the look in his eyes as he stared at the doll.

As baby dolls went, it was perfect. She'd been thrilled when she'd found it. It came in a little cane carry basket with a pink quilted lining and there was also a feeding bottle and a change of clothes.

"You have quite a treasure trove here," he said.

"I need to negotiate a bank loan every year just to cope with Christmas," she joked.

"Six brothers and sisters…"

"Mrs Bligh told you that too?"

He nodded and smiled, then looked back at the bed. "I'd pay you anything for that doll."

Jo thought of Ivy. She was such a sweet little thing and for a fleeting moment she almost weakened. But then she came to her senses. "Sorry. Not possible. That's earmarked for Tilly." She reached for a fluffy lavender-hued unicorn. "What about this? Unicorns are all the rage with the pre-school set."

One dark eyebrow lifted. "I would never have guessed. I'm completely out of my depth when it comes to little girls."

"Or there's this—" She reached for some multicoloured plastic bangles, but stopped when she heard the sound of giggling on the other side of the door. Her stomach plunged.

Tiptoeing to the door, she listened. Yes, there was another burst of giggles.

Carefully, she opened the door a crack and found Tilly and Eric crouching there, their eyes dancing with merriment. "Get lost, you two."

"Bill says you've got a man in there," said Tilly.

"That's none of your business. Now run away."

Eric bumped against the door as if he wanted to push it open, but Jo blocked it with her hip.

"Is he your boyfriend?" asked Tilly.

"No, of course not. Now scram, both of you!"

Face aflame, Jo slipped back through the narrow opening, slammed the door shut and locked it again. Embarrassed, she rolled her eyes to the ceiling, hardly daring to look at Hugh, but when she did she saw that he was standing in the middle of the room with his hands thrust in his trouser pockets, wearing an expression that was a complicated mixture of amusement and impatience.

"I do appreciate your efforts." He gallantly remained silent about the antics of her siblings. "But I think I'd better be off."

"Yes," she said. "Will you take the unicorn?"

"Are you sure you can spare it?"

"Absolutely. Right now, I'd be happy if you took all the presents. I might yet disown my entire family."

He flashed her a smile. "Just the unicorn would be terrific, thank you."

Jo thrust the fluffy toy into a non-see-through pink plastic bag and handed it to him. "Done."

As she hastily transferred everything back into the suitcase and dropped the lid, Hugh reached for his wallet again.

"No." She shook her head. "No money. It's for Ivy." Quickly she opened the door.

"I must say I'm terribly grateful to you," Hugh said. "I would have hated to turn up at Agate Downs on Christmas Eve without the right gift."

His smile and his confession, delivered in his beautifully modulated, polite English voice, had the strangest effect on Jo. She had to fight off a weird impulse to bar the door so he couldn't leave.

"Well," she said, pushing such silliness out of her head and turning briskly businesslike again. "I mustn't keep you any longer, Mr Strickland. I'm sure you need to be on your way and I'd better relieve Bill in the shop."

He hurried off then. After delivering one last quick but sincere thank you he made a hasty farewell, heading out the front door in record time.

Leaping into his vehicle, he pulled out from the kerb at the same reckless speed with which he'd arrived.

And Jo was left feeling strangely deflated.

Her thoughts returned to where she'd been before he'd arrived. Remembering her friends at the office Christmas party in the city, all having a ball.

While Hugh Strickland, possibly the dishiest man in the world and as close to Prince Charming as Jo was ever likely to meet, was riding off in his glittering coach—well, OK, his four-wheel drive. Roaring down a bush track.

Never to be seen again.

Chapter 2

Bindi Creek had its last-minute pre-Christmas rush shortly after Hugh left. It seemed to Jo that almost every household in the township, as well as some from outlying properties, suddenly remembered that the shop would be closed for the next two days and that they needed items vital for Christmas.

No doubt it was paranoia, but Jo couldn't help wondering if some of them had come to the shop just to spy on her. At least two of the local women hinted—with very unsubtle nudges and winks—that they'd heard from Hilda Bligh about Jo's *special* visitor. One of them actually said that she'd heard the Martens were expecting a visit from Ivy's father.

Jo pretended she had no idea what they were talking about.

Apart from these awkward moments, she was happy to be kept busy. The work kept her mind from straying Hughwards.

Brad and Nick, two of her brothers who worked further out west on cattle properties, arrived home around eight. They came into the shop and greeted her with hugs and back slaps and they hung about for ten minutes or so, catching up on her news. Then they went back into the house for the warmed leftover dinner Mum had saved for them.

Jo ate a scratch meal at the counter and she was tired when it was time to close up the shop. She went to lock the front door and looked out into the street and took a few deep breaths. It was a hot, still summer's night and the air felt dry and dusty, but despite this she caught a hint of frangipani and night-scented jasmine drifting from nearby gardens.

Overhead, the Christmas Eve sky was cloudless and clear and splashed with an extravaganza of silver-bright stars. Grace and Tilly would be watching that sky from their bedroom window, hoping for a glimpse of Santa Claus and his reindeer. And Mum would be warning Eric and Bill not to spoil their little sisters' fantasies.

What would little Ivy be doing out at Agate Downs? Had she received her present? Had she liked the lavender unicorn? For a moment Jo let her mind play with the mystery of Hugh Strickland and this child. She could picture him very clearly as he climbed out of his vehicle with the toy unicorn clutched in one hand. Goodness, she should have put it in something more attractive than a plastic bag.

Thinking about him and his mysterious errand caused an unwelcome pang around her heart. She shivered and rubbed her arms to chase away goose-bumps. What was the point of thinking over and over about Hugh? Perhaps she was getting man-crazy. It was six months since she'd broken up with Damien.

She locked the doors, pulled down the blinds, locked the till and turned out the lights in the shop. It was time to slip into her bedroom to wrap her presents. Once the children were safely asleep, she would have fun setting the brightly wrapped gifts under the Christmas tree in the lounge room.

The Berrys enjoyed a no-frills Christmas Eve. She'd have a cup of tea with Mum and they'd both put their feet up. The older boys would sit out on the back veranda with Dad, yarning about cattle and drinking their first icy-cold Christmas beer, while she and Mum talked over their final plans for the festive meals tomorrow.

She hadn't quite completed the gift-wrapping saga when there was a knock on her bedroom door. "Who is it?" she called softly, not wanting to wake her sisters in the next room.

"It's Mum."

"Just a minute." Jo had been wrapping her mother's presents—French perfume and a CD compilation of her mum's favourite music from the sixties and seventies—so she slipped these quickly under her pillow. "I'm almost finished."

When she opened the door her mother looked strangely excited. "You have a visitor."

"Really? Who is it?"

"An Englishman. He says his name's Hugh Strickland."

An arrow-swift jolt shot through Jo. "Are you sure?"

"Of course I'm sure." Margie Berry's brow wrinkled into a worried frown. "Who is he, love? He seems very nice and polite, but do you want me to send him away?"

"Oh, no," Jo answered quickly. "He's just a customer. He—he was in the shop this afternoon."

"Yes, he told me that. He said you were very helpful." Margie looked expectant, but Jo was reluctant to go into details.

Her mind raced. Why was Hugh here? He was supposed to be at Agate Downs. "Wh-where is he?"

"I found him on the back veranda, talking to Dad and the boys, but it's you he wants. He asked for you ever so politely, so I told him to wait in the kitchen."

"The kitchen?" Her bedroom had been bad enough and Jo winced when she tried to picture Hugh Strickland in their big old out-of-date kitchen, cluttered this evening with the aftermath of Mum's Christmas baking. Somehow the image wouldn't gel.

Jo was gripping the door handle so hard her hand ached as she let it go. This didn't make sense. "Did you ask him why he wants to see me?"

Margie gave an irritated toss of her head. "No, I didn't."

Jo wished she had a chance to check her appearance in the mirror, but her mother was waiting with her hands on her hips and a knowing glint in her eyes. Besides, what was the point of titivating? Hugh Strickland had already seen her today and she would look much the same as she had earlier. Her smooth brown hair was cut into a jaw-length bob that never seemed to get very untidy and she wasn't wearing make-up, and there wasn't much she could do to improve her plain white T-shirt and blue jeans.

Just the same, she felt nervous as she set off down the passage for the kitchen, as if she were going to an audition for a part in a play but had no idea what role she was trying for.

Hugh was standing near the scrubbed pine table in the middle of the room and the moment she saw him she went all weak-kneed and breathless.

And that was *before* he smiled.

Oh, heavens, he *was* good-looking. She'd been beginning

to wonder if perhaps her imagination had exaggerated how gorgeous he was.

No way. His dark hair was still spiky, but that was part of his appeal, as was the five o'clock shadow that darkened his strong jaw line. And beyond that there was a subtle air of superiority about him—a matter of breeding perhaps, something unmistakable, like the born-to-win lines of a well-bred stallion.

But behind his charming smile she could sense banked-up emotion carefully held in check. What was it? Anger? Impatience? Dismay?

She wondered if she should ask him to sit down, but his tension suggested he'd rather stand. Why had he returned so soon?

He answered that question immediately when he held out the pink plastic bag she'd given him. "I came to return this."

Frowning, Jo accepted it. She could feel the shape of the fluffy unicorn still inside. Her mind raced, trying to work out what this could mean. "Couldn't you find your way to Agate Downs?"

"I found the place," he said. "Your directions were spot on."

"So what happened? Weren't the Martens home?"

"I turned back without seeing them." A muscle worked in his jaw and he dropped his gaze. His face seemed to stiffen. "I had second thoughts. It's the wrong time."

"Oh." What else could she say? This was none of her business. "That's a—a pity." A few hours ago it had been vitally important that Hugh made a good impression on the child. And it had seemed important that it happened *today.* Jo pressed her lips together, fighting the impulse to interrogate him.

He looked up briefly and she caught a stronger flash of emotion in his intense gaze before he looked away again. Was it anger? "I didn't want to spoil Ivy's Christmas. I—I mean—her guardians knew that I was on my way, but I realised it would be intrusive."

She wondered how Hugh Strickland would react if he knew that the locals were gossiping about him.

His eyes sought hers again. "I suddenly thought how it would be for Ivy to have a strange man turning up on her doorstep on Christmas Eve, claiming—" He broke off in midsentence.

Claiming...what? Jo's tense hands tightened around the package and the unicorn let out a sharp squeak. She was so uptight that she jumped.

"So what will you do now?" she asked.

"I've found a room at the pub."

"Oh...good."

"I'll stay there till Christmas is over and I'll go back to the Martens' place on Boxing Day."

Jo thrust the unicorn back into his hands. "If you're still hoping to see Ivy, you must keep this. You'll need it."

Their hands were touching now, and as they both held the package she was exquisitely aware of Hugh's strong, warm fingers covering hers.

"No," he said. "I came here tonight because I wanted to give this back to you in time for your family's Christmas. There won't be the same pressing urgency for a gift for Ivy once Christmas is over. And this was really meant for one of your sisters."

He was looking directly into her eyes and making her heart pound.

Their gazes remained linked for longer than was necessary, and Jo knew she would always remember the shimmering intimacy of his green eyes as he looked at her then, and the heated touch of his hands on hers.

It was almost depressing to realise that memories of this handsome stranger were going to haunt her nights and linger in her daydreams...for ages into the future...

"Please keep the unicorn." She felt so breathless her voice was hardly more than a whisper. "Believe me, little girls always like presents."

He sent her a quick smile. "If you insist. I'll trust your deep understanding of what little girls like. The only one I know well is my goddaughter, but she's only six months old, so our communication has been somewhat limited."

"Believe me, where presents are concerned, little girls are no different from big girls; they never get tired of receiving gifts."

His eyes flashed confident amusement.

"But I'm sure you already know that."

"Indeed."

But then he seemed to remember something else and almost immediately his smile faded.

And the spell that had kept their hands linked was broken. Jo stepped back, leaving him with the unicorn, and Hugh looked away.

She drew a quick nervous breath. *Calm down, Jo. Stay cool. You're getting overheated about nothing. Nothing. He hasn't come back to see you and he'll be leaving again any moment now.*

"There's another thing I wanted to ask you, Jo," he said softly.

Her head jerked up.

"I wonder if I can possibly impose on you one more time?"

Caught by surprise, she found herself blustering. "How? Wh-what would you like me to do?"

"I want you to come with me when I go back to Agate Downs."

Crumbs. "Why me? I don't understand."

"You already know Ivy—and you have so many brothers and sisters. I have no experience with young children. I can't even remember what it's like to be five."

She tried to speak as casually as he had. "So you think I can help you somehow?"

A muscle in his throat worked. "Yes—if you could spare the time. I get the impression you've hit it off with Ivy already."

"I'm afraid I'm not an expert at managing small children," she warned him. "You've seen how naughty Tilly can be."

"But you're used to them. You're relaxed around them."

"Well…" Jo's immediate impulse was to help him, but a nagging inner warning was hard to ignore. "It might be helpful if I understood a little more about this situation," she said carefully.

He nodded and then he looked directly into her eyes again. "The situation's quite straightforward really. Ivy's my daughter."

Right. Jo tried to swallow. So now she knew for sure. Did this mean Hugh was married? She glanced at his hands. The only ring he wore was the signet ring on the little finger of his left hand.

Sensing the direction of her gaze, he smiled wryly, lifted his hand and waggled his bare fourth finger. "No, I'm not married. I only dated my daughter's mother for a while. And…her mother is dead."

"Oh, how sad." This changed everything. All at once Jo was adrift on a sea of sympathy. She said quickly, "Why don't we sit down for a bit?"

He pulled out a wooden chair on the other side of the kitchen table. "If I'm asking you to help with Ivy I should be perfectly honest with you," he said. "I only learned of her existence a short time ago."

Jo watched the barely perceptible squaring of his shoulders and she sensed that he was working very hard to keep his emotions under control. "That must have been a terrible shock." Her kind-hearted urges were going into overdrive now. "How come you only learned about Ivy recently?"

Hugh stiffened and she guessed she was delving deeper than he wanted to go. But he met her gaze. "Her mother wrote a letter but it never reached me and she died shortly after Ivy's birth."

Jo thought of the dear little bright-eyed Ivy who'd danced about their shop like a winsome fairy while her guardian had selected groceries. How sad that her mother never knew her.

How sad that Hugh still hadn't met her. Jo blinked away the threat of tears.

"It gets worse." Hugh spoke very quietly. "Apparently Linley suffered from severe postnatal depression and—and she committed suicide."

"No!" A horrified exclamation burst from Jo. "I'm so sorry," she added quickly. Then she asked gently, "And you never knew?"

"I thought she had died in a car accident," he said. "There was never any mention of a baby."

Jo wondered if he was being so forthright to draw her into the task of helping him. Well, it was working. It would be hard to turn him down now, especially when his eyes held hers with such compelling intensity.

"Ivy's grandmother died recently and she left instructions in her will, demanding that I claim my daughter," he said. "Of course I wanted to do the right thing by the child, so I came dashing over here. But I've realised now that my timing is off. On Christmas Eve children are expecting Santa Claus, not strange men claiming to be their father."

"Ivy might like you better than Santa Claus," Jo suggested gently.

He sent her a sharp, searching look. "So you think I've done the wrong thing?"

Jo gulped. This gorgeous, confident man was acting as if he really needed her advice. She sent him an encouraging grin. "No, I'm sure you've made the right decision. I always believe it's best to follow your instincts."

"So will you come with me when I collect Ivy?"

Her instincts screamed yes and Jo didn't hesitate to take her own advice.

"Of course I will. I've got a real soft spot for Ivy and, as you said, with six younger brothers and sisters I've got to be something of an expert with kids."

"Absolutely." Hugh glanced at the clock on the wall near the stove and jumped to his feet. "It's getting late and I've taken up far too much of your time."

Jo wondered if she should warn him about Ivy's scars, but perhaps that would only make him more anxious about meeting her. Or maybe he already knew. It might be best not to make a big deal about them.

Standing, she shoved her hands into the back pockets of her jeans and shrugged in an effort to look unconcerned. "So we have a date for Boxing Day?"

He nodded stiffly. "Thanks. I'd really appreciate your help."

Then he turned and walked to the kitchen door. Jo followed.

"I hope you'll be comfortable at the pub," she said as they stepped into the hallway. "It's not very flash."

"It looks perfectly adequate."

"A bit lonely for Christmas."

"I'll be fine." Suddenly he looked very English, sort of stiff-upper-lipped and uncomfortable, as if he couldn't stand sentimental females who made fusses about Christmas.

Her mother appeared in the hall. "Did I hear you say you're staying at the pub, Mr Strickland?"

Jo wanted to cringe at her mother's intrusion, but Hugh didn't seem to mind.

"Yes. It's basic but quite adequate."

"You're not having Christmas dinner there, are you?"

"They've booked me in. Why? Is there a problem?"

"Oh, not the pub for Christmas." Margie sounded shocked and she thumped her hands on her hips in a gesture of indignation. "We can't let you do that."

"I'm sure the food will be fine." Hugh was beginning to sound defensive now. "I'm told they do a fine roast turkey."

"But you'll be all on your own. At Christmas."

Jo could tell where this was heading, but it would look a bit weird if she suddenly leapt to Hugh's rescue by insisting that he would be fine at the pub.

"And you're so far from home," her mother said. "No, Mr Strickland, I won't hear of it. You must join us tomorrow. I know we're not flash, but at least there's a crowd of us. You won't feel lonely here and we're going to have plenty of food. I hate to think of anyone being alone at Christmas."

Hugh's expression was circumspect—a polite mask—and

Jo waited for him to excuse himself with his characteristic, well-mannered graciousness.

But to her amazement, he said, "That's very kind of you, Mrs Berry. Thank you, I'd love to come."

Hugh arrived punctually at noon the next day, bearing two beautifully chilled bottles of champagne.

Jo's dad, who drank beer, eyed them dubiously, but her mum was effusive.

"Nothing like a glass of bubbles to make the day special," she said, beaming at him. "But don't let me have any till I've got all the food on the table or I'll forget to serve something. Nick," she called to her eldest son, "can you find a bucket and fill it with ice? We don't want to let these bottles warm up and there's not a speck of room in the fridge."

Jo had given herself several stern lectures while getting ready that morning. She'd chosen a cool summery dress of fine white cotton edged with dainty lace, and she'd applied her make-up with excruciating care. But, in spite of her efforts to look her best, she was determined to stay calm and unaffected by Hugh's visit.

She was so busy helping her mother to get all the food out of the kitchen and onto the table that she had to leave Hugh to the tender mercies of her father and brothers, but she heard snatches of their conversation as she went back and forth.

"Hugh Strickland," said her dad. "Your name rings a bell. Should I have heard of you?"

"I shouldn't think so."

"What line of work are you in?"

"I'm in business—er—transport."

"In the UK?"

"That's right."

Her dad mumbled knowingly. "I almost got a job in transport once—driving buses—but I wasn't fit for it. My chest was crushed, you see. Mining accident. Lungs punctured, so they pensioned me off."

Hugh made sympathetic noises.

Jo chewed her lip and wondered if she should try to butt in and change the conversation. Her dad tended to carry on a bit.

But if Hugh was bored, he showed no sign. He was fitting in like a local. Clutching his beer in its inelegant Styrofoam cooler, he relaxed in a squatter's chair and looked surprisingly comfortable.

The family always gathered for Christmas lunch on a screened-in veranda shaded by an ancient mango tree. This was the cool side of the house, but Jo wondered if an Englishman would realise that. It was still very hot, even in the shade.

"Now, Hugh," said Mum after everyone had found a place to sit and the family had been through the ritual of pulling crackers and donning unbecoming paper hats. "You'll see we don't have a hot dinner."

"That's perfectly understandable." Hugh smiled bravely from beneath a pink-and-purple crêpe paper crown, which should have made him look foolish but somehow managed to look perfectly fine.

Her mum waved a full glass of champagne towards the table. "There's four different kinds of salad and there's sliced leg ham, cold roast pork and our pièce de résistance is the platter of prawns and bugs."

"Bugs?" Hugh looked a tad worried.

"Moreton Bay bugs," Jo hastened to explain, pointing to the platter in the table's centre. "They're a type of crayfish. If you like seafood, you'll love these."

Hugh did like them. Very much. In fact he loved everything on the table and ate as much seafood and salad as her brothers, which was saying something. And then he found room to sample the mince pies.

And, not surprisingly, he was an expert dinner party guest, an interesting conversationalist, who also encouraged Nick and Brad to regale them all with hilarious accounts of the antics of the ringers on the cattle stations where they worked. And he enjoyed listening while the younger children chimed in with their stories too.

Knowing how tense Hugh had been yesterday, Jo was surprised by how relaxed he seemed now. No doubt he was charming her family to ensure her commitment to helping him.

She decided to relax. She'd been working hard all year in the city and had put in long hours in the shop during the past week and now she decided to let go a little and to enjoy the fine icy champagne. How in heaven's name had Hugh unearthed such lovely French champagne in the Bindi Creek pub?

Everyone raved about Jo's Christmas pudding of brandy-flavoured ice cream filled with dried fruit, nuts and cherries, and afterwards her mum announced that she was going to have a little lie down. And everyone agreed that was exactly what she deserved.

"Jo, you take Hugh out onto the back veranda for coffee," she suggested, "while this mob gets cracking in the kitchen."

With coffee cups in hand, Jo and Hugh retired to the veranda. They leant against the railing, looking out over the tops of straggly plumbago bushes to the sunburnt back paddock and it was good to stand and stretch for a while; Jo felt she had eaten and drunk too much.

The air was warm and slightly sticky and it hung about them like a silent and invisible veil. Jo would have liked to run down to the creek, to shed her clothes and take a dip in the cool green water. She'd done it often before, in private, but she found herself wondering what it would be like to skinny-dip with Hugh. The very thought sent her heartbeats haywire.

They didn't speak at first and she felt a bit self-conscious to be alone with him again after sharing him with her noisy family. The slanting rays of the afternoon sun lit up the dark hair above his right ear, lending it a gilded sheen and highlighting his cheekbone and one side of his rather aristocratic nose.

Eventually he said, "Your family are fascinating, aren't they?"

"Do you really think so? It must be rather overpowering to meet them all in one fell swoop."

He smiled as he shook his head. "I think you're very lucky to have grown up with such a happy brood. They're so relaxed."

She shrugged. "They have their moments. Christmas is always fun."

"I'm impressed that they'll take in a stranger, knowing next to nothing about him."

Too true, she thought. Hugh had shared rather personal details about Ivy in his bid to enlist her help, but she knew next to nothing about the rest of his life.

"You don't come from a big family?" she asked.

"Not in terms of brothers and sisters. I'm an only child. I guess that's why I'm always fascinated by big families."

"Sometimes I envy only children. It would be nice, now and then, to have that kind of privacy. Then again, I spend most of my time these days working in the city."

His right eyebrow lifted, forming a question mark, but, unlike her, he didn't give voice to his curiosity, so there was an awkward moment where they were both aware that the rhythm of their conversation had tripped.

Hugh stood staring into the distance.

"Are you thinking about Ivy?" Jo asked.

At first he seemed a little startled by her question, but then he smiled. "How did you guess?"

"Feminine intuition." She drained her coffee cup. "Seriously, it must have come as a shock to have a five-year-old dropped into your life."

"It was a shock all right." Taking a final sip of coffee, he set his empty cup and saucer on a nearby table and, with his usual gentlemanly manners, he took Jo's cup and set it there too.

"I feel so unprepared for meeting Ivy," he said. "I don't like being unprepared. How the hell does a bachelor suddenly come to terms with caring for a child?"

"He hires a nanny?"

"Well, yes," he admitted with a wry grimace. "A nanny will be essential. But I'll still have to do the whole fatherhood thing."

"At least Ivy's not a baby. She can talk to you and express her needs. I'm sure you'll become great mates with her."

"Mates?" He couldn't have looked more stunned if she'd suggested that Ivy would take over as CEO of his business.

"Good friends," she amended.

"With a five-year-old little girl?"

Jo thought of the warm lifelong friendship she'd shared with her mum. "Why not?"

Hugh shook his head. "A boy might have been easier. At least I have inside knowledge of how little boys tick."

"Don't be sexist. There are lots of little girls who like the same things as boys. Grace and Tilly love to play cricket and go fishing. So do I, for that matter."

"Do you?" He regarded her with a look that was both amused and delighted, but then he frowned and with his elbows resting on the veranda railing he stared down into the plumbago bush. "But what if Ivy turns on a horrendous scene? It would be horrible if she cried all the way home on the flight back to London."

"Goodness," cried Jo. "You're a walking advertisement for the power of positive thinking, aren't you?"

For a moment he looked put out, and then he smiled. "You're right. I'm normally on top of things, so I guess I should be able to handle this." He sent Jo an extra devilish smile. "With a little expert help."

Gulp. "Just remember Ivy is your flesh and blood," she said. "She's probably a chip off the old block."

"Which would mean she's charming and well-mannered, even-tempered, good-looking and highly intelligent."

"You missed conceited."

Hugh chuckled softly and then he glanced up and seemed suddenly fascinated by something above her head. "Is that mistletoe hanging above you?"

Jo tipped her head back. Sure enough there was a bunch of greenery dangling from a hook in the veranda roof. "I can probably blame one of my brothers for that." She rolled her eyes, trying to make light of it, but as she looked at Hugh again his smile lingered and something about it sent shivers skittering through her.

How silly. This reserved Englishman had no intention of kissing her. And, even if he did, why should she get all shivery at the thought of a quick Christmas peck?

But her jumping insides paid absolutely no attention to such common sense.

Hugh gave an easy shrug of his shoulders and his eyes held hers as he murmured ever so softly in his supersexy English voice, "Tradition is terribly important, Jo. And you're under the mistletoe and it *is* Christmas."

Her stomach began a drum roll.

Chapter 3

Something deep and dark in Hugh's gaze made Jo's pulses leap to frantic life.

Oh, for heaven's sake, calm down, girl.

Why was she getting so worked up about a friendly Christmas kiss?

Because Hugh is gorgeous!

She took a step closer to him and Hugh's hand cupped her elbow as if to support her. She hoped he didn't notice that she was trembling.

And then, without warning, he dipped his head. "Happy Christmas, Jo."

She pursed her lips for a quick peck and let her body tilt forward. But the anticipated peck didn't take place.

Instead Hugh's lips settled warmly on hers and suddenly he was kissing her. Properly. Or she was kissing him? It no longer mattered. All that mattered was that it was a full-on kiss.

She could blame the champagne. Or the heat. No, she would blame Hugh, because he was far too gorgeous and far too expert at kissing. There had to be some logical reason to explain how a simple mistletoe kiss became so thorough and lasted for such a long and lovely time.

Yes, she would blame Hugh because at some point his hands slipped around her waist, and then it was incredibly easy and seemed perfectly OK to nestle in against him. His arms bound her close against his strong, intensely masculine body and his mouth, tasting faintly of coffee, delved hers expertly and with daring intimacy.

Without warning, a flood of unexpected yearning washed over her. Her insides went into meltdown. Soft, hungry little sounds rumbled low in her throat as she pushed closer into Hugh.

Oh, man. Never had she experienced a kiss that was so instantly shattering.

The sound of footsteps brought her plummeting back to earth. With a little whimper of disappointment, she broke away.

Hugh let her go and he stood very still with his shoulders squared and his hands by his sides, watching her intently and not quite smiling. Only his accelerated breathing betrayed that he'd been as aroused by the kiss as she had.

Taking a deep breath, Jo shot a scowl back over her shoulder to see who'd interrupted them.

It was Bill and Eric and their mouths were hanging wide open.

"What's eating you two?" she demanded angrily. "Haven't you ever seen someone get kissed under the mistletoe before?"

Eric's face was sheepish. "Not like that."

"Get lost," she said, feeling flustered. "Finish those dishes."

They vanished. Which left her with Hugh, who'd gone quiet again. In fact he was looking so uncomfortable that she wondered suddenly if he regretted the kiss. Damn him. He'd probably only kissed her to get closer to her—to ensure that she would accompany him to Agate Downs.

But he'd been so passionate, so *involved*.

Good grief. She was trying to read too much into the kiss. Hugh had simply reacted to the Christmas tradition. And she'd been carried away. Look how calm he was now.

Nevertheless, their easy conversation was over. They carried their coffee cups back to the kitchen and soon afterwards Hugh said polite farewells and set off for the pub. He left without any special word for Jo.

She was left to be plagued by annoying doubts. And no matter how many times she told herself to be sensible, confusion about the passion in Hugh's kiss kept her churning for the rest of Christmas Day.

Hugh was nervous.

He hated feeling nervous. It was so alien to his nature. Normally he was always in control, but in all his adult life he couldn't remember feeling so helpless.

As he drove with Jo to Agate Downs, he had to keep taking deep, slow breaths to remain calm. Even so, emotion clogged his throat and he kept swallowing to be rid of it.

Jo seemed subdued too, and he wondered if she was remembering the kiss they'd shared yesterday. The chemistry of it had been rather sobering. It had caught him completely by surprise. He'd anticipated a harmless exchange beneath the mistletoe and had found himself launching a full-fledged seduction.

He might have taken things beyond the point of sanity if her brothers hadn't arrived on the scene.

The rough outback track reached a rusty old iron gate where Hugh had turned back two days ago. Jo pushed open the passenger door. "I'll get the gate."

About ten minutes later, after they'd traversed a long paddock dotted with rather scrawny-looking cattle, the homestead emerged through the trees.

Jo frowned. "I haven't been out here for years. This place is looking very run-down, isn't it?"

Hugh nodded. He tried to picture his daughter living here. The yard around the homestead was weedy and parched, with no sign of a garden, and as far as he could see there weren't any playthings to amuse a child—no tricycle and no swing hanging from the old jacaranda tree.

He felt a rush of adrenalin as he parked the car. Within a matter of minutes he would see Ivy, the unknown daughter he was to take home with him, the child he must adjust his whole life to accommodate.

He no longer doubted that he wanted her. Since he'd learned of her existence he'd developed an astonishing deep-seated longing to see her and at some unfathomable soul-level he knew he already loved her.

But who was she? And how would she react to him?

Jo touched him on the shoulder and, when he turned, she handed him the unicorn, wrapped now in brightly coloured Christmas paper and topped by a crimson bow sprinkled with silver glitter.

"Don't worry about this, Hugh," she said. "Just be yourself. Believe me, Ivy is a very lucky little girl to have a father like you. She'll love you."

A grim smile was the best he could offer.

At the front door they were greeted by a dark scowl beneath thick bushy eyebrows. Noel Marten stared glumly at Hugh. "You must be Strickland."

"Yes." Hugh extended his hand. "How do you do?"

"Hmm," was all Noel Marten said and his handshake was noticeably reluctant.

"I telephoned to say I'd be here on Boxing Day," Hugh added.

"Who is it?" called a voice from deep inside the house.

Noel called over his shoulder. "It's him—Strickland."

"Oh." Ellen Marten came hurrying down the central passage, wiping her damp hands on an apron.

Behind her, at the far end of the passage, a small, impish figure peered around a doorway. Hugh's throat constricted. There she was. Ivy. His little girl.

Jo reached for his hand and gave it an encouraging squeeze.

"Do come in, sir," said Ellen Marten, but then she glanced at Jo and looked a little confused.

Jo beamed at her. "Hi, Ellen. I don't suppose you were expecting me. Hugh's been telling me how excited he is about meeting his daughter at last." She offered both the Martens her warmest smile.

"I invited Jo because she knows Ivy and she's had much more experience than I have with children," Hugh explained rather stiffly.

"Right," said Ellen, nodding slowly.

The far end of the hallway was quite shadowy, but when Hugh glanced that way again he saw the silhouette of a little girl jigging with excitement. His heart began to pound. The child's mother had been beautiful with a slim, pale fragility, luminous brown eyes and a halo of soft, golden hair.

Whose looks had Ivy inherited?

Ellen followed his glance back down the hallway. "The little monkey; I told her to wait in the kitchen."

"I don't want to wait," shouted a very bossy little voice.

Ellen sighed. "I'm afraid she's quite a little miss. There are times when I don't know what to do with her."

"That's because you won't listen to me," growled Noel. "I know exactly what she needs."

By now the little girl had sidled along the wall until she was halfway down the passage. She was wearing a pink gingham sundress and no shoes. A handful of pebbles lodged in Hugh's throat. He could see that her hair was a mop of curls as dark as his and she had a pale heart-shaped face with big, expressive eyes—green eyes that were dancing with mischief.

Her nose, mouth and chin were exceptionally dainty and feminine. Strong dark eyebrows and lashes gave her character, as did the intelligence shining in her eyes. He felt an astonishing surge of pride. She was his daughter. She was wonderful.

Ellen called to her, "Come on then, Ivy. Come and meet your visitor."

Your father, Hugh wanted to add, but he held his tongue. He stood very still, feeling terrified and trying very hard to smile, but not quite managing.

As if sensing his tension, the little girl came to a standstill. She pressed herself against the wall with her hands behind her back and she let her head droop to one side, suddenly shy.

"Come on now, Ivy," Ellen Marten said sharply. "Don't keep the man waiting."

"No." Ivy pouted. "Won't come."

Hugh's stomach sank. Ivy didn't want to meet him and he had no idea how to entice her. No doubt his friends in

London would be amused by the fact that he, who could charm twenty-five-year-old females with effortless ease, had no idea how to win the heart of this five-year-old.

Ellen rolled her eyes and sighed again. Noel brandished a fist in the air and Hugh cast a desperate glance in Jo's direction.

And Jo, bless her, was the only person in the room who seemed quite free from anxiety. She flashed a cheery grin across the room to the child. "Hi there, Ivy."

"Hello," came the almost sulky reply.

"I've brought you a special visitor."

Ivy listened carefully, but she didn't budge.

"Don't you want to come and see the lovely Christmas present Hugh has brought for you?"

"What Christmas present?" Ivy inched forward a step.

"This one," said Hugh nervously as he held out the bright package. Then, copying Jo's example, he squatted beside her.

"What is it?" asked Ivy, coming closer by cautious degrees.

Hugh hesitated and looked again to Jo. He had no idea about the proper protocol for divulging the contents of gifts to children.

But Jo didn't hesitate. "It's a beautiful unicorn."

Ivy came still closer. "What's a unicorn?" she asked.

"It's like a pony," said Jo. "A magic pony."

That did the trick. Ivy closed the gap.

Hugh was transfixed. Here she was—his flesh-and-blood daughter, perfect in every way, with his hair colour and his green eyes. And ten neat little pink toes.

"Are you going to open this?" His husky voice betrayed his emotion and he was sure there were tears in his eyes.

Little Ivy stood staring at the package with her hands

clasped behind her back. Her eyes shone with curiosity, but she shook her head. "You open it."

"OK." Hugh began to rip at the paper and his daughter leaned close, her face a pretty picture of concentration. And, as the paper fell away, the unicorn was revealed in all its fluffy lilac glory.

Ivy's eyes widened. "Is it really magic?"

"Ahh…" Hugh had no idea how to answer her.

Jo came to his rescue. "See this?" she said, patting the pearly horn on the unicorn's head. "This is what makes it magic."

One little hand came out and Ivy touched the tip of the horn with a pink forefinger. "How is it magic?"

"It brought your daddy to you," said Jo.

If it was possible Ivy's eyes grew rounder and she looked at Hugh. "You're my daddy, aren't you?"

He was bewitched, his eyes locked with hers. Ivy was a miracle.

Jo dug him in the ribs with her elbow and he remembered his daughter's question.

"Yes," he said, swallowing hard. "I'm your daddy." Then, balancing on his knees, he leaned forward and kissed her very gently on her soft pink cheek.

Beside him Jo made a low snuffling sound that was suspiciously like a sob.

"Give your unicorn a hug," she suggested in a very choked-up voice.

A dimple bloomed in the little girl's cheek as she smiled with excitement and then her arms came out to embrace the unicorn. And that was when Hugh saw…her left arm.

Oh, dear God. The little girl's arm had obviously been very badly burned and it was a mass of terrible scar tissue from her shoulder to her wrist. Some areas were bright pink and shiny and others were a heartbreaking criss-cross of thickened lesions.

A ragged cry burst from him. How in hell's name had this happened? Rioting emotions stormed him. Without a care for the surprised bystanders, he swept Ivy into his arms and hugged her and the unicorn to his chest. Then, cradling her close, he scrambled to his feet.

With his cheek pressed close to Ivy's, he squeezed his eyes tightly closed to stem the threat of tears and he kissed his daughter's cheek and then her hair.

"My little girl," he whispered.

His heart almost burst when Ivy flung her little arms around his neck.

"My daddy," she said softly and then she kissed his cheek.

Behind him, Hugh heard Jo's happy sigh of relief.

"I must say I've never seen her take to anyone so quick," Ellen remarked.

Almost reluctantly, Hugh lowered Ivy back to the floor and then he turned to Jo. "I need to speak with the Martens," he said. "Would you mind entertaining Ivy for a few minutes?"

"Not at all," she said brightly. "Come on, Ivy, let's take your unicorn for a flying lesson."

As they left, Hugh took a deep breath and directed a searching look at the Martens. "Right," he said. "I want straight answers. I want to know exactly what happened to Ivy. I need to know where and why, and I insist on knowing what's being done about it."

For the first time in days he felt he was back in control.

When it was time to say goodbye to the Martens, Jo felt that they'd been genuinely very fond of the child, despite

Noel's gruffness and Ellen's admission that caring for Ivy really was becoming too much for her. And, although they had prepared themselves and Ivy for the parting, they had shed tears at the farewell.

But the bonding between Hugh and his daughter was the real surprise. There was no problem about Ivy leaving. In fact she was excited about going away with her newfound father.

Now, as they bumped down the track back to Bindi Creek, Jo patted the unicorn. "So, what are you going to call this fellow?" she asked in her brightest manner.

Ivy, who was sitting between Jo and Hugh, frowned and studied the fluffy animal carefully, turning it over and upside down. "Is my unicorn a boy or a girl?"

Over Ivy's head, Jo and Hugh exchanged amused glances. "What would you like it to be?"

Ivy giggled and rolled her expressive eyes as she gave this deep consideration. "I think he's a boy. Like Daddy."

"So do I," said Jo. "And now you can give him a nice boy's name."

"Hugh?"

"Well…it might be confusing if Daddy and the unicorn both share the same name."

"What about Howard?" suggested Hugh.

"Howard?" Jo gave a scoffing laugh. "For a little girl's toy?"

"I like Howard," insisted Ivy. "I want to call my unicorn Howard."

Hugh sent Jo a smug wink. "You see? I know more about naming toys than you realised."

"Howard he is then," Jo replied with a wry smile.

Ivy grinned up at Hugh and her little face was a glowing picture of adoration.

Jo wanted to cry for them. It was just so sweet the way Hugh and Ivy were so delighted with each other.

By the time they reached Bindi Creek's main street Ivy had nodded off with her head resting against Jo's shoulder.

"Would you like to bring her back to my place?" Jo asked. "It mightn't be very suitable for her at the pub."

"I've imposed on your family too much." He glanced at the sleeping Ivy, still clutching Howard. "But I know what you mean about the pub. I'm sure a child would be much happier at your place."

"She wouldn't be any trouble. We can put up a little stretcher bed in the girls' room. She'd love it."

Hugh smiled just a little sadly. "She might love it too much. I might never be able to drag her away in the morning."

"Oh, I hadn't thought of that." Jo thought about it now and was hit by an unexpected deluge of sadness. She'd been trying not to dwell on the fact that Hugh and Ivy would soon disappear from her life. "I guess you'll want to try to book a flight home," she said.

"That's already arranged."

"Really?" He must have organised it during one of the dozen calls he'd made from Agate Downs on his cellphone. "So when are you going back to England?" She tried to sound casual, as if she didn't actually care, but she wasn't successful.

"Tomorrow."

"Heavens." *For crying out loud, Jo, don't sound so disappointed.* "You were lucky to get a flight so quickly."

"I know people in the industry."

"Oh, yes, of course. I forgot you're in the transport business. So do you get mates' rates?"

"A-ah, yes, something like that."

"Well, don't worry about Ivy," she said with a brave smile. "She already adores you and she understands she's going to England with you. She'll be fine."

Hugh reached his hand past Ivy and gave hers a squeeze. "Thanks, Jo."

She tried to smile.

Tilly and Grace had seen Ivy a few times when she'd been in the shop but they'd never spoken, so they were a little overawed when the beautiful little girl arrived with Jo and Hugh. But their surprise didn't stop them from asking awkward questions.

"What happened to your arm?" Tilly asked almost immediately and Jo wanted to gag her.

But Ivy was matter-of-fact. "It got burned."

"Does it hurt?"

"Not really. Not any more. It just looks different, that's all."

"I asked Santa for a unicorn," Tilly said next. "But I got a baby doll instead. Do you want to see her?"

After that, the children got on with the fun of dressing up and playing with Howard and the doll and Ivy was in seventh heaven.

In the kitchen, Hugh said to Jo, "How private are we here? Is this conversation likely to be overheard?"

"Very likely, I'm afraid." She wondered what he wanted to discuss.

"Do you think you could come up to the pub with me, for a quick drink and a chat?"

She made the mistake of looking into his eyes and she felt a swift ache deep inside, which warned her that she shouldn't go anywhere near the pub—or anywhere else—with him.

For Hugh, taking her to the pub was a purely practical arrangement—probably to discuss something about Ivy. While she—fool that she was—would be madly wishing it could be a date. And that was crazy.

Then again, what good reason could she give for refusing to go?

"I'll ask Mum to keep an eye on Ivy for us," she said.

They found a table in a corner of the tiny beer garden, tucked between the side of the pub and the butcher's shop, and covered by a green shade cloth that did little to relieve them from the sweltering heat.

"You'll be pleased to get back to England's winter," Jo said, pressing her cool glass against her face and neck.

Hugh chuckled. "Give me two days in gloomy London in late December and I'll wish I was back here."

"So you live in London?"

"Yes. I have a house in Chelsea."

"Chelsea? That's a very nice area, isn't it?"

"It's quite nice. Very central, handy for everything."

Jo realised how very little she knew about this man, while he knew so much about her; he'd even been inside her bedroom.

"So," she said, after she'd taken a deep sip of wine, "what did you want to talk about?"

"Ivy," he said simply.

Of course. Jo sent him her warmest smile. "She's a darling."

"She is, isn't she?"

"Absolutely. She's bright and spirited, with the potential to be naughty, I'm sure, but she's incredibly sweet and beautiful."

Hugh smiled and then his face grew sombre. "I thought

my heart was going to break when I saw the scars from her burns."

Ellen Marten had told Jo about Ivy's burns as the two women had packed the last of Ivy's belongings. At the age of two Ivy had been living at her grandmother's Point Piper mansion in Sydney where Ellen and Noel had been servants, and somehow she'd escaped from her nanny and toddled into the kitchen where she'd pulled a pot of boiling water from the stove.

She'd spent a lot of time in hospital and had had several skin grafts.

Jo reached across the table and laid her hand on his. "Ivy will be OK, Hugh. She has you now. Don't feel too sorry for her. You're going to be a wonderful father. She's a very lucky little girl."

"I'll make sure she has the very best medical attention. Luckily, I have an old school friend who's a top burns specialist."

Hugh looked at her hand covering his and something in his expression made Jo suddenly nervous. She retracted her hand and picked up her wineglass.

Hugh stared hard at the white froth on the top of his beer. "I want you to come back to London with us," he said.

Her heart took off like a racing car.

"I know this is short notice and probably very inconvenient, but I would pay you well. The thing is, Ivy's obviously expecting you to be around. And you're so very good with her and once I'm back at work I won't be able to spend all my time with her."

Crash. Jo's heart skidded straight off the track and into a barrier. He wanted her as a nanny.

Well, of course, what else did you expect, you dreamy nitwit?

She lifted her glass and took a gulp of wine. "I'm sorry, Hugh," she said, not quite looking into his face. "I can't manage it. I've already got a good job in Brisbane." Then, with a haughty tilt of her chin, she looked him squarely in the eyes. "And I have a career plan. I've worked hard to get where I am. I'm afraid I can't just abandon everything here."

He nodded thoughtfully, lifted his beer as if he was going to drink, and then set the glass down again. "I'm sorry, I should have asked before this. What sort of work do you do?"

She hitched her chin a notch higher. "I'm an accountant."

He smiled. "I'd never have picked you as an accountant. You seem too—"

"Too what?" she snapped.

His smile broadened to a grin. "I was going to say relaxed."

"So you're another one."

"Another?"

"One of the millions who like to stereotype accountants."

"Oh, touchy subject. My apologies." Hugh lifted his beer again and this time he drank half of it quickly. As he set the glass down, he said, "You're not accounting at the moment."

"No," she admitted. "That's because I've taken my annual leave over the Christmas and New Year period, but I have to be back at work in a little over two weeks."

Without hesitation, Hugh said, "What about those two weeks? What are your plans for them?"

She was surprised by his persistence. "I'm here to help Mum out with the shop—and to spend time with my family."

Hugh nodded and his face grew serious.

Jo fiddled with the stem of her wineglass. She thought of what it would be like for Hugh on the long flight back to

London with Ivy. How would he go about settling his little daughter into a big strange city like London?

Her natural inclination to be helpful kicked in.

"Do you have friends or family in London who can help you with Ivy?" she asked. "What about a—a girlfriend?"

"My parents live in Devon. I have friends, of course, but—" He paused and sighed.

Jo waited…and an annoying anxiety twisted inside her.

"My girlfriend and I broke up recently," he said at last.

Jo kept a very straight face.

"Actually, we broke up because of Ivy."

"Really?" This time it was hard to hide her shock.

Hugh shrugged. "No big deal. We were heading for the rocks anyway, but the crunch came when I found out that I had a daughter."

"Perhaps if she met Ivy she might change her mind," Jo suggested.

He shook his head. "Not this woman. The point is that none of my friends would understand Ivy the way you do. It's not just that you have sisters her age. She's really taken to you and, besides, you understand what she's used to, and what she'll find strange about London."

He was right, of course. She was sure Hugh could manage quite adequately without her, but she also knew she could be very useful. She could help to make the big transition smoother for Ivy.

"Do you have a boyfriend who'd object to your going away?" Hugh asked.

Jo gulped. "'Fraid not. I'm—um—between boyfriends at the moment." There'd been no one else since Damien, but there was no need to mention that to Hugh.

Should she seriously consider his request? Should she do it for Ivy's sake? Could she go to London for just two weeks until Hugh found a really good nanny? "How much would you pay me?" she asked.

She spluttered into her wineglass as he named a sum. "For two weeks? That's out-and-out bribery."

He smiled. "I know."

"What sort of transport business are you in?"

"Aeroplanes," he said quickly, as if he wasn't eager to divulge details. "There'll be no problem in getting you a seat on our flight."

"I'll have to think about it." Jo drained her wineglass and took a deep breath. She was determined not to be impulsive this time. She wasn't rushing anywhere simply because this charming Englishman had asked for her help.

Just the same, his offer was very tempting. If she tried to balance the pros and cons, there were so many pros… Two weeks in London…all that money…doing a good deed for Ivy's sake…

What about the cons? There had to be cons. She would be leaving her mother in the lurch, but Christmas was over. Besides, she deserved a bit of a holiday. What else? There had to be more reasons why she shouldn't go.

Hugh.

Hugh and his gorgeousness. Two weeks with him and she'd be head-over-heels in love with the man. Even though he would remain polite and simply treat her like a nice nanny, she would fall all the way in love and she'd come home an emotional wreck.

"Sorry, Hugh," she said grimly. "I'd like to help, but I can't. I really can't."

He looked so disappointed she almost weakened.

So she jumped to her feet. "What time will you call in the morning to pick up Ivy?"

"I'll collect her now," he said crisply. "There's no point in her spending any more time with you. She'd only get too attached."

"What's the matter, love?" her mother asked as Jo returned to the house just before dusk. She'd taken a long walk by the creek after Hugh and Ivy had left and she'd shed a tear or three.

The silliest thing was that she'd been crying for Ivy as much as for Hugh. The thought of the two of them...

Enough. She had made her decision and it was time to forget about them. They were starting a new life together and she had to get on with *her* life.

"I'm just a little tired," she said vaguely.

"Tired my foot," scoffed Margie. Steam rose as she lifted the lid on a pot of vegetables boiling on the stove. "You've done something silly, haven't you?"

"No, Mum." Jo's voice developed an annoying squeak. "I've been excessively sensible."

"You've turned Hugh Strickland down."

Jo gasped. "How did you—?" She bit her lip hard. Turning away, she pulled out a chair and flopped into it and rested her elbows on the kitchen table. "Yes," she said. "Hugh offered me money to help Ivy settle in London and I turned him down."

Her mother replaced the lid on the saucepan and lowered the heat before taking a seat opposite Jo. "You should have gone with him, Jo."

"Of course I shouldn't. You need me here."

"We'd manage without you."

"Well, that's gratitude for you."

"I'm grateful, love. You know that, but I'm sorry you didn't grab the chance to go with him. It would really make a difference for that little girl to have a friendly face among all those strangers in a foreign city."

"I'm almost a stranger to her."

"But already she's very fond of you."

Jo sighed. "Ivy will be fine, Mum. London's crawling with nice Aussie girls looking for work as nannies. Hugh will find one at the drop of a hat."

Her mother's chest rose and fell as she released a long slow sigh. "I thought you had more courage."

"Courage? I'm not scared. What would I be scared of?"

"Hugh."

A kind of strangled gasp broke from Jo. "Don't be silly. He's a gentleman."

"Of course he is. A very handsome and charming gentleman. That's why you're scared."

"Mum!" Jo jumped to her feet. "I don't want to talk about this. What would you know?"

"More than you could imagine," Margie said quietly.

About to flounce out of the kitchen, Jo stopped. Her mother was looking...*different*...kind of wistful and sad... and Jo felt her heart begin a strange little wobble.

"There was a man, Jo—before your father."

Jo was quite sure she didn't want to hear this.

"I've never forgotten him."

Appalled, Jo wanted to leave, but was transfixed by the haunted regret in her mother's eyes.

"I was madly in love with him," Margie said. "And he wanted me to sail across the Pacific with him on a yacht."

"Did you go?"

Her mother shook her head slowly. "I wouldn't be telling you this story if I'd gone. I reckon I'd still be with him."

A stab of pain pierced deep inside Jo. "You don't know that. It mightn't have worked out."

Her mother smiled sadly. "Then again, it might have been wonderful. I'll never know."

It was too awful to think of Margie Berry with another man. Jo thought of her mother's hard life—with an invalid husband and so many children.

"I don't regret my life," her mother said. "But I wish now that I'd gone. I might have been disappointed, but then... you never know."

Margie had never given a hint that she wasn't happy, but the expression on her face now was like a window on another world. So many possibilities promised and lost...

Jo's throat was so tight she could hardly speak. "But—but Hugh isn't asking me to go with *him*. He just wants a hand with Ivy." She swallowed again. "I'm not in love with him."

"Pull the wool over someone else's eyes." Margie stood and crossed the room and slipped her arm around her daughter's shoulders. "I think you should go to London, Jo. You'll definitely be good for Ivy and, as for what else might happen, be brave, honey, and take the risk. At the very least it'll be a jolly sight more interesting than hanging around here for the rest of your holidays. And, believe me, you don't want to spend the rest of your life wondering what might have happened."

The light was out in Hugh's hotel room when Jo gave a tentative knock at a little after eight. If he was already asleep she would slip away.

No chance.

The door opened quickly. And by the dim light of a fluorescent tube halfway down the veranda, she saw that he was shirtless, with a pair of unbuttoned jeans hanging loose around his hips, as if he'd just dragged them on.

"Hello, Jo." His greeting was polite but lacking his usual warmth.

"Hi." She swallowed and tried not to stare at his rather splendid shoulders…or at the dark hair on his chest, trailing down… "I'm sorry to disturb you."

"I wasn't asleep." He cocked his head back towards the darkened room. "But Ivy is." Stepping out onto the veranda, he closed the door gently. "What did you want? Is anything the matter?"

"I—I wondered if it would be all right if I changed my mind—about coming to England."

Hugh didn't answer straight away and he was standing close to the wall where his face was in shadow, so Jo was left hovering, filled with sudden doubts. Why on earth had she listened to her mother? This was crazy.

"I'd like to help you with Ivy," she added.

"What made you change your mind?"

"I—I started thinking about her. She's had such a tough life, poor kid. I know everything's going to be fine for her now she has you, but if I can help you to smooth the way for her, right at the start—"

Again there was silence. Hugh's eagerness to have her help seemed to have vanished.

"Are you quite certain your family can spare you?"

"Yes, I've discussed it with Mum. She's actually keen for me to go."

"Is she now?" For the first time, Hugh sounded faintly amused. "Well, then."

"Is—is your invitation still open?"

"It is," he said at last.

Jo waited, feeling dreadful.

"So you're sure you'd like to come?"

"Yes."

"You have a passport?"

"Yes, I do. I went to a conference in Singapore last year."

"That's terrific," he said and his smile was cautious as he extended his hand to shake hers.

That was all? A handshake?

Jo was horribly deflated as she walked home again—down the quiet main street, past the familiar, shabby little cluster of buildings that was her home town. The thought of swapping it for London had been so exciting. She'd been so worked up about reaching her decision and going to Hugh to tell him.

But somehow she'd kind of been expecting a little more enthusiasm from him. Another kiss perhaps…to continue what they'd started under the mistletoe.

Now she wondered if that had been the first and last kiss she'd ever share with Hugh. And an inner voice warned that trying to get close to Hugh Strickland would be dangerous.

In the middle of the street she stopped and she looked up at the vast star-speckled sky stretching overhead and she wished she'd stuck to her original decision.

Why on earth had she listened to her mother's fantasies about a might-have-been romance?

Chapter 4

Hugh was worried. Not about Ivy—his first fears had been for her, but she was travelling like a veteran. However, there was something not quite right with Jo.

It wasn't her initial hesitation over coming to England that bothered him; she'd been happy enough when they'd left Bindi Creek and she'd laughed at her father when he'd warned her not to expect too much of England.

"England's a good place for the English," he'd joked and she'd dismissed his gloomy cautions with a good-natured grin and an expressive roll of her eyes.

"Say what you like, Dad, you won't put me off. I'm going with an open mind."

The change began in earnest when they reached Mascot Airport in Sydney and Jo realised that they weren't flying in a regular commercial jet.

"You're worried my plane won't keep you in the air?" Hugh suggested when he saw her pale face.

"No, it's not that. It's just that I've never known anyone who owned his own jet, let alone his own airline company. I hadn't realised you were quite so—so seriously wealthy."

He'd expected to be interrogated. A straightforward girl like Jo would demand that he laid all his cards on the table. But, to his surprise, she'd backed right off.

She was subdued on the flight—although she was wonderful with Ivy—reading to her, helping her with a colouring-in book, being excessively patient when Ivy insisted on colouring horses purple and chickens bright blue. And, when Ivy had had enough, Jo found a suitable movie from the video collection and she made sure the little girl was perfectly comfortable when it was time to sleep.

He'd thought that they might spend much of the flight chatting, getting to know each other better, even flirting a little, but Jo kept her distance. She seemed determined to stick to her role as nanny and nothing more—which was no doubt very sensible—but it left Hugh feeling strangely dissatisfied.

She seemed happier when they finally landed at Stanstead. They were met by Hugh's man, Humphries. And, as they drove across London to Chelsea, both Jo and Ivy peered from the car's windows with identical expressions of wide-eyed wonder. But when they turned into St Leonard's Terrace and pulled up in front of his house, Jo looked worried again.

"This is your new home," she told Ivy. "Isn't it grand?"

"It's very tall," Ivy said, dropping her head back to look up. Then the little girl frowned as she viewed the other houses up and down the street. "Why are all the houses joined onto each other?"

Jo laughed. "So they can fit lots of people into London."

Ivy turned to Hugh. "How many people can you fit into your house, Daddy?"

"Quite a few if I'm having a party, but most of the time there'll just be the three of us. And Humphries. Oh, and Regina, my housekeeper."

"Do you have lots of parties?" Ivy asked, excited.

"Not these days."

At one time there had been an interminable stream of parties, but now Hugh realised with something of a shock that he was looking forward to a quieter life, getting to know Ivy.

And Jo.

He noticed that Jo was shivering in her inadequate jacket. "First thing tomorrow, we buy you and Ivy decent winter coats," he said.

"Don't worry about me," Jo protested. "I won't be here long enough to make it worthwhile."

Her gaze met his and then skittered away. She was definitely tense. It was almost as if she was deliberately distancing herself from him.

Regina greeted them with offers of cups of tea or supper, but neither Jo nor Ivy was hungry.

"You're tired," Hugh said to Jo, noting her drawn pallor. "Let me show you and Ivy to your rooms." Everything should be ready here. He'd telephoned detailed instructions to Humphries and Regina.

"Yes, I want to see my room," cried Ivy excitedly. "Is it pretty?"

"I hope you'll like it. Come on, it's this way. You'll have to climb some stairs. Here, let me help you off with your jacket."

As they mounted the stairs Ivy slipped her trusting little hand inside Hugh's and he experienced an unexpected flood of well-being. This was his little girl and he was bringing her home.

"Here we are," he said when they reached the third floor.

The door to Ivy's room was standing ajar and at the first glimpse the little girl let out a delighted "Wow!" Her eyes danced as she let go of Hugh's hand and crept on tiptoe across the carpet. "It *is* pretty!" she whispered.

Regina had done a good job, Hugh decided, noting the new bedspread and matching curtains in a pale yellow-blue-and-rose floral print. A little student's desk and chair had been set near the window, complete with a box of pencils, note pads, a little pot of glue, a child's scissors and, on the floor beside the desk, a little cradle and—

"A baby doll!" Ivy fell to her knees and her eyes were huge as she stared in wonder. "She's just like Tilly's." She scooped up the doll. "Oh, thank you, Daddy." Then she was on her feet and hugging his legs. "Thank you, thank you."

Hugh blinked back the tears.

Beside him, Jo bent down and picked up the unicorn that had been abandoned in the excitement. "Look, Howard," she said, holding the fluffy toy near the doll. "You have a little sister."

"Yes," giggled Ivy, taking Howard and embracing both toys. "I'm their mummy."

"Now for your room," Hugh told Jo. "There's a connecting door here, but you and Ivy have your own private en suite bathrooms. Is that OK?"

"Is that OK, Hugh?" Jo cried, giving him a strange look. "Are you joking? Of course it's OK. You've seen my family's home."

Remembering how nine Berrys shared one bathroom, Hugh felt his neck redden. He hurried ahead of her. "Well, anyway, here's your room."

Jo followed him slowly, looking about her with a serious, grim little half-smile. She dipped her head to smell the violets and rosebuds in the crystal vase on the dressing table and then she stepped up to the big double bed and traced the pale gold silk of the quilt with her fingertips and then the pillowcases and the pretty trim on the sheets.

"Snow-white sheets with drawn-thread cutwork and embroidery," she said. "I'm going to feel more like a princess than a nanny."

There was a knock on the door and Humphries appeared. "I have Miss Berry's suitcase."

"Good man," said Hugh. "Bring it in, please."

After Humphries had left again, Jo stood staring at her luggage sitting on the carpet at the end of her bed. "I'm afraid my battered old suitcase looks rather dingy in the middle of such a lovely room."

"You can stow it in a cupboard if it bothers you."

"Yes." She took a deep breath and squared her shoulders before looking at him, and her intelligent brown eyes regarded him with shrewd wariness.

"What's the matter, Jo? Is there something not right?"

"Now I see where you come from, I can't believe you fitted in so well at Bindi Creek."

"The differences are superficial," he said. "You'll fit in here too."

Her face pulled into a disbelieving smile. "We'll see."

He was tempted—*very* tempted—to slip a comforting arm around her shoulders, but the look in Jo's eyes prompted him to slip his hands into his trouser pockets instead.

Jo crossed her arms over her chest and fixed him with her steady gaze. "A girl can handle just so many surprises,

Hugh. I think you and I need to sit down and have a serious talk."

"Now?"

"No, we're all too tired now."

Hugh was feeling more wired than tired, but he said, "OK, I'll leave you to make yourself comfortable. My room's further along the hall."

Her face broke into an unexpected grin. "I bet the master bedroom is really something."

His body reacted in an instant. "You're welcome to come and take a look, if you like."

"Oh, no," she said quickly. Too quickly.

"It'd be a fair exchange, Jo," he responded flippantly. "You've shown me yours, so I'll show you mine."

It was meant as a joke. No matter how much he'd like to have Jo in his bed, now wasn't the right moment. But, to his surprise, instead of accepting the joke and smiling, or telling him to drop dead, she looked upset and blushed brightly.

He felt a surge of dismay. What had happened to the light-hearted, level-headed Jo Berry? The sight of her blush bothered him and, damn it, *stirred* him, arousing the very desire he wanted to quench.

While he struggled to think of a way to lighten the moment, a plaintive cry came from Ivy's room.

"Jo, where are you?"

"I'm here," Jo called.

The sound of a sob reached them and she quickly hurried back through the connecting door. Hugh followed.

Ivy had abandoned her toys and was huddled on the floor in the middle of her bedroom with tears running down her face. When she saw Hugh and Jo, she began to sob loudly and Hugh felt a panicky rush of alarm.

"What's the matter?" Jo said, dropping to her knees beside the weeping child.

"I don't know," Ivy wailed. "I got scared."

"It's OK, you're just tired," Jo said, hugging her. "And everything here's a bit strange for you. What you need is to get into your pyjamas and then into your lovely bed. You'll feel better in the morning."

"Would a cup of warm cocoa help?" asked Hugh, desperate to help.

Jo sent him a grateful smile. "That would be lovely, wouldn't it, Ivy?"

His daughter gave her eyes a brave scrub and then nodded and Hugh dashed downstairs to the basement kitchen—a man on an urgent mission. By the time he returned, Jo had changed Ivy into a frilly white nightgown and the little girl's face looked pink and white and clean as if Jo had washed her as well.

Hugh held out the mug of cocoa.

"It's not too hot, is it?" asked Jo.

"I don't think so," he said, but he wasn't sure. "See what you think."

He watched with interest as Jo tested the mug against her inner arm, then frowned and took a tiny sip. There were so many things to remember about caring for a child, especially this child who'd already experienced one horrendous accident. He wondered how many mistakes he would make. He felt again completely out of his depth.

"This is fine," Jo said. "Yummy, in fact."

Ivy accepted the mug, drank deeply and beamed at him. "It's very yummy, Daddy." But she only drank half before her eyelids began to droop.

Jo was sitting on the edge of Ivy's bed and she gently took the mug from her loosening grip and set it on the bedside table. Scant seconds later Ivy's head reached her pillow and she looked as if she'd fallen asleep.

Hugh began to tiptoe away. "I'll just be—"

Ivy's eyes flashed open and Jo frowned at him and set a silencing finger against her lips. Chastened, he stood very still.

"Don't go away, Daddy," Ivy demanded.

"Don't worry, Ivy. Daddy will stay right here till you're sound asleep," Jo reassured her and Ivy's eyes closed again.

Somewhat gingerly, Hugh sat at the end of the bed. "I'm here, poppet."

With her eyes still closed, Ivy smiled and she looked so sweet and angelic he felt a surge of pride. Emotion lodged in his throat as a rock-hard lump. Good God, he was turning as hopelessly sentimental as his elderly Aunt Daphne.

And yet…

There was nothing sentimental about the way he felt when he looked at Jo.

As they sat together in the lamplit silence, Hugh let his mind play with the fantasy of helping Jo out of her clothes and into bed. He wondered what the chances were that the light tan on her arms and legs extended to her thighs and stomach…

"She's such a beautiful little girl."

Jo's soft voice intruded into his pleasant musings.

Hugh smiled. "I'm dreadfully biased, but I'm inclined to agree with you."

"I'd say she's sound asleep now."

But Jo didn't move and neither did Hugh. They continued to sit very still, superconscious of each other's proximity as they watched Ivy.

"I imagine her mother must have been beautiful."

"Linley? Yes, she was." He sighed. "But I'm afraid she

was rather like a beautiful soap bubble or a butterfly. I felt as if I never got to the essence of her."

"Oh." Jo seemed to consider this as she watched Ivy thoughtfully. "I don't think Ivy's like that."

"No," Hugh agreed. Even at the tender age of five, his daughter possessed an inner strength he'd never sensed in Linley.

Jo turned to him. She looked calmer now and she smiled sleepily.

"You look tired," he murmured.

"Mmm. I am rather." A wing of her hair fell across her cheek and she tucked it behind her ear.

In the past few days Hugh had seen her do this many times. He knew that before long her silky brown hair would slip forward again and he couldn't resist reaching out now to touch the soft curve of her exposed cheek. Her skin was as soft as a rosy-gold peach. "Thanks for coming here, Jo."

"I suppose I should be thanking you. I've never basked in so much luxury."

"Treat this place like it's yours. Take whatever you like."

She looked a little startled and Hugh couldn't resist leaning forward to drop a kiss on her surprised pink mouth. He heard the sharp intake of her breath and it sounded so sexy and her open lips were so warm and sweet that he kissed her again.

She had the loveliest mouth.

"Welcome to Britain, Jo Berry," he murmured as he tested the soft, lush fullness of her lips.

"I'm very happy to be here," came her breathless, throaty reply.

Hugh couldn't resist deepening the kiss and her lips drifted apart in open invitation. He reached for her hands and as he rose from the bed she came with him, moving slowly, languidly, almost floating, as in a dream. Next to the bed he drew her close and kissed her again and then he slipped his arm around her shoulders and she drifted beside him as he guided her to the doorway.

No sooner were they were out of Ivy's room and in the hallway than they fell into each other's arms and in a heartbeat their lips and tongues were sharing secrets they hadn't dared to speak of.

Hugh knew he was sinking fast. Jo was so sexy. She sounded and looked sexy and she tasted and felt incredibly sexy...

His hands explored the gorgeous curves of her bottom, the soft slenderness of her waist and then they found her breasts—beautifully full and soft and round—their tight peaks straining against the flimsy lace of her bra. With a soft, voluptuous moan she arched, pressing her breasts into his hands.

Rampant need inflamed him. He was losing control...

But then he realised Jo was pulling away from him.

She gasped, pressing her hands to her cheeks. "This can't be real. I must be more jet-lagged than I realised."

No.

He was about to haul her back into his arms, to hurry her away with him to his bedroom, but her dark eyes looked directly into his and her gaze was intensely eloquent, as if she were pleading with him, commanding him to agree that their kiss had been a mistake.

Had it been a mistake? *Had it?*

His tormented body cried *no*!

But as Jo backed further away from him he knew that yes...it probably had been ill-advised.

Things could get very complicated if he dragged her to his bed the very minute he got her inside his front door.

"I'm going to follow Ivy's good example and get to sleep," she said.

Hugh took a deep, still-ragged breath. "I'll ask Regina to bring a light supper on a tray to your room."

"Thank you. Some cocoa and a sandwich would be lovely." Without looking his way again, she walked quickly away from him and into her room.

Next morning Jo and Ivy appeared in the dining room just as Hugh was helping himself to bacon and eggs. He'd spent a restless night—the combined result of jet lag and Jo.

But he was relieved to see that both Jo and Ivy were looking more chipper. Jo was looking exceptionally pretty, dressed in cream corduroy trousers and a soft wool sweater in a very fetching shade of deep pink. It seemed the perfect complement for her nut-brown hair and eyes.

She made Hugh think of…wild roses…on a summer's afternoon…

In fact, he found that he was staring.

"So that's what a full English breakfast looks like, is it?" she asked, eyeing his loaded plate.

He grinned, relieved that she seemed to take last night's incident in her stride. "If you want the works you get sausages and baked beans as well. Of course, you don't have to have anything cooked."

"Can I have some orange juice?" asked Ivy.

"Say please," Jo reminded her.

"Please, Daddy?"

"Of course."

"I'll just start with a cup of tea," Jo said, helping herself to a cup and saucer as Hugh poured orange juice from a glass jug. "I love this pink-and-white-striped china. You have so many lovely things, Hugh."

His mother had given him the china. At the time he'd thought it was a strange choice for a bachelor's pad, but whenever he'd brought young women home they'd adored it, and so he'd decided it was a definite asset.

Jo smiled when she lifted the teapot from the sideboard. "Silver. I should have guessed."

"Are you sure you wouldn't like something to eat?" he asked. "Scrambled eggs or poached, or—?"

Behind him a door banged.

And a sharply elegant blonde, wearing an ankle-length silver fox fur coat, swept into the dining room.

Oh, God, no. Priscilla.

Hugh had no chance to recover from the shock of seeing his former girlfriend before she flung herself at his neck.

"Darling, I heard you were back. I've missed you so-o-o-o much."

Her arms latched around him and he was enveloped in fox fur as she pressed herself against him and kissed him on the mouth.

Stunned and angry, he struggled to extricate himself from her embrace. "What are you doing here?" he gasped.

"What a silly question, Hugh, darling. I just had to be here to welcome you home."

Hugh sent a quick glance in Jo's direction. She was looking as stunned as he felt. But Priscilla managed, very deftly, to ignore Jo. Her gaze—perfect blue, but crystal-cold—flicked rapidly over her as if she didn't exist, before settling rather nervously on Ivy.

"And this is your little sweetheart," she said, smiling a very forced, awkward smile.

Hugh glared at her. How could Priscilla do this? She'd

broken up with him the minute she'd learned of Ivy's existence.

"You can't have us both," she'd told him when she learned he was going to Australia to claim his daughter. "Who will it be, Hugh—the child or me?"

"She's my flesh and blood," he'd reminded her. "My responsibility."

"But you can't drag her into our lives now." Priscilla had made his daughter sound like something the cat might bring back from a night's hunting. "What would everyone think, Hugh? I'd be a joke!"

It was the last in a string of disappointments he'd experienced during their relationship. He'd had enough of Priscilla Mosley-Hart's tantrums and was more than glad to be rid of her.

He made no attempt to introduce Ivy, and so Priscilla bent forward stiffly, from the waist, and bared her teeth as she tried again, unsuccessfully, to smile at the child.

"What's your name, sweetheart?"

Ivy didn't answer.

Priscilla's plastic smile slipped, but she tried another tack. "We'll be seeing a lot more of each other from now on, sweetheart."

But Ivy had the good sense to remain silent and she watched Priscilla through narrowed eyes, as if she sensed she was in enemy territory.

"Oh, well," said Priscilla with the air of someone who'd done her very best and couldn't be expected to succeed when a child was so obviously uncooperative.

Not for the first time, Hugh regretted the manners that had been hammered into him from birth. Unfortunate rules about the way a gentleman treated a lady prevented him from grabbing Priscilla by the scruff of her extravagant coat and marching her back through the front door.

He pressed a bell for Regina and his round-faced, middle-aged housekeeper appeared at the door. 'Regina, would you mind taking Ivy to the kitchen and fixing her some breakfast?'

"I'd love to." Regina beamed at Ivy. "Come with me, ducks. Come and see all the lovely things I have for you. You must be so hungry after flying all the way from Australia."

To Hugh's relief, Ivy seemed happy to escape downstairs.

"I'll go, too," said Jo.

"No," commanded Hugh sharply. Then, more gently, "Please stay, Jo." He wanted her to hear firsthand that his relationship with Priscilla was over.

"*I* think the nanny should leave," Priscilla said with a sniff.

Hugh ignored her. Under no circumstances was she going to win this round. He said, "Let me introduce Joanna."

"Joanna?" Priscilla seemed to freeze and she turned to Jo with some difficulty.

Hugh took Jo by the elbow. "This is Joanna Berry. She has come over from Australia and has very kindly—"

Priscilla let out an uncertain titter. "What a sensible idea to bring an Australian nanny with you. She can do everything for Ivy before you find a school to send her to."

How had he ever thought he was attracted to this woman? She was getting more ghastly by the minute.

Jo was standing very still with her eyes downcast, studying an antique table napkin. In one hand she held her cup and saucer, but she seemed to be paying great attention to the monogram on the napkin, running her fingertip over and over the embroidered initial R.

Priscilla gave a toss of her head. "Now can we have some privacy, Hugh?"

"Why on earth do we want privacy?" Hugh injected a thread of menace into his voice—one Priscilla couldn't miss.

"What's the matter with you? That's a strange thing to ask your fiancée."

"My *what*?"

Priscilla's smile was very brittle. "Hugh, dear." She lifted her left hand and pushed at a wing of her expensive hair and an enormous sapphire and diamond ring glinted on her fourth finger.

"Bloody hell, Priscilla, what game are you playing?"

Holding out her left hand, she waggled her fingers at him, making the sapphire and diamonds sparkle. She pouted. "Our engagement is hardly a game, Hugh."

"Our engagement? Have you gone mad? What's this ring?"

"I bought it at a sale at Sotheby's. Do you like it? It's just like the one we planned."

"Like *hell*. We never planned any such thing."

Beside him, Jo set down her cup and saucer and stepped away. "I'm out of here," she muttered, but Hugh moved quickly and reached for her arm and, at his touch, she froze.

Clearly put out, Priscilla fiddled with the ring, twisting it back and forth on her finger.

"Just tell me whatever it is you have to say, Priscilla."

Ignoring Jo as best she could, she said, "I know you want to forget my silly little outburst about dear little Ivy. I don't know what got into me. I was shocked. I was shaken. I wasn't thinking straight and it was all a mistake. Of course I didn't mean it when I said I wanted to break up."

"I'm sorry, Priscilla," Hugh said quietly, while he held

Jo's arm in a tight grip. "It's too late to change your mind. You gave me an ultimatum. I was to choose between my daughter and you, and I made my choice."

"But darling, I wasn't thinking straight. Of course you have to have your daughter with you."

"Our relationship is over."

"Like hell it is!"

"That's my final word."

Priscilla gaped at him and then she pouted coyly like a spoilt little girl. "But I'm planning to marry you, Hugh. Surely you always knew I would. I've booked the church."

"Cancel it."

A breathless silence filled the room. Hugh could feel white-hot anger sluicing through his veins.

Priscilla's eyes narrowed then and she directed a venomous glare at Jo, before swinging a blistering glance back to Hugh. "This is *her* fault. She's got to you, hasn't she?"

"Stop right now." Hugh spoke through gritted teeth. He'd known Priscilla had her imperfections, but he'd never seen this side of her before. Had she hidden it, or had he been blinded to it? "Of course this isn't Jo's fault."

He was surprised by the force of the rising anger surging through him and by his overpowering desire to protect Jo.

A kind of light-headed wildness overcame him and he slipped a possessive arm around Jo's shoulders.

The simple gesture had the desired effect. Priscilla sagged in horror as if she'd been kicked in the chest by a kung fu expert.

But she quickly rallied. Hatred flashed in her eyes. "I can see she's got her nasty little claws into you already."

"I'd advise you to shut up, Priscilla."

She ignored him and directed her glare straight at Jo.

"You might be sleeping with him, but don't fool yourself that he would ever consider marrying you."

Hugh felt a violent shudder pass through Jo and something inside him snapped. He had to defend her from this assault, even if it meant fighting dirty.

"That's exactly where you're wrong, Priscilla." Hugh paused for dramatic effect.

Jo gasped.

And Priscilla screamed. "You're not planning to marry *her*? You're mad. This is crazy. Your father will disinherit you."

"Rubbish. He's delighted."

"Now just hang on a minute," interrupted Jo. Obviously embarrassed, she wrenched her arm out of Hugh's grasp. "This is getting totally out of hand." Outrage flashed in her eyes. "I've had enough of listening to you two fight. I've more important things to do. I'm going to check on Ivy."

With that she stormed out of the room—determined not to be involved in their little game.

Priscilla's lips curled into a sneer as she watched Jo leave. "She might be a fast worker, but she's timid and flighty. She'll be the same as Linley Quartermaine. One thing's for sure, she won't last—not as your nanny—or as your fiancée."

"It's time you left," Hugh told her coldly. He should have chucked her out twenty minutes ago.

In desperation, Priscilla tried again to smile. "You don't mean that, Hugh. I came here to tell you—"

"Leave right now, Priscilla. You've said more than is wise."

She rolled her eyes. "Don't you believe it; I've hardly begun." And then, with a chilling, calculating smirk, she turned and sailed out of the opposite door from the one Jo had used.

Moments later Hugh heard the sharp click of her high heels in the marbled entry hall and shortly after that the front door slammed. And Jo came back upstairs.

She marched into the dining room, her face tense and tight and her hands planted on her hips, ready for battle.

"How's Ivy?" Hugh asked her quickly.

"She's fine—eating you out of house and home. I'll join her just as soon as we've had our little *chat*."

"Jo, I'm sorry about that. Priscilla was abominable."

"Yes, she was. But what are you up to, Hugh?"

He flinched.

Momentarily, her face crumpled. "Why on earth did you let her think we're getting married?"

She looked so wretched a stab of pain pierced him in the chest.

To defend you and help me, he thought. "To get through to her. To finish it," he said.

"Surely you can wriggle out of a sticky situation with an old girlfriend without dragging me into it?"

"I know it was reckless of me, but at the time I was so furious with her."

Jo glared at him. "You didn't even deny that we're having sex." She gave an accompanying stamp of her foot to show how very mad she was. "You more or less said, 'Yeah, it's a red-hot relationship and we're going to get married'."

"That's not what I said at all."

"It's what you implied."

Hugh felt a surge of annoyance. He'd just had one woman take centre stage when he should have dropped the curtain on her. Now here was another!

He sighed. "I was trying to defend you. I'm sorry."

"It's a bit late for apologies. Priscilla's walked out of here convinced that we're having sex—which is dead wrong!

And she thinks we're going to be married. Wrong again! What have you achieved? I can't see that you've done me any favours."

Feeling cornered, he scratched the back of his neck. "You have to admit, it was almost worth it to see the look on her face when she thought we were going to be married."

Jo rolled her eyes to the ceiling, but a moment later a little smile tweaked the corner of her mouth. "She did look like she'd been slapped in the face with a kipper."

But then she gave an annoyed toss of her head. "Don't try to sidetrack me, Hugh." Eyeing him warily, she added, "Just make sure you tell Priscilla the truth and tell her soon."

The phone rang in the next room and he ignored it.

But Jo dived for the door. "That might be Mum. I couldn't ring her last night because of the time difference, but she's expecting to hear if I've arrived here in one piece."

She dashed to answer it, but she was back in less than a minute. "It's your father," she said, looking and sounding shaken.

Bloody hell.

"He's just congratulated me on my engagement to his only son. He was very polite and charming, but somehow I don't think he sounded too happy about it."

Hugh groaned. The minute Priscilla had been out of the door she must have rung his father on her cellphone.

"You'd better sort it out, Hugh. I'm not prepared to continue this charade just so you can keep your Priscilla at arm's length."

"Yes, you're right. I'll explain."

The strange thing was, he thought as he headed to the phone, that for one reckless moment marrying Jo had seemed to make perfect sense.

Chapter 5

What a mess! What a dreadful, dreadful mistake she'd made by coming to England—to Chelsea—to this house, Hugh's house. She should never have listened to her mother.

As Hugh went to answer the phone, Jo was awash with tears. The door closed behind her with a gentle click and she stumbled across the room to put as much distance as possible between herself and Hugh's conversation with his father.

She felt terrible. She'd already been tired after the long flight and a long, restless night of tossing and turning as her mind wove fantasies about her and Hugh and now—*this*.

Priscilla was ghastly.

Of course she was rather beautiful in a plastic, ultraexpensive, super-model kind of way. And men fell for that sort of thing—but how could Hugh have ever liked her?

But then she knew nothing about him really. *Nothing*. Well, one thing. She knew that he had to be seriously wealthy—or seriously in debt. He apparently owned his own aviation company and this house was five storeys tall and in one of the swankiest parts of London.

But that was all she knew and there were so many questions screaming around inside her.

And the biggest question was how he could so casually claim to be marrying her. It made a complete mockery of her deepening feelings for him.

With an angry little huff, she looked out through the dining room window—actually, it was a pair of full-length French windows—and they opened onto a little balcony edged with a dainty wrought-iron railing. Elegantly decorated porcelain pots on the balcony had been planted with carefully pruned topiary trees, each tree consisting of three neatly clipped balls.

Around each trunk a large red bow had been tied, presumably to provide a touch of Christmas. She wondered if they'd been Priscilla's idea.

Outside the house, the sky was winter-white. Across the street there was a row of tall trees so bare that she could see right through the branches to a large playing field and a big, rather grand old building.

"That's the Royal Hospital."

Hugh's voice sounded close behind her.

Jo's heart leapt as she swung around. "I didn't hear you come in. That was a quick conversation."

"Charles the Second had the hospital built for returned soldiers," Hugh said. "It was designed by Christopher Wren."

Why was he suddenly talking about hospitals and history? "What's the matter, Hugh?" He looked rather pale. "Did you explain to your father that the engagement was all a mistake?"

He looked a little ashamed and awkward but, to her relief, he nodded.

"Thank heavens for that."

"But I wasn't able to talk him out of coming up to London. He and Mother are coming up from Devon soon."

"Well... I suppose they want to meet Ivy."

Hugh sighed. "Yes." Turning back to the table, where his bacon and eggs still lay cold and untouched, he said, "I've rather lost my appetite. Why don't I ask Regina to do something quick and easy—some fresh tea and hot buttered toast? Would that suit you?"

"Yes, of course, thank you."

He disappeared and was back in a matter of minutes. "Breakfast is on its way."

"Hugh, before Regina and Ivy get here, *I'd* like to get a few things straight."

Hugh flexed his shoulders, squared his jaw and then grinned at her.

Jo wasn't in a grinning mood, but his smile wrought its usual havoc on her heart. She tried to hide her distress behind a small smile. "I think it's only fair that I know exactly who I'm dealing with while I'm working here," she said.

"You're not working here, Jo. You're my guest."

"If I'm not working, why did you offer me a great deal of money?"

Hugh didn't seem to have an answer.

"So," Jo resumed, "I'd appreciate it if you'd answer a few questions."

"What would you like to know?"

"What school did you go to?"

He looked taken aback. "Why do you need to know that?"

"*Please*… I'd just like to know."

"OK, I went to Eton."

"Right." She'd been afraid that would be his answer. "And that signet ring on your little finger. It has a crest that matches the one on the teapot and the teaspoons."

"You're very observant."

"Is it a family crest?"

He glanced idly at his little finger. "Yes."

Jo picked up a starched linen table napkin. "What about this initial R? Is it significant?"

"Jo, you've missed your calling. You should drop accountancy and take up law. I feel like I'm being cross-examined."

"And I feel like a mushroom."

"A what?"

"Someone who's deliberately kept in the dark."

With a helpless shrug, he said, "The *R* stands for Rychester. My father, Felix Strickland, is the Earl of Rychester."

Oh, my God.

Jo's face flamed as she thought of how well Hugh had seemed to fit in at Bindi Creek, eating a Christmas dinner of cold salads on the veranda with her family, listening politely to her dad's corny jokes and her brothers' risqué campfire stories.

She gulped. "Does that mean—it doesn't mean—you're not related to the Queen, are you?"

"Good heavens, no."

"So, what are you called? Does an earl's son have a title?"

"In formal circles they stick a Lord in front of my name, but you don't have to worry about that."

Oh, heavens. What had Lord Hugh Strickland really thought of her family?

She remembered the wistful, dreamy look on her mum's

face when she'd urged her to go to London with Hugh. Poor Mum. If she'd been hoping for a romantic outcome from this venture, she was in for a major disappointment.

What a joke. What a disaster! How had Jo Berry from Bindi Creek entertained even the tiniest romantic fantasy about an involvement with an heir to a British earldom?

Far out! Her fledgling dream seemed so foolish now. She was such a child. "I wish you'd told me, Hugh."

"But I wasn't keeping it a secret. I just didn't see the need to make a big deal about my family. It's only a title."

Taking a deep breath, she folded her arms across her chest. "What about your parents? I bet they're not as low-key about all this as you are. I'm sure your father was very relieved to hear that you haven't rushed into an engagement with the hired help."

Hugh gave an exasperated shake of his head. "If it's any consolation, my father has never liked any girl I've introduced to him. Priscilla was at the top of his list of pet hates."

Jo awarded Hugh's father a mental tick for his good taste. "And, speaking of Priscilla, what about her? Does she have blue blood too?"

"Her father has a minor baronetcy."

Damn! Somehow, Jo hadn't expected that. Silly of her, but she'd hoped to hear that Priscilla was *nouveau riche*— with a father who'd made all his money doing something that was generally frowned upon—like robbing banks or making pornographic movies.

But Priscilla was an aristocrat. All Hugh's circle were probably aristocrats—a club of exclusive peers of the realm. Jo's sense of alienation, her hurt and simmering anger, erupted. Tears threatened, stinging her eyes. "I can't believe I let myself get into this mess."

"Jo, don't be upset."

"Why not? I have every right to be upset. Maybe it doesn't bother you that your old girlfriend is running all over London spreading the word that you're sleeping with your daughter's nanny—or worse, that you've got yourself engaged to a money-grubbing nobody from Australia."

"I doubt Priscilla has the energy to stir up trouble."

Jo didn't believe him. After four years working in a city office, she'd witnessed enough broken affairs to know that a woman scorned had masses of energy and could cause all kinds of damage.

What a mess. If she wasn't very careful she would start crying, but she was too proud to break down in front of Hugh, so she squeezed her eyes tightly shut and took so many deep breaths she was in danger of hyperventilating.

"Jo, I really am very sorry to have caused you this distress." Hugh's voice sounded worried. His hand touched her cheek.

Her eyes flew open.

His face was very close to hers and he was looking at her so tenderly she almost broke into very noisy sobbing. And then he gave her his endearing, crooked-sad smile. "I can't bear to see you upset," he said ever so gently. "You're such a sunshiny girl. I want you to be happy here."

She blinked—twice—and forced a watery smile. Hugh's gentle concern was breaking her heart. "Don't worry about me," she said, holding bravely on to her smile. "I'm fine."

"No, you're not."

"Then I'll *be* fine, very soon."

Hugh leant just a little closer and dropped a quick, warm kiss on her forehead. It was just a brotherly kiss, but it was very nice. Jo drew a deep breath. And then suddenly Hugh's hand was at her waist and he dropped another kiss onto her cheek.

A second kiss was *not* brotherly. A flash of awareness zigzagged through her—and an unbearable longing for him to kiss her again.

But she knew she shouldn't let that happen. Not again. She should step away from him. Right now. Even if he wanted to, she mustn't let him kiss her the way he had last night. She mustn't submit. Hugh must realise how susceptible she was to his—

Oh, man. She'd hesitated too long.

His lips were already on hers. His hands were bracketing her face and he was taking a delicious sip at her top lip, and now, oh, *yes*, he was tasting her lower lip, drawing it gently between his teeth. And there was no way she could ask him to stop—especially when his hands shifted to her hips and, with a soft sound that was half a sigh, half a groan, he covered her mouth with his.

Her legs turned to liquid as he drew her against him. She could feel the hardness of his arousal and he began to kiss her with a thoroughness that stole her breath. His lips and tongue were hot and demanding—delving the soft, warm recesses of her mouth.

His hands slipped under her sweater to touch her bare waist and, just as it had last night, a wild longing broke loose inside her and he went on kissing her, as if he needed her desperately, as desperately as she needed him.

"Look what I found."

A voice sounded in the doorway.

Breathless, stunned, they sprang apart. Jo's heart was going haywire.

Ivy came into the room with a huge fluffy marmalade cat in her arms. "I found this pussy cat," she said with a beaming smile.

Jo's head and heart were still spinning and she couldn't

think of a thing to say. And then she felt a rush of shame. What must Ivy be thinking?

Hugh recovered first. "Well, hello there." His greeting sounded just a little breathless and he sent a quick side-ways glance to Jo before he addressed his daughter. "So you found Marmaduke?"

"Yes, I've been exploring and I found him under the stairs."

"He's Humphries's cat, so be gentle with him."

"And guess what else I found?"

Hugh glanced Jo's way again and he sent her a quick, worried smile. "What else did you find?"

"Your Christmas tree, Daddy. Come and see, Jo, it's beautiful."

"Hang on," said Hugh. "Here's Regina now with Jo's breakfast."

As Hugh hurried to help his housekeeper with the heavily laden tray, Jo took a deep, steadying breath. The after-shock of Hugh's kiss seemed to reverberate all the way through her.

But thank heavens Ivy hadn't been upset by the sight of them pashing each other to oblivion.

Hugh looked particularly light-hearted as he joined her at the table. His eyes held Jo's for a shade longer than was necessary. Why? Was he flirting? She couldn't bear it if he was playing games with her.

She thought again of her mum and suddenly remembered her promise to phone her. "Excuse me," she said, jumping to her feet. "I need to telephone home. Mum will be frantic."

"By all means."

"I'll be back in a minute."

She supposed it must have been jet lag that hit her as she dialled her home phone number. She felt vague and disoriented and teary. But at least she managed to convince her mother that everything was absolutely fine and that she was very, very happy. However, she found the white lie exhausting and it was a relief to hang up.

Just as she did so, the phone rang again.

Jo started. Heavens, she was jittery. And then she stared at the phone, wondering if she should answer it. What if it was Priscilla, or Hugh's father?

She took a step back and looked through the doorway to the dining room. Hugh was busy showing Ivy how he liked to cut his toast and he paid no attention to the phone.

Her hand shook a little as she lifted the receiver. "Hugh Strickland's residence," she said and her voice came out squeaky and thin.

"Oh," said a male voice. "You must be Jo."

"Yes, that's right." She wondered nervously how this person knew about her. She thought of Priscilla and her stomach clenched.

"It's Rupert Eliot here," the voice said. "I'm a friend of Hugh's."

He had a very nice voice, cultured and beautiful like Hugh's, and just as warm and friendly.

"Would you like to speak to Hugh?"

"No, that's not necessary. Hugh's coming to our party on New Year's Eve and Anne and I were hoping you could come too."

He must have made a mistake. Surely he mustn't know she was the hired help. "I'll—er—tell Hugh straight away," she said.

"We're looking forward to meeting you, Jo," Rupert added. "Hugh rang me from Australia and said you were helping him with little Ivy. Make sure Hugh brings Ivy too. There'll be other children here and they'll be good playmates for her, so the sooner she gets to meet them the better."

"That sounds lovely," Jo said, feeling dazed. "Thank you. Thank you very much."

"We'll hope to see you on Friday then."

Back in the dining room, as Hugh poured Jo a lovely hot cup of tea and plied her with toast, she told him of the phone call and he wasn't the least surprised.

"Rupert's my oldest and best friend," he told her. "His six-month-old daughter, Phoebe, is my goddaughter."

She must have looked worried because Hugh rushed to reassure her. "You'll really like Rupert."

"He isn't a Lord or a Duke or anything, is he?"

Hugh grinned. "He's an Honourable, but honestly you'd never know. He doesn't have a snobbish bone in his body."

"He did sound rather nice on the phone."

"Anne, his wife, is really wonderful. She's a mad keen gardener and just dotes on Phoebe." Almost wistfully, he added, "Rupert and Anne fell in love when they were both eighteen and they're as happy as pigs in mud."

Jo decided she very much liked the sound of Rupert and Anne. But what on earth would she wear to their party?

Hugh, however, was one step ahead of her. He'd already made plans for a shopping expedition.

And later Jo decided she must have fallen under some kind of spell because, for the rest of the day, she had let Hugh lead her and Ivy to shops and exquisite boutiques all over Chelsea and Knightsbridge.

There had been a great deal of dashing about, jumping in and out of tall, sturdy, square-looking black taxi cabs, which Hugh had said was easier than taking his car and trying to find parking spaces.

The prices of the clothes were high enough to send Jo

into credit cardiac arrest, but Hugh had taken complete charge of the purchasing and wouldn't listen to any of her protests.

By the time they'd arrived home, she and Ivy had an astonishing number of purchases, including beautiful winter coats for them both and a gorgeous, utterly *divine* red evening gown for Jo from a shop in Sloane Street.

"You'll need something glamorous to wear to the Eliots' party," Hugh had insisted.

And, as she hadn't packed anything remotely formal, she'd had to agree.

Hugh had taken charge of the whole thing. He'd pointed the gown out to the assistant. "I want Miss Berry to try that one. Take her away and if it fits and she likes it, we'll have it."

"Would you like to see the young lady in the gown?" the assistant had asked.

"No," he'd replied, sending Jo an unexpected wink and one of his bothersome smiles. "Keep it as a surprise."

There had been just one sticky moment when Ivy had spotted the toy department in Harrods and Hugh had been eager to rush in there and buy her the lot.

But just as he'd been about to dive inside, Jo had stopped him. "I wonder if that's a good idea," she'd said.

"Don't be a spoilsport, Jo." She suspected that his look of stubborn resistance was one his own nanny must have endured on many occasions when he was a boy. "It's not as if Ivy has a houseful of toys."

"But already this week you've given her Howard and the baby doll and her beautiful new bedroom with all those school things and now an entire wardrobe of lovely clothes…"

"You think my money will spoil her?"

"If she gets too much too quickly."

His eyes had twinkled as he smiled another charming smile. "I've turned out OK, haven't I?"

Jo gave a roll of her eyes. No way would she comment on that. "Ivy's not used to luxury." As she said this, Jo had wondered if it was her own reaction she was talking about. It was hard not to feel uncomfortable about being surrounded by such wealth. It was such a far cry from home.

But then Hugh had let out an exaggerated, moody sigh and grinned. "You're probably right. Women always know best."

By then Ivy had already wandered right inside the toy department and she was entranced by a wind-up pig chugging across the floor.

"Can I have him, Daddy?" she'd asked as Hugh approached.

"Maybe not today, poppet."

"But I want a pig!"

Hugh shot a here-we-go glance back to Jo. "If you're very good I promise I'll buy you a pig another day," he'd said as he reached down and scooped her up.

She'd begun to protest.

"It's time to go home to Howard and baby doll," he'd said.

"And Marmaduke?" she'd asked, her eyes brightening quickly.

"And Marmaduke," Hugh had agreed.

"Yes, let's go home. I love your home, Daddy."

Hugh's eyes had gleamed with a suspicious sheen. "It's your home too, poppet."

As Jo slipped into her sumptuous bed that night, she was exhausted but almost too excited to sleep. A whole day with Hugh had been intoxicating. He'd been so much fun, so generous, so solicitous, and so full of compliments, both for her and for Ivy.

She knew that the inevitable was happening; she couldn't help herself. Even though she'd started out by trying to resist Hugh, she was falling way past head over heels and into the deepest depths of being hopelessly in love with the man.

And all the time they'd been shopping—when she'd been under his spell—and remembering his kisses—a romantic future beyond the brief two weeks had almost—*almost*—seemed possible.

The problem was that now, as she lay alone in the dark, listening to the muffled sound of distant traffic on the King's Road, the happiness of her day with Hugh seemed unreal.

Of course she would be going back to Australia at the end of the two weeks. Hugh had his little daughter. He and Ivy were wrapped up in each other.

They didn't really need Jo at all.

Chapter 6

"Daddy?"

Ivy's voice came through the darkness just as Hugh passed her room.

Her door was halfway open and he gently pushed it further. "Did you want something, poppet?"

"Can you tuck me in?"

"Yes, if you like."

A newly purchased night-light in the shape of a toadstool stood on Ivy's bedside table, casting a warm pink glow across her bed, making her look rosy and prettier than ever, and Hugh felt a swift clutch of emotion.

"You look rather nicely tucked in to me," he said, eyeing her neat bedclothes. "What would you like me to do?"

"Daddy," Ivy scolded. "Tucking me in doesn't just mean tucking me in."

"It doesn't? What does it mean then?" He felt lost again for a moment.

Ivy's bottom lip stuck out and her dark brows drew down into a stubborn frown. "You should know."

"Should I?" He swallowed a constriction in his throat. For the life of him he couldn't ever remember his own father tucking him into bed when he was a youngster. His mother had...but mothers and nannies were different, weren't they...and he'd been sent away to school when he was quite young. "I'm sorry, Ivy. I've never had a little girl before."

She turned her head to the side and looked towards the door that led to Jo's room. "Jo knows what to do."

"Well, yes." Hugh sighed. "That's because—because she has little sisters." As Ivy continued to look sulky, he said, "I'd love to tuck you in properly, sweetheart."

"Don't call me that word."

"Sweetheart? Why not?"

"That's what *she* calls me."

"Who? Jo?"

"No. Gorilla."

Gorilla? She meant Priscilla, of course. Hugh had difficulty suppressing his smile.

"I promise never to call you the *S*-word again," he said solemnly. "Now, tell me, what Jo does when she tucks you in."

Ivy patted the bed. "She sits here."

"Oh, yes, of course," said Hugh, lowering himself onto the edge of the bed.

"And she tells me a story, but you don't have to tell me a story."

That was a relief. Hugh knew he wasn't much of a story-teller.

He watched Ivy looking up at him with trusting expectation and he realised with a rush of happiness that there was no need to ask her what Jo did next. "I've just worked out what a daddy should do now," he said.

"What?" she asked, her green eyes sparkling suddenly.

Hugh picked up her hand. "I should eat you up, starting at the fingertips." He growled playfully as he began to nibble.

"No," Ivy squealed, delighted.

"No? Then I should tickle you," he suggested, tickling her ribs.

"No, no," she protested amidst a flood of giggles.

"Have I still got it wrong?" He gave a deep, exaggerated sigh. "Then, there's nothing for it, I'll just have to cuddle you and kiss you goodnight."

"Yes!" With an excited cry she held out her arms.

And Hugh gathered her up.

His heart swelled. She was his little girl. His very own. She felt so tiny and warm and she smelled of clean nightgown and the delicately scented special soap Jo used to bathe her sensitive skin. And she clung to him, her little heart beating against his. He kissed her cheek.

"I love you, Daddy."

"I love you too, poppet."

He hugged her again and then released her and she sank happily back onto her pillow.

"I like that name."

"Poppet?"

"Yes."

"Good. I like it too. It's my special name for you." He kissed her forehead.

"I'm so glad you came and founded me. Ellen told me you would come and I've been waiting for you for so-o-o long."

Hugh's heart ached for her. "I'm glad I found you too. Now, goodnight, sleep tight."

"I will."

Ivy reached for Howard and closed her eyes and Hugh's throat tightened with a welling of emotion, stronger than anything he'd thought possible. He was astonished and deeply moved by how quickly and completely his little girl had opened her heart to him.

As he watched her, she hugged the unicorn closer and the sleeve of her nightgown bunched, revealing the terrible burn scars on her arm, and he felt a sharp, savage twist to his heart, so intense that he thought he might actually cry. Fearful that Ivy might open her eyes and see his distress, he turned and walked quickly to his own room. What fierce, sweet agony it was to be a father. He wondered if he was adequate for the task.

He slumped onto the side of his bed and began to unbutton his shirt, lost in thought. So much tragedy had clouded his daughter's early life.

And yet in spite of that she was such a lively, spirited, loving little thing. But she had big battles ahead of her.

No matter how carefully he chose her school there would be inevitable taunts about her burned skin from some of the children. And in the future, as she grew, she would have to face more trips to the hospital and more painful skin grafts.

If Ivy was going to remain lively and spirited and grow into a happy, well-adjusted adult, she needed strong, positive, loving forces in her life.

Was he man enough for the task?

Until very recently he'd been a rather selfish man, but now he had little choice; he had to change. As his father had been telling him for years, he had to take life more seriously. The thing was, he found running a business and making money relatively easy. Personal relationships were more problematical.

His friendship with Rupert and Anne Eliot had been one of his sounder personal choices. His selection of women, on the other hand, had been lots of fun but less prudent. His girlfriends usually proved to be more decorative than reliable.

Priscilla was a prime example.

Damn.

The shoe he'd just removed fell to the floor with a thud as he remembered. He'd promised Jo he would phone Priscilla and set the record straight. But he'd had so much fun taking Jo and Ivy shopping today he'd forgotten.

He would have to plan his speech very carefully before he rang. It was important to hit exactly the right note and it wasn't going to be easy. First he had to squash Priscilla's assumption that he'd been sleeping with Jo; and then he had to confess that he'd lied about asking Jo to marry him; and finally he needed to block any opportunity for Priscilla to belittle Jo in any way.

Rather a tall order—especially when he also had to ensure that Priscilla was left in no doubt that he wanted her out of his life—and he most definitely didn't want her anywhere near his daughter.

It was midafternoon the next day before he made the call. He was at his office in the city, where he'd been attending to urgent business that couldn't be left until after the New Year weekend. But his guilty conscience was nagging him and at last he punched Priscilla's speed dial number into his cellphone.

She recognised his number even before he spoke. "Hello, Hugh," she purred. "What a delightful surprise. What can I do for you, darling?"

He thought he'd prepared for this call, but suddenly his

concentration—superfocused when dealing with business matters—was distracted by a kind of sixth sense, a vague feeling of unease, a suspicion aroused by the fact that Priscilla sounded far too relaxed and happy.

Was she plotting something?

"Darling?" Priscilla's voice repeated.

She'd never called him darling when they'd been a couple, and the hollow meaninglessness of the endearment set his teeth on edge now. "Good afternoon, Gorilla, I hope you're feeling calmer today."

"I beg your pardon?"

"I said I hope you're feeling—"

"Not that. What did you call me?"

"I don't know. I called you Priscilla, didn't I?"

"It sounded like Gorilla."

Had he really made that slip? "Good God, no," he protested. "Impossible. So, how are you?"

"Calm as a millpond. We're having an absolutely fab time—afternoon tea at The Ritz."

"How nice." It had been raining heavily since lunch time and taking tea in one of the city's grand hotels while the rain fell on others less fortunate outside was a predictable, Priscilla-style activity.

He could picture her adopting her Marie Antoinette pose as she lifted a crystal champagne flute or a teacup—azure blue with a thick gold rim—or took a leisurely nibble at a dainty cucumber-and-smoked-salmon sandwich. Yes, she *would* be at The Ritz; he could even hear a string trio playing Mozart in the background.

Somewhat reassured that she was out of harm's way, Hugh refocused his attention on his line of attack.

"You'll never guess who's here with me," she said.

Distracted, it took a moment or two for her question to register. "Oh?"

"Jo and Ivy."

"What?" Fine hairs rose on the back of Hugh's neck. His gut clenched as he leapt from his swivel chair. Jo and Ivy had gone sightseeing today.

Priscilla chuckled. "Isn't it a lucky coincidence?"

Like hell it was.

"I ran into the poor things just as they were leaving Hyde Park."

It was more likely that she'd been stalking them.

"Hugh, you should tell your international visitors never to go out in London without an umbrella. The poor darlings were absolutely drenched and it was freezing cold. Poor little Ivy could have caught pneumonia. Of course I insisted on giving them a lift to The Ritz to dry off."

By now Hugh had grabbed his coat and was shrugging his shoulders into it as he clutched his cellphone to his ear. "How are they?" he barked as he rushed out of the office.

"They're absolutely peachy *now*, darling. Jo's enjoying a cup of Earl Grey and Ivy's stuffing herself with scones and strawberry jam and cream."

Hugh knew this pretence at cosiness was nonsense. There was no way Priscilla would make such an about-turn without a reason. A rotten, sneaky reason.

He was absolutely certain she hadn't extended such a conciliatory gesture to Jo out of the goodness of her heart. As the lift shot him to the car park in the basement, he tried to think of a way to keep the conversation going. He needed to distract Priscilla from whatever she had planned.

But, just as he reached his car, Priscilla said, "Oh, sorry, Hugh. We have an emergency. Ivy needs to go to the ladies' room." And she hung up.

He considered calling straight back again, but chances were she wouldn't answer and he decided instead to concentrate on his driving. He needed to make his way through the rain and the traffic as quickly as possible.

He felt ill with dread as he steered his car through driving sheets of rain, but as he turned down Piccadilly, he tried to convince himself his fears were illogical.

Priscilla might have turned nasty, but she wasn't evil. And what could happen to Jo or Ivy at The Ritz? The place was swarming with staff trained to watch over their patrons and to attend to their every whim.

Swerving into Arlington Street, his tyres sent up a spray of rainwater and another shower as he came to a halt quite close to The Ritz's commissionaire. But the good fellow, dressed in his greatcoat and top hat and armed with a huge black umbrella, greeted him with his customary courteous smile.

"Would you like us to park your car, Lord Strickland?"

"Thanks," Hugh muttered, tossing the keys to him. He had no time for their usual exchange of pleasantries as he dashed through the rain to the huge revolving doors.

Where were Jo and Ivy?

His gaze darted everywhere as he strode through the spacious lobby. He had no idea if Priscilla was here or in The Ritz's famous Palm Court restaurant. Most people needed to make a reservation for afternoon tea in the Palm Court and Priscilla might have done so but, then again, she was a notorious queue jumper.

One thing was certain; when Hugh found her, he was going to make sure that the first message she got was to get the hell out of his life. He wasn't prepared to have her anywhere near his daughter—or Jo!

And then suddenly he saw Priscilla, walking through

the lobby, looking about her in much the same manner as he was. Alone.

Surprised to see him, she blinked. "Hugh, what are you doing here?"

"I came to have a word with you."

Something in his tone must have alerted her. She looked suddenly wary. "Hold it, Hugh. Don't say a thing you might regret. The most important thing right now is to find your daughter."

"What?" Hugh felt as if he'd been slugged. "What the hell do you mean?"

"The poor little sweetheart. I'm trying not to think the worst, but dear little Ivy has disappeared."

"How could she?" Hugh roared so loudly that several heads turned their way. "What have you done?" He couldn't bear this. He grabbed Priscilla's arm. "Where's Jo?"

"Who knows where Jo is? She panicked and took off. She's no good in a crisis."

That was rubbish but he didn't have time to argue. "Where was Ivy when you last saw her?"

Priscilla shrugged. "She went to the ladies' room and didn't come back."

"Where? Which ladies' room? Have you searched every cubicle?"

She slipped her arm through his and snuggled against him. "Come with me, darling. I'll do my best to show you where she was last seen."

Hugh shook her off. "Just lead the way and be quick about it."

As they rounded a corner Jo came towards them. And, in spite of Hugh's terror, he felt an immediate lift in his heart. But, to his surprise, she was walking at a sedate pace and she didn't seem particularly distressed.

"Have you found Ivy?" he demanded. But it was a foolish question. Surely if she'd found the child she wouldn't be alone.

"Not yet," she said calmly. "But I'm sure she'll turn up soon."

Her composure annoyed him. "How can you be so sure? Have you alerted the staff?"

"Yes, and I'm sure they'll find her. She must have gone exploring."

"What about the police?"

"The police, Hugh?" Her brown eyes rounded with surprise. "No. I didn't want to overreact."

Hugh ploughed frantic hands through his hair. "I can't believe this." He reached for his cellphone.

"What are you doing?"

"Calling the police, of course."

Jo laid a restraining hand on his arm. "Just a minute, Hugh. Calm down. Ivy has been missing for ten minutes. Isn't it a bit early to call the police? We don't want to make a fuss about nothing. I'm sure she'll turn up any minute now."

What had happened to warm, caring Jo? "How can you be so damn casual?"

"This is a big hotel and a little girl has wandered off," she said. "But, for goodness' sake, the place is full of very nice, charming people, who will be only too happy to help her to find us."

Her forehead creased as she peered at him more intently. "Do you really think London is a mass of kidnappers just waiting to jump on her?"

Yes, he wanted to shout. A part of him knew he was overreacting but he just didn't know what a father should do in a situation like this.

But, at that very moment, Jo glanced past his shoulder and smiled. "Look, just as I thought. Here she is."

Hugh spun around and a desperate, choking little laugh broke from him. There was Ivy walking along the corridor, holding hands and chatting happily with an elegantly dressed, sweetly smiling elderly lady.

The moment she saw him, Ivy let go of the woman's hand and rushed forward excitedly.

"Daddy!" She hurled herself at his waist. "What are you doing here?"

Hugh was so overcome, so suddenly confused, he couldn't speak. He simply patted Ivy's head while she clung to him and, although his heart was galloping like a steeplechaser, he noted that her hair was only a little damp and her clothes weren't wet at all. Obviously Priscilla's claim that she'd been drenched was an exaggeration.

He heard Jo thanking the elderly woman profusely and he took a deep breath and blinked several times to try to clear his eyes.

Jo knelt in front of Ivy. "Where were you? We've been searching everywhere. You gave Daddy a terrible fright."

Ivy gave a puzzled shrug. "Gorilla took me to see the big Christmas tree and told me to hide there. She said it was a game and I had to wait there for you to find me, Jo. But you didn't come."

"That scheming—" Hugh spun around, looking for Priscilla, and realised that Jo was doing the same.

"Where is she?" they both asked simultaneously.

But it was rather obvious that she'd taken off.

Jo's lip curled into a very un-Jo-like malicious sneer. "She plotted this." She shook her head in disbelief. "She was trying to make me look bad—trying to prove that I don't know how to look after Ivy."

"I can't believe you got in the car with her."

Jo sighed. "She made me feel terribly guilty about having Ivy out in the rain. But Ivy's coat has a hood. She was fine, really." She darted Hugh a shrewd glance. "How did you get here so fast? Did Priscilla phone you?"

"No," he said. "As a matter of fact *I* was ringing *her* to—" He broke off, not keen to admit that he still hadn't carried out his promise to set Priscilla straight.

With one arm around Ivy, holding her close, he watched the play of emotions on Jo's expressive face as she stood regarding him with her arms wrapped over her middle.

"You haven't spoken to her yet, have you?"

"I was about to." He knew that was the lamest excuse under the sun.

"No wonder she tried to quiz me. She still doesn't know, does she? It's your job to set her straight, Hugh, not mine."

"I'm sorry." He chanced a smile. Jo was looking very fetching in an ivory-cream sweater, tweed skirt and knee-high brown leather boots that he'd bought her in Knightsbridge yesterday. "What did you tell her?"

"Oh, what does it matter?" she cried angrily. "I should never have spoken to her. I shouldn't have let her persuade me to come here with her."

He stepped towards her and reached out to pat her shoulder, but she jerked away quickly and sent him a sharp *hands-off* look.

He had to hand it to Priscilla. She'd managed to upset everyone.

"I'll take you home," he said.

"Goody." Ivy beamed.

Jo merely nodded. And then, "I'll fetch our coats."

As they approached the heavy revolving doors, Jo took Ivy's hand and Hugh let them go ahead. Through the glass, he could see a policeman on the footpath, talking to someone. And then, as the door rotated and he stepped into the next available space, Jo and Ivy reached outside.

Hugh shoved at the door and pushed his way forward.

The policeman turned. "Lord Strickland?"

"Yes?" Hugh snapped. "What do you want?"

"We've received a report that your little daughter is missing."

Damn.

Chapter 7

Jo woke to the shrill ringing of a telephone.

She lay in the semiparalysed state of the still-half-asleep and it seemed to take ages for her mind to kick into gear. When it did, she remembered that she'd been dreaming about phone calls...lots of phone calls...*weird* calls...from home, from Priscilla, from her boss in Brisbane, even one bizarre call from Queen Elizabeth the Second.

As she pushed her bedclothes aside and swung her feet over the edge of the bed, the phone downstairs rang again, and she wondered if it had been ringing a lot this morning. Perhaps it was the sound of many phone calls that had penetrated her sleep and prompted her strange dreams.

Had something happened? Some kind of emergency?

Her mind flashed back to last night. Hugh had been moody and distracted, but he hadn't wanted to talk about it with her. In fact he'd gone out.

Ivy had been dog-tired and had fallen asleep quite early,

but Jo hadn't been able to sleep till after midnight. She hadn't heard Hugh come home.

Again the phone rang. What was going on? Her feet sank into the deep pile carpet as she hurried to check on Ivy. She was gone.

Her first reaction was to panic, but then she told herself that was silly. Nevertheless, she washed her face quickly and dressed in haste, paying no more attention to her hair than to drag a quick brush through it before she rushed downstairs.

And, of course, there had been no need to panic.

Ivy was at the dining table, still in her pyjamas and with her hair a mass of sleep-tousled curls, and Hugh was helping her to take the top off a boiled egg that sat in a bright red hen-shaped eggcup.

He offered Jo a rather grim smile as she hurried into the room. "Good morning."

Ivy waved a gleeful spoon at her. "We started breakfast without you."

"Sorry, I slept in."

"That's no mean feat, considering all the phone calls," said Hugh.

So she'd been right. There had been a lot of calls even before she had woken. "Why so many? What's happened?"

Hugh shrugged as if to make light of her query, but then his face twisted into an angry scowl. "Have a cup of tea before you try to face the day."

"What does that mean?" she asked as she lifted the silver teapot.

He didn't answer, but his scowl remained stiffly in place as he watched Ivy dip a finger of toast into her softly boiled egg.

"Come on, Hugh, tell me what's happened." The worried tension in his eyes frightened Jo. "Does it involve me?"

"I'm afraid so." His glance shifted to a folded newspaper lying on the dining table.

Jo's teacup rattled against its saucer and she set it down quickly. She felt ill. "Don't tell me there's a story in the paper. Priscilla hasn't run to the press?"

"Don't worry, it's a load of nonsense. And this is a discredited rag. No one takes any notice of it."

"If no one takes any notice, why have there been so many phone calls?"

Even as she spoke, the phone rang again in the next room. She glanced expectantly at Hugh. "Are you letting the answering machine deal with them?"

"Humphries is handling all the calls," he said. "He's doing a sterling job, diverting press enquiries to my PR fellow and vetting the private messages. I'll deal with those later."

Jo's gaze flashed back to the newspaper—a potential time bomb just sitting there on the table—looking innocuous in the middle of all the breakfast things.

Hugh leaned closer to Ivy. "Poppet, how would you like to have breakfast down in the kitchen with Regina again?"

She grinned. "And Marmaduke?"

"Yes, Marmaduke will be there too."

"Can I take my egg?"

"Of course."

"Is Jo coming?"

"No, Jo and I need to talk about something."

Hugh's ominous tone caused a lead weight to settle in the pit of Jo's stomach. She reached for the paper as soon as he and Ivy left the room, but she didn't want to read whatever was printed there.

And yet, if it involved her…and if the entire London populace already knew what it said…she had to face the worst.

The paper shook in her hands as she unfolded it and scanned the headlines. At first she couldn't see anything except general news stories. But then she saw a column—*Nelson's Column*—down the left-hand side and Hugh's name jumped out at her.

Sinking into a chair, she began to read.

The Lord's Love-Child

Publicity-shy and supposedly squeaky-clean Lord Hugh Strickland, only son of the Earl of Rychester, has finally blotted the family's impeccable copybook.

Not one to do things by halves, the charming Lord Hugh is now at the centre of a growing scandal featuring the suicide of an abandoned lover and the sudden appearance of an illegitimate child, flown from Australia earlier this week.

Obviously the powerful and influential family went to great lengths to keep this a dark secret, particularly the fact that Strickland's love-child, a sick and delicate little girl, has a severe deformity.

No! Oh, God, no! Dropping the paper, Jo covered her face with her hands. How could they say something so terrible about Ivy? This was much worse than she'd feared. She wasn't sure she could bear it.

Could it get any worse?

Sick with dread, she forced herself to read on…

And it could have remained a family secret but for the bungling of an unqualified Aussie nanny who lost the child on her first outing in London yesterday.

A lost child sparks a call to the police, which in turn alerts the media (to keep you fully informed of the scandalous facts, dear reader)…and, as usual, this column is delighted to provide a vital link in the info chain.

How does a nanny lose a child on a visit to one of London's grandest hotels?

Perhaps it's not surprising when the attractive but totally disoriented nanny only has eyes for Lord Hugh...

The nanny, one Jo Berry, has no training or qualifications for the task (her previous experience has been with cattle, sheep and wombats) but apparently she's the hottest thing that the dashing Lord set eyes on when he made a mysterious visit to the wilds of the Australian outback recently.

It is obvious that the relationship is much more than nanny to Strickland's love-child and a source close to the family reports that an engagement has been announced to shocked family and friends.

But perhaps we shouldn't be too harsh on poor Miss Bindi Creek (Yes, dear readers, there is such a place, I assure you).

It's no wonder she forgot she was guarding a defenceless little girl whose medical condition requires constant attention.

Jo Berry probably had stars in her eyes, visions of diamond rings, a society wedding and a honeymoon spent rolling naked in the Rychester estate money.

But here's some free advice for little Miss Bindi Creek:

"You can lose the diamonds, darling, or even the engraved family silver...but not the daughter of the heir to the estate of the Earl of Rychester."

The fiery old Earl himself is about to intervene and even this intrepid reporter wouldn't want to be around when that happens!

So, readers, stand by for official denials about any impending marriage and watch for the imminent return of Miss Bindi Creek to her distant native soil.

Jo thought she might throw up.

Each sentence was like a knife thrust. She couldn't bear it. She'd heard of gutter press but she'd never imagined such awful journalism was possible. There were so many lies. Every word was a lie.

Unable to bear the sight of that ghastly print, she closed her eyes, but from beneath her lids tears spilled down her cheeks. Hurt and indignation welled in her throat.

"Jo, it's a beat-up column by a broken-down hack."

Hugh's voice startled her. She hadn't heard him return.

Looking up, she slapped at the newspaper in her lap. "This is Priscilla's work, isn't it? This is all because of that stupid smokescreen engagement."

"Yes," he admitted. "I didn't expect her to be so quick off the mark—or so vicious."

Tears blinded her. She was trembling with anger and outrage.

"Jo, I promise you, I've dealt with Priscilla now. Last night. She won't cause you any more problems."

"She doesn't need to! She's already done her worst." With an angry yelp, Jo tossed the paper onto the floor and stomped on it. "How can any journalist write such filth? Everything in it's a lie. They're all vicious lies. It's totally, totally despicable. One hundred per cent wrong. It's vile."

Pressing her fingers against her lips, she tried to stop her mouth from twisting out of shape.

But she couldn't stop herself from crying. She felt violated. Betrayed.

Hugh reached for her and she tried to bat him away, but he drew her close and she was too overcome, too helpless to hold back. Her head fell onto his strong, bulky shoulder and she clung to him as she sobbed her heart out.

"I'm sorry, Jo," he said in a husky whisper. "I'm really sorry that this has happened."

She wanted to be mad at him. She *was* mad at him. But he sounded so genuinely sorry that she found herself forgiving him.

And, as her sobbing slowed, she realised that it was rather comforting to nestle into his reassuring strength, to feel his protective hand stroking her head. He was actually being rather patient with her. He wasn't annoyed by her tears as many men might be. He held her as if he had all the time in the world.

He held her as if he cared. Really cared. And that made such a difference.

When at last she felt calmer, she lifted her head. "This must be awful for you too, Hugh."

But all he said was, "I'm furious and incensed for you and for Ivy."

She stepped away from him and her eyes searched his face, trying to read his true feelings beneath the calm, handsome façade. "I guess this is what people with high profiles have to put up with."

"Yes, it goes with the territory. But don't worry, this will backfire on Priscilla. She'll be *persona non grata* among our friends."

There was a careful knock on the door behind them.

Hugh turned. "Yes, what is it?"

Humphries took two steps into the room. "I have a message from the QC you asked me to contact."

"Good man, what did she say?"

"She's afraid that a successful action is unlikely, sir—and going to trial would be very messy and distressing."

"I see." Hugh's green eyes were thoughtful as he stood with his hands on his hips. "I can't say I'm really surprised."

"Why not?" Jo couldn't help asking. "There isn't a grain of truth in that column. Surely you can sue them? The whole thing's a stack of garbage."

"Yes, it's a stack of garbage, but unfortunately it's garbage piled on top of some basic facts."

"Facts?" she cried. "There's nothing factual."

"Thank you, Humphries," Hugh said and, with a courteous bow of his head, Humphries left them.

Hugh turned back to Jo. "I'm afraid we're just going to have to ride this out. There's no point in getting tangled up in a long and drawn-out court case and having the media stirred into a frenzy."

Jo frowned. "What did you mean before—about facts? Where were the facts?"

Letting out his breath slowly, he leant a hip against the table and folded his arms over his chest. "Well, there's Linley's suicide…"

"OK," she said slowly. "That might be true, but I didn't lose Ivy yesterday. And to say that Ivy is deformed! That's a terrible thing to say about such a beautiful little girl."

"I agree totally." Hugh ran a hand down his face and released a long sigh. "But can you imagine the pain of arguing in court about whether Ivy was lost or hiding—or—or whether she's beautiful or deformed?"

"No," Jo admitted, shuddering. Hugh was right. It would be horrendous. "And I guess I'll just have to live with all that rubbish about Bindi Creek and the claim that I wouldn't know how to care for anything except wombats. But it—it's—"

She clamped her mouth shut to stop herself from swearing. If she wasn't careful she would be in tears again.

"I doubt anyone will believe that about you, Jo."

"But then there's the problem of the engagement announcement," she said. "I assume you set Priscilla straight last night, but what about everyone else? What are you going to tell them?"

"About our plans to marry?"

The question seemed to resonate in the room as if a gong had been struck. Hugh continued to lean against the table, not moving at all.

But a tiny smile sparked in his eyes.

And a sudden shiver rippled down Jo's spine.

"I don't know," he said at last, letting the words roll out slowly. "Maybe we shouldn't get too uptight about denying our wedding plans. After all, it's New Year's Eve."

Jo gulped to try to rid herself of the sensation that she'd swallowed a marble. "What's New Year's Eve got to do with it?"

His eyes shimmered with an intensely intimate glow.

And for some inexplicable reason Jo couldn't breathe.

This was ridiculous. Anyone would think she and Hugh had something going—an *understanding*—that they were actually contemplating marriage.

And, just to make things worse, her skin flashed hot and cold as she remembered the way he'd kissed her, the way she'd kissed him back.

His mouth tilted into his familiar heartbreaking smile. "Today marks an important milestone. We've known each other for an entire week, Jo."

A week. Had it only been such a short time? She felt as if she'd known Hugh for ever.

He was still smiling. "So it wouldn't be rushing things if we made our engagement official, would it?"

Of course he was teasing her. He had to be. *The cad.* She wasn't in the mood for playing games.

It wasn't very sporting of him. Even if he was the future

Earl of Rychester and the best-looking man in Greater London, and even if his ancestors had been bedding their serving wenches for centuries, Lord Hugh Strickland should know better than to play around with his daughter's twenty-first-century nanny.

Her emotions were already fragile this morning and now she could feel her anger shooting high—volcano style. It would serve Hugh right if she called his bluff.

Come to think of it, why shouldn't she? It would do him the world of good if he got some of his own back.

With a coolness that reflected nothing of the havoc inside her, she threw back her shoulders and looked straight into his cheeky smiling eyes. "What a terrific idea, Hugh. We can make a formal engagement announcement at your friend Rupert's party tonight. Actually, why stop there? I'll alert the Country Women's Association in Bindi Creek to be ready to cater for our wedding reception. That would be fine with you, wouldn't it?"

She allowed herself a small, self-satisfied smirk as she waited for his reaction.

But, when it came, it wasn't quite what she expected.

Hugh didn't laugh. He didn't chuckle. He didn't even grin.

He suddenly looked impossibly serious. Colour stained his high cheekbones and he stared at her with a breath-robbing intensity.

For lo-o-ong seconds they stood watching each other, while Jo's heart pounded and her preposterous counter to his joke echoed back at her from every corner of the room.

What was the matter with Hugh? He must know she wasn't serious. He knew she was going home at the end of next week.

Suddenly overcome by the tension that seemed to have

seized them both, she dropped her gaze and stared at her hands instead. For heaven's sake, someone had to break the silence. She took a deep breath. "And if tonight's going to be the big night, you've only got the rest of the day to come up with a spectacular proposal." And then she chanced an anxious glance his way.

And at last he reacted.

For one brief moment he frowned. Then his right eyebrow arched as he flicked back the ribbed cuff of his black cashmere sweater and looked at his wristwatch. "So we have till midnight?" Without warning, he sent her a roguish smile. "That means we still have fourteen and a half hours. Plenty of time for me to propose."

Jo gulped. Was she seriously overreacting, or was this nonsense getting completely out of hand? But as she struggled to think of a response, the front door bell rang.

And Hugh's merriment vanished. "Humphries will get that," he said, suddenly businesslike. "If either of us answers the front door we might find our photo in the paper tomorrow."

"Really?" It hadn't occurred to Jo that there might be paparazzi lurking outside Hugh's house. She was standing near a window where the curtains had been drawn open, and she couldn't resist taking a quick peek.

"Jo, stay away."

Too late! There was a bright flash from the foot path.

She jumped back. "I'm sorry, Hugh. I didn't think they would notice me up here."

From the hall came the sound of the front door slamming, and then a man's voice. "Damned press. Every last one of them should be hanged, drawn and quartered."

"But not by you, Felix," a woman's voice said. "There

was no need to swing at that young man with your umbrella."

"Ah," said Hugh with a strange look that expressed a mixture of pain and virtuous duty, as if he'd swallowed unpalatable medicine that he'd been told was good for him. "Now you'll have the pleasure of meeting my parents."

"Already? I thought they were coming up from Devon?"

Hugh managed a tight smile. "By helicopter."

Oh, good grief. Jo pressed damp palms against her thighs and found herself standing to attention. She didn't feel ready to meet the earl and his wife. Not before breakfast.

To add to her surprise, Hugh crossed to her side and slipped a friendly arm around her shoulders. "Don't look so worried, Jo. They'll love you. You're the daughter-in-law they've always wanted."

"Stop it, Hugh. How can you keep joking about that?" She was furious that he could be so playful about such a serious subject. How insensitive of him to tease her now, when he must know she was stressed to the max!

Even if Hugh's parents hadn't read the column in the paper they were sure to have heard about it. They would know by now that she was the incompetent, careless nanny who'd managed to lose their grandchild between bouts of leaping into bed with their son.

If only she could scurry downstairs to join Ivy and Regina in the kitchen.

"Oh, God, Hugh," she whispered in sudden panic. "How do I address your parents?"

"Call them Felix and Rowena," he whispered back.

"Hugh!"

He grinned. "Or Lord and Lady Rychester—whichever takes your fancy."

She half-expected Humphries to come to the door and

announce the earl and his wife, the way butlers did in movies, but when the door opened a somewhat matronly woman hurried into the dining room and Jo had no chance of getting her knocking knees under control.

"Hugh, darling."

"Mother."

Holding out her arms, the woman gave Hugh a kiss and an enthusiastic motherly hug.

Jo bit back an involuntary gasp of surprise. She wasn't sure what she'd expected Lady Rychester to look like— probably someone with a regal air and a haughty, cold beauty like Priscilla's. She certainly hadn't anticipated a woman who was shorter than herself, almost plump, with soft salt-and-pepper curls and warm, smiling brown eyes.

Hugh's mother even had an outdoorsy glow about her. She was not unlike how Jo's own mother might look if Margie Berry ever had the funds to dress in classic black trousers, a cream silk blouse teamed with an Hermes scarf, and pearl studs in her ears and a single strand of perfectly matched pearls at her throat.

Jo had barely got over that shock before Hugh's father, who'd been having a word with Humphries, strode into the room.

The earl was a different story—a taller, thinner, more stiff-upper-lipped version of Hugh. His eyes were very dark, almost piercing jade-black, and they made him look more than a little frightening.

Lord Rychester greeted Hugh with a grunt and a hand-shake. "Had to fight through a pack of vultures to get to your front door," he grumbled.

And then he fixed his sharp-eyed attention squarely on Jo.

Chapter 8

Hugh intervened quickly. "Mother, Father, I'd like you to meet Joanna Berry. As you know, she's kindly come with me from Australia to help Ivy settle in. I couldn't have managed without her."

Hugh's mother clasped Jo's hand between hers. "I'm delighted to meet you, Joanna. It's so kind of you to help Hugh."

"How do you do, Lady Rychester?" Jo said and she wondered if a curtsey was in order.

"Pleased to meet you, Joanna," the earl said more formally.

Jo offered her hand. "How do you do, Lord Rychester?"

Oh, heavens, this felt seriously scary.

How had a chance meeting with Hugh in her family's humble shop in Bindi Creek lead her to this?

"My dear, I can't imagine what you must think of our

outrageous British press," said Hugh's mother. "I'm so sorry."

Jo could have kissed her. "Thank you. It's very kind of you to say so."

"We've had a dreadful morning," admitted Hugh.

"Damn tabloids," muttered the earl and his piercing gaze speared Jo. "Don't give them a victory, lass. You're not going to charge off home to Australia because of this, are you?"

"Not yet, sir."

"Jo hasn't even managed so much as a cup of tea this morning," said Hugh.

"Can't have that," said his father. "Let's get a fresh pot. I could do with a cup."

Hugh smiled. "I'll organise fresh provisions."

Lady Rychester was casting a curious glance towards the door leading upstairs. "I'm dying to meet Ivy," she said. "Is she awake?"

"She's in the kitchen," Hugh told her, "eating a soft-boiled egg with toast soldiers."

His mother's eyes shone. "Oh, the little darling." She turned to Jo. "Is she very shy?"

"No, not really." The eager light in the other woman's eyes touched Jo's heart. She'd been so caught up with feeling nervous that she'd temporarily forgotten how important this meeting must be for Ivy's grandmother. Now she felt a rush of empathy for her.

"I'll fetch Ivy, shall I?" asked Hugh with a proud smile that advertised how very much he was enjoying his new role as a father.

"Darling, please do."

It was only after Hugh had left that Jo remembered Ivy

was still in her pyjamas. Worse, her hair wasn't brushed and her face was probably covered in egg.

Cringe. Hugh's parents might be prepared to overlook the preposterous claims in the newspaper, but they would be less charitable when they saw evidence of the nanny's incompetence with their own eyes.

Nervously, she asked them if they would like to sit down. But they had only just taken their seats when a piping voice could be heard coming up the stairs.

"Have I really got an English grandmother, Daddy?"

"Yes, don't you remember? Jo and I told you about her yesterday. She's upstairs."

"Is she a fairy grandmother?"

"No, just a regular grandmother."

"A hairy grandmother?" Ivy was giggling at her own joke.

Jo held her breath. When Ivy got overexcited she could be quite silly.

"A scary grandmother?" Ivy giggled again as she and Hugh walked into the room, hand in hand.

Despite the pyjamas and the tumbled curls, Jo thought the little girl looked very appealing. Her face was scrubbed clean. *Thank you, Regina.* Her lively eyes were dancing with merriment and no amount of stray curls could mar her exquisite features.

But when Ivy saw Hugh's parents she came to a halt and Jo was reminded of the morning when she and Hugh had arrived at Agate Downs and the child had been overawed to see strangers.

"Ivy," she said, holding out an encouraging hand. "Your grandmother and grandfather have come all the way to London especially to meet you."

But Ivy seemed to have frozen to the spot. She clung to

Hugh's hand and eyed her grandparents from a safe distance, assessing them with solemn, frowning wariness.

Hugh looked a little out of his depth. "Come on, Ivy, say hello."

"Hello," she said and then she lowered her gaze and dropped her bottom lip.

Sensing an awkward moment that could escalate into an uncomfortable scene, Jo jumped to her feet. "I have a good idea. Why don't we take Grandmother upstairs to show her your new bedroom? You can introduce her to Howard and Baby and you can show her some of your nice new clothes." *And I can tidy you up and get you dressed.*

Ivy seemed to think this over.

The little minx, thought Jo. She's playing with us.

But suddenly the little girl took a delighted skip forward. "Yes," she said, eyes twinkling once more. "That's a very good idea." She held out an imperious hand to a rather bemused Lady Rychester. "Come on, Grandmother. Come with Jo and me and we'll show you my lovely new bedroom."

"Well done, Jo. I couldn't have managed without you. I categorically *could not* have survived this day without your help."

It was midafternoon and Hugh was sprawled on a sitting room sofa, where he'd collapsed the minute his parents had left to visit friends in Mayfair.

Jo, curled in an armchair opposite him, was rather stunned by the enormous relief Hugh had expressed.

"I can't believe they took Ivy with them," he said.

"They want to show off their granddaughter," she responded. "They're absolutely smitten with her. It's wonderful, isn't it?"

"The amazing thing is the adoration seems to be mutual. Ivy really took to them, didn't she?"

"That's not so surprising, Hugh. I thought your parents were rather sweet. I was afraid of your father at first, but he's a softie underneath that upper-class crust."

"He's a softie around *you*," Hugh amended. "You have no idea how differently my father behaved today compared to the way he usually treats my women."

"Perhaps that's because I am *not* one of your girlfriends." Jo hurled a cushion at him.

Hugh caught it and hugged it to his chest and then he grinned at her. "You might not be mine yet." He glanced at the clock on the mantelpiece. "But it's half past three. Only nine hours left till midnight. Time's running out, Jo."

She let out a wail of impatience. "I'm getting tired of this ridiculous game."

"Then perhaps I should propose to you now."

Yeah, right.

"For heaven's sake, Hugh, give that subject a miss!" She hurled another cushion his way but, to her horror, it went sailing over his head and knocked a beautiful porcelain vase from the sofa table behind him.

She leapt to her feet, appalled by the mess she'd made. The vase had broken into three pieces and rose petals, flower heads and stems were scattered in a sodden heap. And, of course, there was a pool of water soaking into the white wool carpet.

"I'm so sorry. I'll get something to mop up the mess. Was that vase expensive? It's not Ming or anything is it?"

Hugh jumped from the sofa and caught her hand as she hurried past. "It's Meissen, but don't worry." Holding her hand tightly, he drew her close. Within a heartbeat her face was only inches from his.

"Hugh, I—I've got to get a bucket or—"

"Or nothing."

Jo gulped for air. Up this close, Hugh was breathtaking. Literally. "But the carpet. That stain should be treated quickly."

"There's another matter that requires more urgent attention."

"What—what's that?"

His hand slid down, pressing into her lower back, bringing her pelvis suddenly against his. "I desperately need you, Jo."

Oh, God. His words plunged straight between her legs and she felt a shocking, violent eruption of desire.

With one hand holding her close, Hugh used the other to trace a line with his fingertip along her jaw, down her throat to the V neckline of her sweater, and his green eyes burned with such wicked, devilish heat she felt her breasts swell and her nipples grow tight with unbearable longing.

So quickly. Just like that. She'd become an incendiary bomb about to explode. If Hugh kissed her, if he lifted her sweater, if he touched her anywhere *intimate* she would disintegrate. She'd be lost.

"No," she managed to whisper. "Don't."

"Come upstairs," he urged and his voice was low—a hot chocolate, superseductive rumble. "You want me, Jo. Don't you?"

Of course she did, but that wasn't the point. "Please, no. Let me go." Shoving her hands into his chest, she pushed him away from her.

And to her relief as well as her dismay, he did exactly what she asked. He let her go.

Breathless, panting, she staggered backwards, almost overbalancing.

Hugh looked as if he might follow her and she held up a shaking hand. "Hold it."

His eyes narrowed.

"I think you're getting a little confused, Lord Strickland. I'm here to look after your daughter, not to be your girlfriend."

"Jo, don't be angry. Just be honest with yourself. And with me."

"I'm sorry, Hugh, but why shouldn't I be angry? Sex was not part of our agreement. Maybe you're used to having the pick of whichever English girl you fancy, but despite what's reported in newspapers here, Aussies aren't all that impressed by titles."

He stood very still with his shoulders squared. His chest expanded and compressed, as if he was breathing hard. His eyes smouldered with dark, banked heat. "What if I were to tell you that I think I love you?"

Oh, no, don't do that to me. Jo gaped at him, too stunned to come up with an answer.

In his eyes she saw naked emotion that made her want to cry.

How had this happened? Something was wrong. She was the vulnerable one. She didn't have the power to hurt Hugh Strickland. But he could break her heart.

On the verge of tears, she pressed her lips tightly together as she tried to get her emotions in check. "Why? Why do you have to be who you are?"

"What the hell does that mean?"

She released a desperate strangled sigh. "If you were an everyday, average Englishman, it would be different."

"You mean you might be upstairs naked and in bed with me right now?"

Jo gulped. "Yes…perhaps."

His frown was accompanied by a troubled smile. He scratched the back of his neck. "Excuse me, Miss Berry, but aren't you contradicting yourself?"

It was Jo's turn to frown. "No, I don't think so."

"But one minute you're telling me you're not impressed by titles and the next you're saying that my title is so damned impressive it's scaring you off."

Finding herself suddenly at sea, she flapped her hands helplessly. "There's no point in discussing this. I'm going upstairs. To *my* room. I—I need to paint my nails for tonight."

"By all means." A weary smile flitted across Hugh's face. "You'll want to look your very best for tonight."

Confusion stormed inside her as she hurried upstairs. What was the matter with her? In her secret heart she'd been hoping for a romance with Hugh, and now that she had the chance she was running scared like a terrified child.

Running scared because Hugh thought he might love her—which was exactly what she'd hoped, but had never dreamed was possible.

It wasn't possible. Hugh was confusing lust with love. Very soon he would come to his senses and realise his mistake and she would be grateful for her lucky escape.

In her room, she took out the small bottle of dark berry-red nail polish to match the beautiful dress Hugh had bought her. One thing Hugh had said was right. Tonight she needed to look as glamorous as possible if she was to have any hope of measuring up to his friends. But her hands were still shaking so badly she had no chance of applying the polish.

Ivy and Hugh's parents would be home soon and then she would be busy getting Ivy ready for the party and she'd have no time for herself.

Acting on a sudden desperate whim, she snatched up the bottle and tore back downstairs, not glancing to the sitting room where she'd left Hugh but continuing all the way to the kitchen, where Regina was ironing and listening to the radio.

"I'm sorry to bother you, Regina." Jo held up the little red pot of polish. "I was wondering if you could lend me a steady hand."

"Heavens, love, it's a while since I painted a fingernail, but I'll give it a try. It makes a change from ironing."

After switching off the iron and lowering the volume on the radio, Regina pulled out a chair at the kitchen table. "Let's see if I still have the knack."

"It's so good of you. I'm too nervous and shaky," Jo admitted.

"Don't be nervous about going to Rupert's house," Regina said as she shook the bottle. "He's the loveliest, kindest man." Regina sent Jo a sudden shrewd glance. "That Priscilla Mostly-Tart won't be there, will she?"

"Priscilla *who*?"

"Mosley-Hart. Sorry, Jo. I know I have a hide to call her names."

But Jo couldn't resist a small smile. "I don't think she'll be there. She's out of favour. If she turns up, Hugh will have her clapped in irons and taken to the Tower."

"About time Hugh came to his senses." Regina painted a steady stripe of crimson onto Jo's thumbnail. "You have lovely hands."

"Thank you."

As she finished the first nail, the housekeeper let out a laughing shout of triumph. "Look at that. Perfect. I haven't lost my knack." She dipped the little brush back into the polish. "Just relax and enjoy yourself tonight, ducks. I have a very good feeling in my bones. I think you'll come home on cloud nine and won't that be a wonderful way to start the New Year?"

Chapter 9

Hugh had never felt more uptight than he did that evening as Humphries drove him with Jo and Ivy to the Eliots' house. His feelings for Jo had thrown him into a complete tailspin. He'd never been so undone.

He'd fallen in love—*really* in love—and it was no fun at all. He couldn't imagine a condition that rendered a man more helpless. More joyous. More tormented.

He was racked by gut-wrenching pre-party nerves and he hadn't felt this tense about taking a girl to a party since his teenage years.

During the past week there'd been times when he'd convinced himself that his feelings were returned. He'd caught Jo looking at him with a special soft light in her eyes. He'd seen the way his sudden appearance in a room could make flushes of colour come and go in her cheeks. And when he'd kissed her, her lips and limbs had responded with a trembling, sweet desperation that couldn't be faked.

She was such a contrast to Priscilla who'd been so in love with his title and money that she'd been willing to gamble everything in a bid to win him as a husband.

What bitter-sweet irony it was that Jo had thrown his riches and privileges at him as her reasons for keeping him at bay.

"Oh, look." Jo was craning her neck to look out through the car window. "I think I can see snow." She turned back to him, her eyes shining. "Is it, Hugh? Is it snow?"

He blinked and saw fluffy white flakes spinning and gleaming in the glare of street lights and headlights. "That's snow all right. Haven't you ever seen it?"

"No," Jo and Ivy answered together and they gave little squeals of delight as they leaned forward, watching with mouths and eyes wide open.

"It's just beautiful," said Jo.

But her happiness depressed Hugh. He glared at the pretty flakes. In his current mood the snow seemed to emphasise the vast differences between Jo's world and his.

"I'm afraid most of the snow we get in London usually melts or turns to slush almost as soon as it reaches the road," he felt compelled to warn her.

But she wasn't going to be put off.

"It doesn't matter." Her face was flushed with the enchantment of it all. "Look Ivy, it's real snow. Now I'll be able to tell everyone at home that I've seen it."

Hugh swallowed a sigh.

When they arrived at the Eliots' the white flakes were still drifting softly about them and as they stepped out of the car the scene before them was picture-perfect—the Eliots' lovely house with lights glowing from every window, the falling snow outside and the promise of warmth and gaiety within.

And then the door opened and a blast of music from a dance band greeted them and Rupert, who'd beaten his butler to the door, was grinning broadly and urging them to hurry in out of the cold.

Inside, they were immediately surrounded by a grand and welcoming spectacle—warmly tapestried walls, dazzling chandeliers, glittering mirrors and pieces of silver, beautiful flower arrangements and polished parquet floors designed especially for dancing feet.

Introductions were made amidst a great deal of laughter and happy chatter accompanied by hugs and kisses. The Eliots' butler hurried to help Ivy and Jo with their coats. Jo smiled as she thanked him and then she turned slowly, looking a little overwhelmed as she took in her surroundings. And Hugh felt as if he'd turned to stone.

He stood stock still, rooted to the spot by the sight of Jo in her lovely red dress.

She was beyond beautiful.

The deep crimson gown was perfect for her. Its colour offset her dark brown hair and eyes and highlighted the rosy tints in her complexion and the delicious deep red of her mouth. The dress's fabric was soft, skimming close to her figure without clinging. The cut was daring, with a deep plunging back and a tantalising low neckline, which somehow, mercifully, kept Jo's modesty intact.

The combination of boldness and decorum sent fire shooting to his loins.

"Is something the matter, Hugh?" High colour sprang into her cheeks. "Don't you like the dress?"

He tried to answer, but his heart seemed to fill his throat.

"What about my dress, Daddy?" demanded Ivy, not to be outdone. "Do you like it?"

He dragged his gaze from Jo to his daughter in her new

winter dress of emerald-green velvet that matched her sparkling green eyes. "It's beautiful, poppet. You both look—" He had to take a breath. "You both look like princesses." He turned to his best friend. "Don't they, Rupert?"

"Absolutely gorgeous." Rupert shot a knowing look Hugh's way. "So gorgeous I'm going to have to ask you both for a dance."

Ivy was suddenly shy and turned to whisper to Jo, who gave her a reassuring pat.

"Ivy's worried because she doesn't know how to dance," she told Rupert.

"Then I shall teach you," he said to Ivy with a charming grin as he held out his hand to her. "Come on, let's go."

Which left Hugh and Jo alone.

A waiter offered them a tray of drinks and they made their selections—champagne for Jo and Scotch for Hugh—and for a short while they stood together without talking, while they watched Rupert take Ivy's hand and spin her around. Within seconds the child was beaming with delight.

"Oh, there you are," called a voice. It was Anne Eliot, so there were more introductions and happy chatter. "I thought we'd let the children party with us for an hour or so and then our nanny will take them upstairs," Anne explained. "Don't worry about Ivy. There are plenty of children here to keep her happy and plenty of beds for when she gets tired."

She dragged them off then, so that Jo could be introduced to other guests and, as Hugh might have expected of guests at the Eliots', no one raised the question of the newspaper column and it was all very pleasant—until Jack Soames asked Jo to dance.

She responded after only the slightest hesitation and as she and Jack headed out onto the dance floor Hugh toyed with the idea of asking one of the other women to be his dancing partner, but he was hopelessly mesmerised by Jo. Leaning against a marble pillar, he clutched his glass of whisky and watched her dancing and smiling—and suffered.

Once or twice, Jo sent a brief, anxious look his way, but on the whole she paid a great deal of attention to Jack and she looked as if she was enjoying herself. Very much. Almost as much as her partner.

"That Jo of yours is charming."

Hugh started as Rupert's voice sounded close beside him. Rupert raised a sandy eyebrow. "You're not yourself tonight, old chap."

Hugh grunted and muttered a deliberately incomprehensible reply.

"You're not letting that idiot from *Nelson's Column* bother you, are you?"

"No, not at all, but it's been hard for Jo. I blame bloody Priscilla for the whole thing."

"I hear old Mosley-Hart's lost all his money," Rupert said. "Some crazy get-rich-quick investment that went belly up."

So that explained why Priscilla had been so dead keen to get herself engaged when he'd returned from Australia, thought Hugh. It was all about money.

"I must say your little Ivy is absolutely delightful," Rupert added in an obvious attempt to soothe his friend.

This time Hugh smiled. "She's fantastic, isn't she? I'm so lucky. I still can't quite believe I'm a father, though. But we've gotten to know each other very quickly. I adore her."

His friend didn't reply at first. "I take it you're referring to your daughter?"

"Naturally." Hugh felt his face flush and shot Rupert a warning look.

"But if I'd been talking about Joanna Berry, your answer would have been the same, wouldn't it?" Rupert said with clear disregard for Hugh's warning.

Hugh opened his mouth to deny it. But what was the point? Rupert was his oldest friend and could read him like a book. "Yes," he said softly and then he downed his Scotch in a swift gulp.

Rupert signalled for a waiter to bring them fresh drinks and, once they'd made their selections, he said, "Unless I've lost my ability to sum up a person at a first meeting, I'd say you've hit the jackpot this time, old fellow."

Hugh frowned.

"Don't pretend you don't know who I'm talking about."

"So you like Jo?" Hugh couldn't resist asking; the question mattered a great deal.

"Yes, and I don't just mean that I like the look of her." Rupert took a sip of wine. "Although it's hard to ignore that lovely figure."

Hugh glared at him. "When will you ever give up? You've been a stirrer since our school days."

Rupert smiled. "Actually, she's very different from the women you usually mistreat. No offence, Hugh, but I consider that a plus."

Hugh knew what Rupert meant. They were both familiar with his tendency to be blind-sided by women of rare physical beauty and his habit of moving on as soon as he got to know them.

But then he'd met Jo and he hadn't been swept away by stunning looks. He'd been pleasantly charmed by a pretty girl with a sweet, warm smile. And now, after a week in her company, he was completely spellbound by her rare and beautiful spirit. For him, Jo's ordinary prettiness had blossomed and deepened into a more stirring, more compelling beauty than any he'd encountered.

"I'll tell you something else I like about your nanny," said Rupert.

"Mention her body again and you put our lifetime friendship in jeopardy."

Rupert chuckled. "Seriously, I like what she's done to you."

"Done to me? I'm a wreck."

"Exactly. And I'm very pleased to see it. It's about time." From behind rimless spectacles Rupert's clever blue eyes shone with a beguiling mixture of sympathy and delight. "You've never felt this miserable over a girl before, have you?"

"No." After a bit, Hugh said, "I love her."

"Does she know how you feel?"

"Yes. No. Sort of." He stared at the drink in his hand. "I've made a complete hash of trying to tell her."

"Well, there's no need to rush these things."

"There is, actually. She's going back to Australia at the end of next week."

Rupert lifted both eyebrows. "I'll admit a deadline injects a certain degree of urgency."

"Yes. I've got to pull a rabbit out of a hat."

Hugh sighed. Rupert and Anne had it all—a relationship that was as secure and constant as it was passionate. And deep down he was certain that he could have that with Jo. If only he could find the right words…

Rupert's hand clasped his shoulder. "Be careful, my friend. A proposal of marriage isn't the same as securing one of your business deals. Women don't respond well to pressure."

Hugh wasn't so sure about that as he watched the couples

out on the dance floor. Hal Ramsay was cutting in to replace Jo's partner and, as soon as she began to dance with
Hal, the music slowed to something soft and bluesy.

Next minute Hal was drawing her in—and his hand,
damn it, was dangerously close to her lovely bare back. For
crying out loud, the man had a wife of his own and Jo was
smiling at him as if he'd offered her the sun and the stars.

What a pity Hugh was spoiling everything.

Jo didn't know what to make of his behaviour tonight.
Why wasn't he dancing and having fun? She'd been sure
that the dashing and charming Lord Strickland would be
the life of the party.

She was having a great time. It was so exciting to be in
such a lovely house, wearing such a beautiful, beautiful
gown. She felt totally welcome. The Eliots were charming
and friendly and so were their guests. No one so far had
been snobbish or condescending. No one had mentioned
Nelson's Column. No one had asked awkward questions
about her relationship with Hugh.

But, instead of enjoying himself, Hugh was standing
aloof, watching her with the frowning stare of an old maidish chaperon.

Well, maybe not old maidish. Not Hugh. He looked far
too manly and gorgeous in his superb black tails. Brooding
and moody might be a better description.

What was the matter with him? Surely he wasn't upset
with her? She couldn't believe that his teasing about pro-
posals and engagements was serious. As for his comment
about loving her—she would be naïve and foolish to think
that had been any more than smooth words rolling off the
tongue of a skilful seducer. They were worlds apart and she
had to remember that.

She was determined to have fun this evening in spite of Hugh's sulky mood. Tonight was a one-off chance for an Aussie chick in London to check out the way the upper-crust partied. She owed it to the girls back in the office to soak up every glamorous detail so she could give them a blow-by-blow report when she—

"Excuse me."

Hugh's voice stopped her thoughts and her dancing midtrack.

Her head jerked up and her eyes met his. Green. Gorgeous. Black-fringed. Oh, man. Her heart began a strange little dance, completely out of time with the music.

Hugh tapped her partner's shoulder. "I'm sorry, Hal, but your time's up," he said, flashing a tight-lipped version of his charming smile. "My turn."

Hot and cold shivers darted over Jo's skin and she felt an urgent need to protest, or to find an excuse to avoid close contact with Hugh. The dance was about to end, wasn't it? Shouldn't she check on Ivy?

But her partner was politely stepping away and within a heartbeat Hugh had usurped his place, taking her hand in his and placing his other at her waist and then drawing her close.

Too close. She couldn't breathe.

The dance was no more than a simple slow shuffle in time to the music. Nevertheless she stumbled.

"I'm sorry," said Hugh. "Did I trip you?"

She shook her head, suddenly too breathless, too anxious to speak. Oh, dear heaven, why did she have to react to Hugh this way? Why couldn't she be calm and sensible, the way she'd been when she'd danced with the other men? She was quite an uninhibited dancer normally. Now, for the life of her, she couldn't untangle her feet.

She bumped into Hugh again and the impact of their bodies was only slight, but that was all it took—a brief brush of his chest and thigh—to set off flashpoints of re-action all over her.

Hugh leaned back a little and studied her face. "You look a little pale, Jo. Perhaps you need a drink?"

"Thank you." It would be a blessed relief to stop danc-ing.

His hand settled at her waist as he steered her from the dance floor and she could feel the burning imprint of his thumb on the bare skin at her lower back.

"Why don't you try a brandy?" He looked about for a waiter. "It's supposed to have medicinal benefits."

But now that he wasn't touching her Jo felt more com-posed. "I don't need brandy, thank you. I'd just like some water, please."

He came back from the bar with a tall crystal tumbler filled with ice and water and, as he watched her drink it, a worried frown creased his forehead.

"That's better," she said, forcing a smile as she finished half of it. "This is a lovely party, Hugh."

He nodded. "Anne and Rupert always put on a good show for New Year's Eve."

Jo looked towards the foot of the staircase where a young fresh-faced woman had gathered several of the children. "I think that might be the Eliots' nanny getting the children ready to go upstairs now. I'll go and find Ivy and make sure she understands what's happening."

"Good idea. I'll come with you."

That wasn't quite what she'd had in mind.

Ivy and another little girl were playing peek-a-boo around a pillar at the side of the dance floor.

"But I'm not ready to go to sleep yet," she protested when she saw Hugh and Jo approaching.

"All the other children are going upstairs now," Hugh told her.

"No, I don't want to!" Ivy's bottom lip projected in a familiar pout.

Time for some gentle coercion, Jo decided. "Wouldn't you like to sleep upstairs with your new little friends?"

"In the same room?" Ivy asked, suddenly interested. "Like Tilly and Grace?"

"Yes," said Jo, although she was quite sure that the Eliots' nursery would be nothing like the humble bedroom her little sisters shared.

Remarkably, that was all it took for Ivy to agree.

"After everything else that's happened this week I'm surprised Ivy remembers Tilly and Grace," Jo said as they watched the chattering children climb the stairs.

Hugh smiled. "You'll have to admit that your family's rather memorable."

Something in the way he said that lifted fine hairs on Jo's skin. She looked up at him and he smiled again, but it wasn't a particularly convincing smile. She was sure she could sense a shadow of sadness behind it.

She was afraid to ask, but then the words spilled out anyhow. "Is something the matter, Hugh?"

His eyes pierced her. "I need to talk to you, Jo."

"OK." She felt suddenly breathless. "I'm listening."

"Not here."

Her heart hammered as she looked about her. The Eliots' nanny and her little flock of children were almost at the top of the stairs. To her right, Anne Eliot was helping an elderly white-haired woman into a chair and offering her a glass of sherry. A couple nearby were sharing an apparently uproariously funny joke. No one was paying any attention to Hugh or Jo. "You can talk here, can't you?"

"No," he said, reaching for her hand. "Come upstairs with me."

"Upstairs?" she squeaked.

"There's a little conservatory on the next floor, and there's something I want to show you."

Rolling her eyes at him, she made a nervous attempt at a joke. "That's not very original, Lord Strickland. What have you got up there? Etchings?"

His mouth quirked as he gave her hand a tug. "I promise this is all above board. It will only take five minutes."

"Oh, very well."

At the first landing, he pushed open a door to the right and they entered a small informal dining room. Hugh didn't turn the light on, but on the far side of the room pale moonlight spilled through a snow-covered glass-roofed conservatory onto potted palms and flowers.

"Wow!" Jo forgot to be nervous as she walked towards the glass-walled room. "This is so pretty." She stepped into the conservatory and was met by the scent of roses. She looked up and saw enchanting little banks of snow lying against the ribs that joined the glass panels—and, higher, the moon shining through a break in the clouds.

But then she turned back to Hugh and in the moon-washed shadows she saw the look of deep intent in his eyes. Her heart leapt. "Oh, God, Hugh, why have you brought me here? You're not going to try to seduce me again?"

He held up his hands. "I'm on my very best behaviour, Jo. I want to ask you to marry me."

She felt a slam of panic. "But you can't. You mustn't keep this silly joke going."

"I love you."

"Don't say that."

"Why shouldn't I love you?" Hugh stepped towards her and his voice was husky with emotion. "You're a miracle, Jo Berry."

She mustn't let herself listen to such temptation. "I'm going home in a week, I'm only here to help you with Ivy."

He took her by the shoulders. "This has nothing to do with my daughter. I want you for myself."

She wanted to cry. Her dream had come true. But now that it had, it felt terribly wrong. She felt a rush of tears. This was so surreal.

"Why can't you believe me?" Hugh whispered.

Wriggling her shoulders out of his grasp, she took two steps back. "It—it's too much like a fantasy—a fairy tale. I'm Jo Berry from Bindi Creek and you're—you're Prince Charming. I shouldn't even be here at this party, dressed in this gorgeous gown and dancing with your blue blood friends. I—I should be with the Eliots' nanny, taking the children to the toilet or settling them down to sleep."

Hugh ploughed a frantic hand through his hair. "You're letting that damned *Nelson's Column* get to you. Either that or you're deliberately underselling yourself."

"I'm being realistic."

"How's this for realism?"

Hugh took something from his breast pocket. It was difficult at first to see what he held in his hand, but then he moved slightly and she caught the unmistakable sparkle of gemstones.

Her heart jumped as if a shot had been fired.

"This was my grandmother's engagement ring," he said. "I've never offered it to another woman, but I very much want you to have it, Jo."

This couldn't be happening. She was dreaming. She had to be.

"There are five stones," Hugh continued in his low, deeply beautiful voice. "Three diamonds and two rubies and, according to the story my grandmother liked to tell, the five stones represent five words. *Will you be my wife?*"

The conservatory seemed to swim before her.

"Jo," Hugh whispered, "please say something."

She blurted the first words that came into her head. "I think you've taken this too far."

"What?" The little jewellery box in his hand shook. "You can't really believe this is still a joke."

She pressed a hand against her clamouring heart. "What else can it be? Think about it, Hugh. You've already hinted at our engagement once when you didn't mean it. That's pretty fast work for a couple who've only known each other a week. Maybe it's getting to be a bad habit—a quick fix solution. How can I be confident that you really mean it this time?"

He gave an impatient shake of his head.

"A marriage proposal! That's for life, Hugh. It would make more sense if you propositioned me again. Can't you see that?"

Surely she'd made perfect sense. Why was he being so stubborn? "Can't you see how rushed this is?" She felt compelled to fling him her trump card. "After all, you still have Priscilla's things in your bedroom."

He frowned. "When were you in my room?"

"This afternoon."

She'd gone there after Regina had painted her nails. She'd felt a sudden need to apologise to Hugh for the immature way she'd rebuffed him. And she'd decided to tell him the truth…that she fancied the pants off him. She could be persuaded to change her mind…

But when she couldn't find him in the lounge she'd gone upstairs and she'd stepped into his bedroom…

"You still have a box of Priscilla's things on the floor just inside your bedroom door," she told him now. "Her name is marked very clearly on the side."

Hugh groaned softly. "Humphries was going to deliver that box to her but with all the phone calls and nonsense in the press he's been distracted. I'm sorry."

"I'm not sorry. It was a timely wake up call for me."

He gave another impatient shake of his head. "I was never in love with Priscilla, Jo. Even before I learned about Ivy, I had realised that Priscilla and I were headed for misery. And that was before she walked out on me at the very time I needed her support."

"Well, I can't help wondering if you'd change your mind about me too," said Jo. "What guarantee do I have that in a month or two there won't be a box of my things waiting for Humphries to deliver to me?"

She swallowed and bothersome tears sprang to her eyes. "I'm sorry, Hugh. I'm not prepared to take a gamble on that."

In the moonlight she saw the way his face stiffened. "Is that your final word?" he asked.

Every part of her wanted to say no.

He remained standing very still. Very British and stiff— and he looked more dashing and gorgeous than ever in his dark formal evening clothes.

"Is it your final word?" he asked again.

She opened her mouth to say yes, and then she shut it. She thought of her mum and the wistful dream that had sent her flying here to London with Hugh. And then she thought of the box of frilly negligées in Hugh's room and she imagined the words *Joanna Berry* written in black felt pen on the side.

"Yes," she said. "It's my final word."

Hugh looked down at the ring in his hand and then quickly closed his fist over it. "Forgive me for taking up your time." With a grim, tight face he slipped the ring into his pocket.

He made a movement as if he planned to take her elbow, but then he thought better of it and, without another word, he turned and walked away from her.

In the moonlit silence Jo watched him disappear and she wondered how on earth she could face the New Year without him.

Jo's mum telephoned several nights later. "So how's it all going, love?"

"Terrific." Jo gulped back the homesick tears that threatened the instant she heard her mum's voice. "I've been having a really good time."

"You don't sound too happy."

"Must be a bad line. I'm fine, Mum. And Ivy's fine. How are you and everyone at home?"

"Oh, we're all chugging along the same as always. Not much news. Eric broke his arm. Silly kid jumped out of a tree, trying to frighten Grace."

"Heavens. Poor Eric. I hope he's not in too much pain."

"He'll live."

"Give him my love. Give everyone my love."

"I will. So…what have you been up to, Jo?"

"Well… I think everything's just about organised for Ivy."

"Organised? How do you mean?"

Being organised and efficient was the way Jo had survived the past week. Luckily, it was how Hugh had chosen to conduct himself as well. They'd both been superorganised, mega-efficient and they'd deflected any superfluous emotion to Ivy.

"Hugh's had Ivy checked out by Simon Hallows, a fantastic burns specialist, who went to school with Hugh. You should have seen how gentle and kind he was with Ivy, Mum. And he's been able to set Hugh's mind at rest about what can be done for her in terms of future surgery as she grows."

"The poor little lamb. She shouldn't have to go through all that."

On the other end of the line there was the sound of a chair scraping and Jo could picture her mother sitting down, settling in for a comfortable chat. "So you went along to the doctor's with them, did you?" Margie asked.

"Yes, Hugh wanted me there."

"That's nice, love."

The sentimental warmth in her mum's voice made Jo nervous. She'd done her best to squash Margie's wistful yearning for a romance between her daughter and the handsome English gentleman. She'd told her about Hugh's money and his aristocratic family and about Priscilla and the havoc she'd caused.

What else did it take to get the message across?

"We've found Ivy a school," she said, hoping to steer the conversation away from uncomfortable topics. "We've spent three days going to inspections at all the schools Hugh's friends have recommended, and he's found a lovely one only a few streets away from his house."

"Sounds perfect. Does Ivy like it?"

"Loves it. Can't wait to start. You should have seen her

face when she saw the little English schoolkids in their uniforms. The girls wear little green blazers and pleated skirts and knee-high socks. And the boys wear the cutest little green peaked caps. I think Ivy wanted to bring one of the boys home to keep him as a pet."

Deep chuckles sounded on the other end of the line.

"And this afternoon we finished the interviews for a new nanny," Jo added quickly.

"Oh?" There was no doubting the sudden tension in Margie's voice.

"It was such a hard choice. There were lots of very suitable girls, but I think Ivy will get on really well with the one we've settled on."

"So you really are coming home?" Margie made no attempt to hide her disappointment.

"Of course I am. My holiday's almost over and I have to get back to work. I've already told you I'm flying out on Saturday."

"I thought Hugh might have persuaded you to stay."

"Well, he hasn't," Jo said sharply, too sharply, but it couldn't be helped. This wasn't her favourite talking point.

"Has he tried?" Margie asked.

"No."

"I don't believe you."

Oh, heck. There was nothing for it but to bite the bullet. "Well, yes, he tried to talk me into staying—and not just as Ivy's nanny. But it wouldn't work, Mum."

"Jo!"

"It wouldn't! Hugh came to his senses and realised his mistake."

Jo was aware of a movement behind her and she turned to see Hugh in the doorway. She felt a rush of panic—her chest squeezed tight and her face felt as if she'd been sun-burned. How long had he been there?

He'd taken up a casual pose, with his hands thrust deeply in his trouser pockets, his shoulder propped against the doorjamb and one foot crossed over the other.

The expression on his face was anything but casual.

Oh, God.

"Are you sure he wants you to go home, love?"

She could hardly hear her mum's voice above the pound-ing in her ears. Snatching her gaze from Hugh's, she twisted the phone cord with frantic fingers. "Y-yes," she said.

It was true. Hugh hadn't once this week tried to convince her to stay. He'd never mentioned the engagement ring or his feelings. He'd been the perfect courteous, polite English gentleman.

Until now. It wasn't very gentlemanly to listen in on someone else's telephone conversation. The way he watched her was downright intimidating.

There was a deep, loud sigh on the other end of the line.

"We mustn't talk for too long now, Mum," Jo said, glanc-ing again briefly in Hugh's direction. "This call must be costing you a fortune."

"Before I forget, can you thank Hugh for the lovely letter he sent?"

Again Jo's eyes flew to Hugh and he regarded her with a dark, brooding vigilance that sent her heartstrings twang-ing. She turned her back on him. "What did you say? Some-thing about a letter?"

"Yes. Hugh sent us the loveliest long letter. He must have written it last week, but it's only just arrived."

"That—that's nice. OK, I'll thank him."

Her mother gushed on. "It was beautifully handwritten and he thanked us for sharing Christmas dinner with him.

Said he'd never enjoyed a Christmas more. And he invited us all to England."

"You're joking."

"No, seriously. He thought we'd love his family's farm in Devon. And he went to the trouble of telling each one of us specific things we'd enjoy."

"What—what kind of specific things?"

"Well…let me see…" There was a crackle of paper. "He said Brad and Nick should try polo because they're such good horsemen…and Bill and Eric could go exploring on the moors…and Tilly and Grace would love the little Dartmoor ponies. And if we go in the spring there'd be wild flowers and market villages that I'd love and he has a good trout fishing stream for your dad."

Jo sent a quick, frantic glance back over her shoulder to the doorway. Hugh had gone again, leaving as silently as he'd appeared. She ought to feel relieved, but she felt strangely bereft. She forced her mind back to the conversation. "Hugh didn't actually name everyone in the family individually, did he?"

"Yes, he did, love. He remembered the names of everyone. I thought he must have checked them with you."

No, no he didn't.

"Wasn't that nice of him?" her mum added.

"Very."

Jo couldn't believe it. None of her friends in Brisbane had ever been able to remember the names of all her brothers and sisters—not even her flatmates—and she'd been living with them for four years and they'd even visited Bindi Creek with her.

She'd known Hugh for two weeks. He'd spent one day with her family. One day and he could remember them all— Nick, Brad, Bill, Eric, Grace and Tilly.

OK, so he had an excellent memory for names. There was no need to get all choked up about a man's memory. "Well, I'm sorry you won't be coming over here now," she said.

"Yeah." Margie sighed.

"Mum, I'm looking forward to seeing you all very soon." There was silence from the other end of the line.

"Mum, are you there? I should say goodbye now."

"All right. Goodbye, love."

"I'll see you really soon."

"Yes, have a safe trip." Her mum sounded so dejected as she rang off that Jo burst into tears.

Chapter 10

"No airport farewells," Jo insisted. "It would be too trau-matic for Ivy."

Somewhat reluctantly, Hugh agreed.

And so the goodbyes took place at St Leonard's Terrace.

He watched the shining dampness in Jo's eyes as she hugged Ivy for the last time. He watched her tight white face as she held out her hand to shake his. He watched her back—ramrod straight—as she walked to the car behind Humphries.

And he saw that she didn't look back and she didn't wave once, not even as the car turned the corner.

The plan was that Humphries would drive her to Heathrow while Hugh stayed behind to keep Ivy entertained with the wind-up pink pig he'd ordered from the toy depart-ment in Harrods.

But how in hell's name was a man supposed to entertain a child when his heart was breaking? Especially when the child persisted in asking awkward questions about when Jo was coming back, or why there had to be a new nanny.

"I don't want a new nanny. I want Jo," she repeated over and over as they sat on the floor in her bedroom and made a poor attempt to play with the toy that had so delighted her a week ago.

"You'll like Sally, your new nanny," Hugh said, wishing he could dredge up an enthusiasm he couldn't feel.

Ivy's lower lip pouted ominously. "But I love Jo."

"Jo explained it to you, poppet. She has to go home to Australia. Now, look at this lovely fat pig. Isn't he funny? He's walking right under your bed. I think we need to get Howard to—"

"I don't want Jo to go to Australia," Ivy said, pushing the treasured toy away. "I want her here."

"Well, aren't you a Miss Bossy Boots?" Hugh wondered how he would cope if his daughter threw a tantrum.

"Why did you let her go, Daddy?"

He wasn't ready for that question. "I don't know," he whispered hoarsely.

Ivy stared up at him with curious green eyes. "Daddy, are you crying?"

"No."

"You are."

"No, no." He blinked hard. "It's just something in my eye."

Scrambling to her feet, Ivy looked worried. She pushed her little face close up to his till their noses were almost touching and she stared anxiously into his eyes. "You *are* sad," she said. "You're very sad."

"Just a little."

"Is it because Jo had to go away? Doesn't she love us?"

"I'm sure she loves us, poppet, but she loves her family too."

"Does she love Tilly and Grace better'n us?"

Hugh forced a smile and he hugged Ivy close. "She couldn't possibly love anyone more than she loves us."

"Don't worry, Daddy. She'll come back."

"No, poppet, you've got to understand Jo's not coming back."

Ivy's eyes were huge. "She's gone for good?"

"Yes." Hugh sighed.

From her lonely seat in the back of the car, Jo watched the streets of London flash past. This was her last glimpse of the famous city. There would be no more chances to visit London's wonderful museums or art galleries, or to go to lovely concerts like the one Anne Eliot had taken her to in St Martin-in-the-Fields.

Never again would she take Ivy for walks along the Thames Embankment, or go to the King's Road to buy sweets from the little shop around the corner.

Worst of all—very, *very* worst of all—there were no more chances to see Hugh and Ivy.

She'd come to the end. The final page. And she'd discovered what she'd suspected all along; her story was a gritty reality drama, not a fairy tale.

She'd accused Hugh of creating a fairy tale but, if that were so, he would have found a way to stop her from leaving. He would have done the Hollywood thing—chased after her and swept her into his arms and vowed his undying love for her. Or he would have found a magical fairy tale way to *prove* beyond doubt that he loved her.

Instead he'd shaken her by the hand.

And he'd said goodbye with a strange little stiff nod of his head. How jolly British!

How bloody awful! Her face crumpled and her tears overflowed and streamed down her cheeks. And her chest hurt with the awful pain of wanting Hugh. It was her fault that she'd lost him. She'd walked away from him. But she loved him! Oh, dear heaven, she loved him so much.

She loved looking at him, she loved talking to him, she loved being with him and she loved making plans for Ivy with him. She loved his friends, his parents, living in his house, his city...

There wasn't a thing about Hugh Strickland that she didn't love.

Another torrent of tears poured down her face and she reached into her pocket for a tissue to stem the flow. Along with the tissue, a stiff piece of paper came out of her pocket and, as she mopped her face, she stared at it lying in her lap.

Actually...it wasn't a sheet of paper; it was an envelope— with a single word written in spiky black handwriting.

Jo.

It was Hugh's handwriting.

Her heartbeats seemed to stop and then they began a querulous thumping. She turned the envelope over and slipped her little finger beneath the flap. *What on earth could it be?*

Inside, there was a single sheet of notepaper and something else. Something small. Her eyes caught a glint of gold and her hand trembled as she reached inside.

A ring! Oh, dear Lord. Hugh's grandmother's engagement ring. Her heart picked up pace until it thundered. Her hands shook so badly she almost dropped the ring, so she slipped it onto her finger for safekeeping and opened the piece of paper to read a handwritten message.

Dearest Jo,

I am desperately in love with you. I know it's hard for you to believe; it's all happened so quickly—how can I convince you?

I feel as if my past has happened in another lifetime, and all I know now is that with you by my side I could live my life as it's meant to be. If you were my wife I would be the happiest man in all history and I would devote my days to making you happy too.

If ever or whenever you decide that you want me, all you need to do is slip this ring on your finger and come back to me and I'll be yours for ever.

If you return the ring I'll know that I've been wrong in thinking you love me too.

I love you.

Hugh

"Pigs don't usually go in the same pen as unicorns," Hugh patiently explained to Ivy.

His daughter frowned at him. "Why not?" She didn't like being corrected.

"They eat different things."

"Unicorns eat grass. What do pigs eat?"

"Oh, grain and scraps—almost anything really."

An impish grin suffused Ivy's face. "Like you."

"Are you calling me a pig?"

She giggled. "Yes, you're a pig, Daddy. You eat almost anything."

"I beg your pardon. I don't think I can let you get away with that. Little girls who call their fathers pigs must be tickled."

"No."

"I'm going to have to tickle you to death."

"No!" Ivy shouted again, but she was giggling too and her fate was sealed.

Toys scattered as the two of them tumbled sideways on the carpet. Next minute Hugh was on his back holding Ivy up in the air at arm's length and the little girl was laughing and squealing.

"Is this a private party or can anyone join in?"

Hugh paused in midtickle. His heart jolted hard. Had he heard what he thought he'd heard?

He turned.

And there was Jo standing at the top of the stairs, just outside the doorway to Ivy's room.

Her face, framed by her neat brown hair, looked pale and yet bright spots of colour stood out in her cheeks. She sent them a rather wobbly smile.

"Jo!" Ivy screamed. "It's Jo, Daddy! I told you she'd come back!"

As soon as Hugh lowered her to the floor Ivy dashed across the room to fling herself at Jo, and Hugh's heart pounded so fiercely he felt it might burst through the wall of his chest.

Jo was back.

Jo, smiling across at him as she hugged Ivy. Jo, with raindrops in her hair and with sparkling, lovely eyes—looking as if she might cry.

Hugh swallowed the painful lump in his throat.

Silver tears glistened on her lashes as she looked at him. "You remembered all their names," she said.

"I did?" He had no idea what she was talking about, but he pushed himself to his feet.

"My family. My brothers and sisters—you remembered their names."

"That's why you came back?"

"It was so sweet of you to remember, Hugh."

She wasn't making sense. Hugh felt his elation falter.

But then Jo held out her hand—her left hand—and he saw the twinkle of rubies and diamonds.

He wasn't sure who moved first, or how they came together. All he knew was that he was holding Jo at last. He was clasping her tight, breathing in the special fragrance of her, feeling her arms around him and her sweet body pressing close, and she was welcoming him with open lips, kissing him, wanting him.

"I love you, Hugh," she whispered against his lips. "I love you. I love you. I love you." She kissed him on his mouth and on his chin, on the underside of his jaw, his throat and then his lips again.

Laughing, he caught her eager face between his hands and held her still so that he could return her kisses, so that he could kiss her soft, warm mouth and her salty tears. And then he hugged her to him, almost afraid that she might disappear.

"Daddy! Stop it, you're squeezing Jo too hard!" Impatient little hands tugged at their clothing.

Breathless, they broke apart and looked down at Ivy as if she'd just arrived from outer space.

"Ah, poppet," said Hugh. "Why don't you run down to the kitchen and see if Regina has afternoon tea ready for you?"

"Has she made chocolate cake?"

"Perhaps. Why don't you go and ask her?"

"OK. See you." At the top of the stairs, Ivy turned back and she eyed them warily. "Make sure Jo doesn't go away again."

"Don't worry, Ivy, I promise I'm here to stay," Jo assured her.

His daughter set off happily downstairs and Hugh took Jo's hands in his and looked again at the ring. It suited her hand beautifully. "I've been so worried," he said. "I didn't know if you would find this, or when you'd find it, or how you'd react, or what you'd do, or whether—"

Jo stopped him by placing two fingers against his lips. "It's OK, Hugh. I'm here."

And then they were lost in another kiss—an unrestrained, lush and lingering kiss—a kiss that released at last all the loving and longing that had lain in their hearts.

It was much, much later that Jo told him her story. "We were on the approach into Heathrow. You know where all those big hotels are. Poor Humphries didn't know what to make of me when I started blubbering that we had to turn around. He was so worried I'd miss my plane. It took me ages to convince him that I *wanted* to miss it. Once he realised I was serious he broke the speed limit to get me back here." She blushed sweetly. "To you."

Just for that Hugh kissed her again. "You do understand that I truly love you, don't you?"

"Yes, Hugh." She lifted a hand to gently caress his cheek. "Yes."

"I'm the luckiest man alive."

She dropped her head onto his shoulder and Hugh pressed kisses to the back of her neck. "I know I've been far too rushed about this, but when can we be married? Is six months too soon?"

"Oh, goodness, six months?" Her eyes danced with silent laughter. "I couldn't possibly wait that long."

Epilogue

From Nelson's Column:

One of the best-kept secrets on the London social calendar last week was the sudden and very private wedding of Lord Strickland, long-time Chelsea bachelor and owner of Rychester Aviation.

Always first with the spiciest news, this column blew the lid off Hugh Strickland's clandestine romance with Australian nanny, Jo Berry.

We made startling revelations and saucy suggestions about what would happen to the unfortunate miss from Down Under.

Humble pie is not usually on the menu in this column. However, dear readers, I will eat a large slice since my predictions about this couple fell so wide of the mark.

Who would have guessed that True Love would play an unexpected hand, and that Miss Bindi Creek would become Lady Joanna Strickland, wife of the future Earl of Rychester?

This columnist was somehow overlooked by the minions who prepared the guest list for the Strickland-Berry wedding, as were most others apart from family and a few close friends, who gathered at the chapel on the Rychester estate in Devon.

However, I can report that the bride looked radiant, the bridesmaid very sweet, and that the post-wedding celebrations continued for several days.

I am reliably informed that Jo Berry's extended family from Australia were flown over on one of Strickland's private jets. No small order considering there are enough Berrys to field a cricket team.

My spies tell me that the honeymooners—with a little companion—have been seen in the French Alps, in New York and in Tahiti...and I have no reason to doubt any of them.

* * * * *

REQUEST YOUR FREE BOOKS!

2 FREE NOVELS PLUS 2 FREE GIFTS!

Harlequin

Desire

ALWAYS POWERFUL, PASSIONATE AND PROVOCATIVE

YES! Please send me 2 FREE Harlequin Desire® novels and my 2 FREE gifts (gifts are worth about $10). After receiving them, if I don't wish to receive any more books, I can return the shipping statement marked "cancel." If I don't cancel, I will receive 6 brand-new novels every month and be billed just $4.30 per book in the U.S. or $4.99 per book in Canada. That's a saving of at least 14% off the cover price! It's quite a bargain! Shipping and handling is just 50¢ per book in the U.S. and 75¢ per book in Canada.* I understand that accepting the 2 free books and gifts places me under no obligation to buy anything. I can always return a shipment and cancel at any time. Even if I never buy another book, the two free books and gifts are mine to keep forever.

225/326 HDN FEF3

Name	
	(PLEASE PRINT)
Address	Apt. #
City	State/Prov. Zip/Postal Code

Signature (if under 18, a parent or guardian must sign)

Mail to the Reader Service:
IN U.S.A.: P.O. Box 1867, Buffalo, NY 14240-1867
IN CANADA: P.O. Box 609, Fort Erie, Ontario L2A 5X3

Not valid for current subscribers to Harlequin Desire books.

Want to try two free books from another line?
Call 1-800-873-8635 or visit www.ReaderService.com.

* Terms and prices subject to change without notice. Prices do not include applicable taxes. Sales tax applicable in N.Y. Canadian residents will be charged applicable taxes. Offer not valid in Quebec. This offer is limited to one order per household. All orders subject to credit approval. Credit or debit balances in a customer's account(s) may be offset by any other outstanding balance owed by or to the customer. Please allow 4 to 6 weeks for delivery. Offer available while quantities last.

Your Privacy—The Reader Service is committed to protecting your privacy. Our Privacy Policy is available online at www.ReaderService.com or upon request from the Reader Service.

We make a portion of our mailing list available to reputable third parties that offer products we believe may interest you. If you prefer that we not exchange your name with third parties, or if you wish to clarify or modify your communication preferences, please visit us at www.ReaderService.com/consumerchoice or write to us at Reader Service Preference Service, P.O. Box 9062, Buffalo, NY 14269. Include your complete name and address.

HDES11B

REQUEST YOUR FREE BOOKS!

◆ Harlequin *Presents*

PASSION GUARANTEED SEDUCTION

2 FREE NOVELS PLUS
2 FREE GIFTS!

YES! Please send me 2 FREE Harlequin Presents® novels and my 2 FREE gifts (gifts are worth about $10). After receiving them, if I don't wish to receive any more books, I can return the shipping statement marked "cancel." If I don't cancel, I will receive 6 brand-new novels every month and be billed just $4.30 per book in the U.S. or $4.99 per book in Canada. That's a saving of at least 14% off the cover price! It's quite a bargain! Shipping and handling is just 50¢ per book in the U.S. and 75¢ per book in Canada.* I understand that accepting the 2 free books and gifts places me under no obligation to buy anything. I can always return a shipment and cancel at any time. Even if I never buy another book, the two free books and gifts are mine to keep forever.   106/306 HDN FERQ

Name _____ (PLEASE PRINT) _____

Address _____ Apt. # _____

City _____ State/Prov. _____ Zip/Postal Code _____

Signature (if under 18, a parent or guardian must sign) _____

Mail to the **Reader Service:**
IN U.S.A.: P.O. Box 1867, Buffalo, NY 14240-1867
IN CANADA: P.O. Box 609, Fort Erie, Ontario L2A 5X3

Not valid for current subscribers to Harlequin Presents books.

**Are you a current subscriber to Harlequin Presents books
and want to receive the larger-print edition?
Call 1-800-873-8635 or visit www.ReaderService.com.**

* Terms and prices subject to change without notice. Prices do not include applicable taxes. Sales tax applicable in N.Y. Canadian residents will be charged applicable taxes. Offer not valid in Quebec. This offer is limited to one order per household. All orders subject to credit approval. Credit or debit balances in a customer's account(s) may be offset by any other outstanding balance owed by or to the customer. Please allow 4 to 6 weeks for delivery. Offer available while quantities last.

Your Privacy—The Reader Service is committed to protecting your privacy. Our Privacy Policy is available online at www.ReaderService.com or upon request from the Reader Service.

We make a portion of our mailing list available to reputable third parties that offer products we believe may interest you. If you prefer that we not exchange your name with third parties, or if you wish to clarify or modify your communication preferences, please visit us at www.ReaderService.com/consumerchoice or write to us at Reader Service Preference Service, P.O. Box 9062, Buffalo, NY 14269. Include your complete name and address.

HP11B

REQUEST YOUR FREE BOOKS!
2 FREE NOVELS PLUS 2 FREE GIFTS!